A DEGREE IN DEATH

RUBY GUPTA

First Impression in December 2012

ALCHEMY PUBLISHERS
4767/23, Pratap Street, Darya Ganj, Ansari Road
New Delhi: 110 002

ALCHEMY is a registered trademark of Mehras
and is licensed for use to Alchemy Publishers.

Distributed by
MEHRAS BOOKS PVT. LTD.
38 A Akshoy Kumar Dutta Sarani,
Second Floor, Kolkata-700 006

4767/23 Pratap Street, Darya Ganj, Ansari Road
New Delhi: 110 002

A-36, Bindal Industrial Premises, Near Samhita Complex,
Saki Naka Telephone Exchange Lane, Vijay Print, Andheri Kurla Road,
Andheri (E), Mumbai - 400072.

NEW INDIA BOOK SOURCE
5/1, Sirur Park B Road, Thanappa Mansion,
Seshadripuram, Bangalore: 560 020

ISBN: 978-81-8046-084-5

Cover design by ART TRICKS;
Layout by Sharmistha De

Printed by M/S Decora Book Prints Pvt. Ltd., Mumbai

This is for you, Dad.

You left fingerprints of grace on my life.

You will never be forgotten…

CONTENTS

CHAPTER – 1

Professor Murlidhar Indresan looked bleary-eyed at his watch. It was 4 a.m. in the morning. His cell phone was vibrating incessantly. As he was a light sleeper, it did not take much to awaken him. Cursing under his breath, he picked it up. "Yeah?" he growled.

"It must be from MIST as usual," his long-suffering wife spoke in a miffed tone.

"Sir! There is an emergency situation in the boys' hostel! Please come immediately!" It was an agitated Mayank on the other side of the line. He was one of the hostel wardens.

"You take care of it for now. I'll come in the morning," Professor Indresan spoke imperiously. These wardens cannot even handle petty issues, he thought disgustedly.

"Actually sir, a... a boy has been found dead!" Mayank squealed in distress.

"What? What are you saying?" Professor Indresan was shocked. "Are you sure?"

"Yes!" Mayank seemed panicky. "He committed suicide... hanged himself," he continued in a traumatized tone.

The warden was telling the truth, the professor realised. This was awful. Who was the poor boy and why had he done this to himself? There was no point discussing all this on the phone, he thought. "Have you informed the chairman?" he asked instead.

"Yes," Mayank said.

"Okay, I'm on my way," Professor Indresan said.

He sprang out of bed. "I'm sorry, I'll have to go," he told his wife. Without a word, she turned away from him. Minutes later, Indresan was driving towards the college.

The Modern Institute of Science and Technology (MIST) was located amidst lush greenery on the outskirts of the sleepy little town of Dehradun. Built upon acres of softly undulating terrain, it was flanked by the majestic Shivalik range on one side and the verdant Doon Valley on the other. The breathtaking location was one of its strongest USPs.

As Professor Indresan's car swung through the tall gates of the institute, the guards stood at attention and saluted. Without stopping at the main building, he drove straight to the hostel premises located behind the academic block of the institute.

All the three hostel blocks were awash with bright lights. Everybody was up. Everywhere he looked, there were huge crowds of boys. How had the ghastly news spread so quickly? Professor Indresan wondered, alarmed.

He observed the chairman's BMW along with several other vehicles parked in front of the third hostel block. Rapidly he lumbered into the foyer.

The first thing he noticed was the annoyed expression of the chairman, G.D Singhal. Next to him was Professor Shantanu Bose, Dean — Research and Development, anxiously talking to the Chief Warden — Col Hari Shankar, while Mayank stood dutifully, listening in.

Just then, G.D Singhal saw him. "Why so late?" he was irritated.

Professor Indresan was apologetic. "Sir, I came as soon as I was informed and..."

"Now you have to see that this does not give us any bad

press," G.D. Singhal cut him in mid-sentence. "Remember, no bad publicity. After a couple of months, admissions will be on. So take care! I'm depending on you." Clearly the incident had made the chairman uncharacteristically jittery.

"Yes sir. No problem. Please don't worry sir," Professor Indresan tried to pacify him.

"This is really terrible. How could such a thing happen at my Institute?" G.D. Singhal looked worried. There was a call on his blackberry. He moved away to be able to talk in private.

Professor Indresan slowly expelled the breath that he had unconsciously been holding in. "Who is the boy?" he asked.

"Vipin of third-year mechanical engineering," Professor Shantanu Bose said.

"But he is...er...was a very intelligent boy, and president of some club. I remember he used to be in my office very often seeking permission for organising some extracurricular activity or for conducting some programme," Professor Indresan said, looking perplexed.

Mayank nodded in concurrence.

"Then why would he commit suicide? He does not seem to be the type to take his own life," Professor Shantanu said to no one in particular.

"Have you informed the parents?" Professor Indresan turned to Col Hari Shankar.

"Yes sir. I got the number from Vipin's roommate and phoned them. They were in the Andamans and are already on their way here. They managed to catch a flight immediately on receiving the news," Col Hari Shankar said. As a retired colonel, he was reputedly efficient.

"I should address the students and then send them back to their rooms," the director of the institute, Professor Indresan continued.

Col Hari Shankar summoned all the wardens and asked them to get all the students to assemble in the basketball court located in front of hostel block two.

G. D. Singhal finished his call and came towards them.

"We will have to call the police. And also lodge an F.I.R.," Professor Indresan was back to his usual pro-active self.

"Yes. You take care of it," the chairman ordered.

Professor Indresan rapidly made a call to the Station Officer, of the nearby Rajpur thana, Inspector Bisht.

"Sir, the students have assembled," Col Hari Shankar told the director.

Rapidly they strode to the basketball court. There were so many students that most of them spilled out on all sides of the court.

"My dear students," Indresan began. "An unfortunate and tragic incident has occurred. We are extremely saddened by this happening. We will immediately look into all aspects of the matter. I request that all of you should co-operate with us and help us take care of the situation. This is the first time that something like this has happened in the history of MIST, and we will take an in-depth look into the cause of this mishap. In the meantime, I request all of you to go back into your rooms and take rest. Thank you."

For a moment, no one spoke. Then, disgruntled voices could be heard from various corners among the students' group. Immediately Col Hari Shankar took matters into his own hands.

"Please, everybody, go into your hostel rooms," he requested. With a flick of his hand, he gestured to the three wardens to escort the students. Mayank started leading the students.

"But sir, we want to know the details of why and how this has happened…," a loud voice emanated from the student group.

Col Hari Shankar responded in a booming tone (reserved for such occasions), "We know how troubled all of you are by this tragedy. However, this is not the time or the place to discuss it. We will look into it and tomorrow we will let all of you know the details."

At this, the students started going into their respective hostel blocks silently. Col Hari Shankar was widely feared by the students. One never knew when — without much provocation — he would suddenly insult someone in public.

"You should have announced a condolence meeting for tomorrow," G.D. Singhal reminded the director.

"Er… yes, well; we will bring out a notice to the effect and announce it in the first period, so that all the students can be informed," Professor Indresan tried to salvage the slight lapse on his part.

"Ah well, alright!" G.D. Singhal was mollified.

All the boys had gone into their hostels. The professors gathered around the chairman. The wardens who were mere lecturers maintained a respectable distance, awaiting further instructions.

"You all must ensure that this situation is not allowed to develop into anything nasty," G.D. Singhal commanded.

"Sir," Col Hari Shankar said loudly.

"What is the status of the police?" Singhal continued.

"They will soon be here," Professor Indresan said.

"Okay, then I'm leaving. Brief me about everything tomorrow morning. I want a complete report about why this has happened," Singhal left.

"We need to discuss the strategy for tomorrow and stay on for a while till all the students have settled down and the police arrive and do whatever they do in such situations," Professor Indresan said.

"Yes sir," Col Hari Shankar agreed.

"Have you seen the er... the body?" asked Professor Shantanu.

"Of course," Col Hari Shankar nodded.

"It must have been dreadful," Professor Indresan spoke poignantly.

"Oh yes. Think of the boy who found him," Col Hari Shankar said.

"Who found him?" Professor Indresan asked.

"His roommate," Col Hari Shankar said.

"But why wasn't the roommate in the room at the time? After all, it must have been the middle of the night," Professor Shantanu Bose queried.

"The roommate was part of a study group. They were studying late into the night in the adjoining apartment. At some point of time, he needed to refer to a particular book. So, he went back to his room for the book, and... found the body," Mayank eagerly exhibited his alertness about the goings-on of the nightlife in the hostel.

"So that means the door was unlocked? Would anyone try to commit suicide without locking the room?" Professor Shantanu

Bose pointed out.

"No. Of course the room was locked," Col Hari Shankar spoke patiently.

"When the door was not opened after repeated knocking, the roommate jumped on to the room's balcony from the balcony of the adjoining room and entered through the balcony door," Mayank explained.

"Oh…," Professor Shantanu nodded.

Everybody was quiet, involuntarily picturing the horrifying scene.

Professor Indresan thought of his own son pursuing engineering at Punjab Engineering College. He shuddered to think of such a thing happening to him. "We must look into the matter critically and find out the cause immediately," he spoke firmly.

"First thing we do tomorrow is call a meeting with all the deans, heads and the wardens," the director continued brusquely. He would not get into wishy-washy sentiments which might hamper his effectiveness, he thought.

The police officer, Inspector Bisht, along with four constables and a photographer, arrived.

Col Hari Shankar apprised them about the situation.

"Let's go and have a look," Inspector Bisht said.

Mayank led the way to the scene of the tragedy.

"I want to have a look as well," Professor Shantanu said, and followed them.

Col Hari Shankar who had already seen everything, stayed back with Professor Indresan who did not wish to see the horrible scene.

The boy had been a third year student, and almost all the third year students were housed on the third floor. Without a word, everyone went up the winding staircase.

"Here we are," Mayank said as they reached a room in the middle of the long corridor on the third floor.

Everybody trooped inside the room.

Professor Shantanu hesitated to enter. He saw a student peeping from the adjoining apartment. Steeling himself, he walked in. Even though expecting the horror of the scene that would confront him, he was unprepared for the ghastliness of the entire spectacle. He had seen such things in the movies and on television; but seeing it with his own eyes was horrendous. Involuntarily, bile rose in his throat. He retched and swallowed. This was too much. He turned away.

"I hope no one has touched the body?" Inspector Bisht asked.

"No. The boy who found it ran out immediately and informed the other boys who, in turn, informed me," Mayank said.

The body was suspended from the fan only a few inches above the bed by a bedsheet. The head was tilted to one side. The face was engorged and purplish-red in colour. The eyes were open, staring and somewhat bulging; the mouth too was open in an ugly manner. He had been a handsome boy but death had turned him into a grotesque shadow of his original self. He was dressed in a pair of low-waist jeans, which were so loose at the waist that they barely clung to his hipbone. His Adidas t-shirt looked crumpled as though he had slept in it.

A wooden stool lay fallen upside-down, a little way from the bed. The bed had been pulled sideways to the centre of the room so that it was beneath the fan. Apparently, the boy had pulled the bed underneath the fan and then kept the stool atop it, in order to reach up to the fan. After tying himself, he must have kicked the stool, Professor Shantanu conjectured. The original position of the bed was adjacent to the wall, a little way from the centre. The other bed in the room was in its original position adjacent to the opposite wall.

"Take photographs," Inspector Bisht instructed.

The photographer clicked several snaps from all angles.

Mr. Bisht noted down all the details he could observe. "Bring him down," he directed.

Immediately two constables climbed on the bed and lifted the body while the third untied the bedsheet. The boy was laid on the bed. The photographer clicked more pictures of the body. For good measure, he took several photographs of the room as well.

It was all too much for Professor Shantanu. He walked out into the balcony adjoining the room. Quickly he gulped in large quantities of fresh air and held on to the railing. He was more shaken than he cared to admit. He looked up at the stars. The stars were still shining; the full-moon was spreading its silvery light in benign blessings; and all seemed well with the world.

"So, the roommate jumped in through this balcony and entered and found the body?" Inspector Bisht shattered the calm as he entered the balcony accompanied by Mayank. He continued to jot down details.

"Yes sir," Mayank concurred.

Mr. Bisht nodded.

Mayank continued, "He went into the balcony of the

adjoining room and from there, jumped onto this balcony." The adjacent balcony was about two feet away. There was a sheer drop in between; but clearly for the daredevil boys, this was of little consequence.

"Was there any suicide note?" Mr. Bisht asked.

"We don't know. Nothing in the room has been touched since the body was discovered," Mayank said.

"In that case, we will carry out a preliminary search of the room and also check his mobile for any messages or last-minute calls that might give us a clue about why the boy did this," Mr. Bisht said.

Everyone went back into the room. Adjacent to the two beds were a couple of study-tables and chairs facing the two opposite walls. There were also two medium-sized almirahs built into the walls. A couple of wooden shelves filled with books hung from the wall above each table. There was a laptop on each table. The room had a medium-sized window that opened into the balcony.

This was an imposing room, Inspector Bisht thought to himself. He went up to the study-table next the bed of the deceased boy. There were no loose papers or anything that might be regarded as a suicide note. He went through all the files and books on the table and the shelf and shook them thoroughly. "Check the boy's pockets for his cellphone," he instructed one of the constables.

Professor Shantanu turned away. This was too gruesome for him.

"There is nothing, sir," the constable responded.

"Well, check everywhere!" Mr. Bisht commanded.

Both the constables started searching the room expertly. They checked the body thoroughly, looked under the bed and searched the almirah and the shelves.

There was neither a cell phone nor a suicide note.

"This is strange," muttered Mr. Bisht.

"Maybe you should look under the pillow," Mayank offered.

Triumphantly, one of the constables pulled out a fancy gadget from under the pillow.

"How did you know where to find the phone?" Mr. Bisht asked a tad suspiciously, whilst writing down more details.

"Er... I don't know; the thought just occurred to me...," Mayank stammered.

Mr. Bisht gave him a sharp look and flipped open the phone. He pressed a few buttons. "This is peculiar. There are no incoming or outgoing calls or text messages," he said.

Everyone was quiet.

Mayank decided not to offer any opinion.

"Maybe the boy deleted everything because he did not want to reveal anything," Mr. Bisht muttered.

"Yes, maybe," Mayank agreed quickly. All this was getting on his nerves and he wanted to get back to his room now.

"Well, it seems to be a clear case of suicide. I have made a record of everything and the panchnama is complete. The body can be kept on ice in an isolated room downstairs till the parents arrive," Mr. Bisht said.

"Er... right," Mayank had no idea what Inspector Bisht was talking about.

Seeing his puzzled expression, Mr. Bisht explained, "Well,

this is standard police procedure. Once the parents arrive and give their consent, only then will the body be taken to the mortuary."

"Yeah that's right," Professor Shantanu felt somewhat choked.

"And the post-mortem will be done after that. But only if the parents want it," Mr. Bisht paused, "or, if foul play is suspected...."

"I don't understand," Professor Shantanu was baffled.

"Don't worry. It's nothing. I will be off now. My constables will ensure that the body is laid on ice. In the meantime, ensure that this room remains sealed," Mr. Bisht spoke rapidly. It had been a long night for him.

"Yes, of course," Mayank said, eager to be able to escape at last.

Mr. Bisht went near the body once again and bent down to look more closely. "Strange! The ligature mark is much lower than usual... it should have been higher, and at an angle...," he mumbled. He seemed to be talking to himself.

"What?" Professor Shantanu was puzzled.

"Oh, it is probably nothing," Mr. Bisht brushed him off. But all the same, he wrote down something in his notebook.

They went downstairs. Mayank stayed back to ensure that the room was sealed after the body was carried out.

Inspector Bisht addressed the director, "I have done the panchnama. Inform me once the parents are here." He spat sideways.

"Yes. Right!" Professor Indresan said. He started to ask him something; but then thought the better of it and simply nodded.

After Mr. Bisht departed, the lights in the hostel rooms began to be switched off gradually. Things appeared to be going back to normal. Professor Indresan prepared to leave. He instructed Col Hari Shankar and Professor Shantanu to stay on for a while to ensure that everything remained in order. After being assured that things would be under control, he left.

The professors left behind decided to take one last round of the hostel and then leave. Everything seemed peaceful. They called the three wardens and gave strict instructions to them to remain vigilant for any untoward incident. They were to take care in case any student complained of uneasiness or any disturbance. Arrangements were made for the deceased's roommate to stay with Mayank for the remainder of the night. The next day, the roommate would be shifted elsewhere.

CHAPTER – 2

It had been a sleepless night for most of the students. The thought of a dead body, and that too of a fellow student, lying within the hostel premises, was just too horrendous. Why had Vipin committed that horrendous act? The thought plagued everybody. They all agreed that Vipin had seemed like the last boy who would commit suicide. He just wasn't the suicidal type. Something really bad must have happened for Vipin to have taken such a drastic step. But what had happened? As far as they knew, there had not been anything untoward in the recent past. And even if it had, then Vipin would have lashed out against the responsible person or thing causing him distress, rather than succumb tamely to the circumstances. He had been a fighter, not an escapist.

These thoughts soon led to distress and trepidation. Some students became traumatized picturing the moment of death. Some became fearful of the deceased boy's soul, which they thought was perhaps wandering in the corridors of the hostel. Some believed that disturbed souls were never at peace and often remained behind at the place of death, as ghosts. By morning, all the students agreed that they should find out what was being done by the director and management to sort out the situation.

At sharp nine, a group of students crowded in the main corridor of the academic block. Agitated, they discussed various aspects of the terrible suicide. The reason behind the suicide was the question that troubled everyone. All kinds of plausible causes were suggested.

"Let's all go to the director's office. The authorities should tell us why it happened and what they are doing about it," Suresh, a budding student leader of sorts, urged everyone.

"Yes, let's go!" Nitish, his most devoted supporter, was vociferous.

"Er, shouldn't we be attending classes?" a diffident girl spoke.

Everyone ignored her plea.

"Anyway, classes should have been suspended. Such a major tragedy has occured and these people are still interested in taking classes!" a boy said.

"Perhaps we should wait," someone cautioned.

"Oh! don't be a sissy. We have a right to know what is happening. And there is no way we will go to class," another urged.

Outside the director's office, the peon told them that a high-profile meeting was on. The door of the office opened and Professor Indresan's personal assistant came out for some work. In that split second, they caught sight of the sombre look on peoples' faces at the meeting that was in progress inside.

"I guess we should wait for the meeting to get over," some boy said grudgingly.

"Mayank sir said that a condolence will be held and then classes will be suspended," a girl spoke.

"O.k. then, let's find out the time of the condolence and then go to the canteen," Suresh said.

"Bhaiya, has the director provided an official notice for the condolence meeting?" one of the boys asked the director's personal assistant who was about to re-enter the office.

The assistant did not answer. As a rule, he kept the students at a distance.

"Oh well. Let's go. In any case, we will come to know once the notice is circulated. The bureaucratic procedures here are worse than those prevalent in apna IAS," Suresh said in disgust.

It was *de rigueur* for the students to criticise the institute now and then. This despite the fact that MIST had been established over 15 years ago and had done exceedingly well from the word go. With faculty at par with that of the IITs and crores worth of state-of-the-art laboratories, MIST had built a formidable reputation in academics and research.

"Was everything all right last night?" Professor Indresan asked.

"Absolutely. I myself took a round around campus to ensure that everything was in order," Col. Hari Shankar said in his usual authoritative tone before anyone else could speak.

All the deans, heads et. al. had assembled for the 9 a.m. meeting in the director's office. Those who had classes in the first period had got some other professor to take their class. Everyone was perturbed by this unprecedented tragedy which threatened to mar the pristine reputation of MIST.

"Mayank, what about later in the night?" Professor Indresan turned towards the warden.

"Yes sir. There was no problem at all," Mayank spoke. A few students kept whining about being scared, and a few talked of management apathy. But such things were normal under the circumstances; so there was no need to mention it, he thought.

"Have you typed the notice for the condolence meeting?" Professor Indresan pulled up his long-suffering assistant.

"Yes sir," he mumbled, whilst taking a printout of the said notice, seated in his designated position in a corner alcove adjacent to the main office.

"Make sure it is circulated everywhere and read out in every class," Professor Indresan continued.

"When are his parents going to arrive?" he switched tracks and addressed Col. Hari Shankar.

"They flew out from the Andamans immediately after hearing Vipin's death. Then from Delhi, they will be flying down here. I think they will reach soon," Col. Hari Shankar replied.

"These parents have more money than can do them any good. Their son had been so troubled and there they were holidaying in the Andamans," the Electrical Engineering Head said in an aside to the Electronics Engineering Head.

"He was troubled, was he?" the Electronics Head asked.

"Obviously he must have been. Why else would he commit suicide?" the Electrical Head responded.

"I have offered my condolences to the parents on behalf of the management," Col. Hari Shankar added rapidly.

"Hmm... well, is the note for the condolence ready?" Professor Indresan asked the Dean of Academics, Professor Girish Shukla, instead.

"Yes sir, here it is," Professor Shukla passed the note to the director sombrely.

Everybody was quiet whilst the director read it.

"I think this is fine. I think all of you should read it and give suggestions if you feel any changes need to be made," Professor Indresan said.

The paper was circulated to everybody. No one made

any comment except for nodding and murmuring that it was perfectly fine.

"I think we should add a line about God granting peace to the departed soul and giving courage to the family to face this loss," the Computer Applications Head spoke up.

"Yes, that would be appropriate," Professor Indresan said.

"Yes sir, I too think this should be added," Dean of Students, Professor Ramesh Bhardwaj agreed. Since the director had agreed to the suggestion, there was no harm in seconding the opinion, he thought.

"Well, in that case, make sure the additional line is also typed in at the appropriate place. And then show it to me," Professor Indresan instructed the Head of Computer Applications.

"Yes sir," the Computer Applications Head left.

"Well, that is done. Now we need to take care of a few more things," the director looked at the points written in his diary and said, "Firstly we need to inquire into the reasons that led to the suicide. Then we need to pre-empt any sort of student reaction to this incident. And lastly we need to ensure that this incident does not result in any sort of bad publicity for the institute."

Everybody remained quiet. The director glanced at the registrar for some kind of backup. The latter promptly obliged. "Yes sir, you are absolutely right. We should, *kya kehte hain,* take care of these three things immediately," he said.

"Well then, what do you suggest?" Professor Indresan asked.

"I think sir, the news is bound to get into the press and you should prepare a formal press note and release it. That way at least we can exercise some control over what is published," Col.

Akash said.

"I should prepare the note?" the director's voice was soft as silk.

"No no sir… what I meant was that we will prepare the note and *kya kehte hain,* it will be released from your office," Col. Akash tried to salvage the situation.

"Yes, you should have it ready in an hour," the director was at his authoritarian best. "Well, that is taken care of. Now about the other two matters…," Professor Indresan looked around expectantly.

Just then, the Computer Applications Head entered and handed over the amended condolence message to the director. The latter started reading it.

"You have done a good job," Professor Indresan commended the Computer Applications Head, who in turn preened at this public praise.

"We should form two committees — one to inquire into the cause of the suicide, and the other to counsel the students," Professor Shantanu Bose, Dean of Research and Development spoke for the first time. This meeting would go on forever and he wanted to finish with it and get back to his research. He was working on a project funded by the Department of Science and Technology, and he hated to spend any moment away from either his project or his teaching. These tedious meetings always got on his nerves. He was a man of pure academics and research.

"Yes. So please suggest names for the committee members," Professor Indresan looked around expectantly.

Everybody avoided his gaze whilst maintaining poker faces. Only the few who knew that they would not be roped into it looked back at him.

Sheesh! These people! thought Professor Shantanu in disgust. "It is very simple sir," he said. "The Proctor, Professor Mrityunjaya Sharma, should head the Inquiry Committee and the Dean of Students should head the Student Counselling Committee. And then they can choose their own members and get the team approved by you."

"Yes. That's right," the director was relieved, but disgruntled. Yet again, Dean of Research had proved that he was the more competent man. Thank god, he was only confined to his lab and books, or else his own job would be in danger. The man's brilliant research in nano-technology and remarkable reputation in academics often made him insecure. Many a time, he had tried to motivate Professor Shantanu to leave, but had not succeeded.

"Sir, it is almost time for the condolence meeting," Col Akash said.

"Er... Yes!" the director felt an inexplicable rush of uneasiness well up within him. "Go and see if all have assembled, and then inform me. I'll be there promptly." He had really been better off as a professor at IIT where he did not have to handle such unexpected things. Immediately he shook his head and tried to squash the thought.

Everybody watched the play of emotions on his face. With his longish salt and pepper hair in disarray around his ear lobes, the director looked extremely disturbed.

"We will continue with this meeting after the condolence. All of you go ahead and ensure everything is in order," Professor Indresan quickly took firm control over himself.

Everybody filed out of the office. The Computer Engineering

Head, Professor Tandon, stayed back with the intention of escorting the director.

"You think the meeting went well?" the director's voice held a note of diffidence.

"Of course, sir. You handled it very well. It was all due to your competence that things have been managed so smoothly," Professor Tandon assured him.

The director gave a grateful smile. Then he took up the condolence message he had to read, whilst coiling a slim lock of hair around his right index finger.

"Sir, please come. Everyone is waiting," Col Akash entered and said.

"Right," the director said and promptly disappeared into the adjoining washroom.

Col Akash and Professor Tandon waited respectfully.

A while later, they reached the auditorium.

The director went up to the dais. All the students and faculty members who had assembled, looked at him expectantly.

The director took out his note and read it through, slowly and sombrely.

There was absolute silence in the auditorium. Obviously, everyone was deeply disturbed by the incident.

After the condolence and the one-minute silence, the director came out of the auditorium.

Professor Tandon said, "That went off very well, sir."

The Heads of Departments and the others who had been a part of the morning meeting headed to the director's office for the sequel. All the others filed out of the auditorium.

The day scholars prepared to go home as the classes had

been suspended. A few hostelers headed back to their hostels; some headed to the canteen, some to the library and others to the computer centre to surf the net.

"Is it an off day for us too?" Vinita, the Computer Applications lecturer asked, as all the faculty members walked towards their respective departments.

"Are you crazy? Why will it be an off day for us?" a Physics lecturer, Punit, responded.

"Yeah, one of us will have to die before we are given a day off," Rakesh, the Electrical lecturer, commented sarcastically.

"Arre, then too it is highly unlikely that we will get the day off," Mona, an Electronics lecturer, commented.

"Yes. Then they will call a condolence meeting at 4:30 p. m. and then declare that the remainder of the day will be an off day for us," Punit spoke disgustedly.

Everybody guffawed.

"So what do we do now that there are no classes?" an over-sincere assistant professor of Maths, Mrs. Nisha asked.

"Arre, you enjoy yourself — surf the net, go to the canteen ... do you need to ask?" Punit replied.

"No; you go and prepare for your next day's lectures," Mona said sarcastically.

"Yes, but first let's go to the cafe for some coffee," Ashish, the Mechanical Engineering lecturer, suggested.

Everyone turned towards the coffee shop.

"But this is a terrible thing," Vinita said.

"Yes, why did he do it?" Punit asked.

"I heard that it was a case of an affair gone wrong," Rakesh spoke in a whisper.

Everybody looked at him with respect. No doubt there was some truth in what he said. He had the inside information on everything that went on among the students.

"Oh really?" Mona was shocked. "What happened?"

"He was involved with this girl for quite some time, a year maybe, and recently they broke off; rather, she broke off with him. Maybe he was depressed about it," Rakesh explained. "Or maybe it was the other way round... yes, yes, come to think of it, it was the other way round..." his voice trailed off.

"So, you mean to say that's why he did it?" Vinita asked.

"Well, maybe..." Rakesh was hesitant. "But if Vipin broke off with her, why would he need to commit suicide? Rather, if she had committed suicide, then it would be understandable," he continued.

"Who is this girl?" Vinita asked.

"Gurpreet," Rakesh said.

"The one in third year Mechanical? But she is a good student. I wouldn't have thought that she would be doing such things," Punit said.

"These students... really! Their parents send them here to study and spend so much money on them and look at what they end up doing!" the conscientious Mrs. Nisha said, shaking her head.

"And not only that — I also learnt that Gurpreet had gone to the boys' hostel last night!" Rakesh said.

"What! What are you saying? That is impossible! No girl is permitted there. Besides, the guards at the hostel gate would have stopped her!" Punit was indignant.

"I'm telling you. She was seen near the third block of the

boys' hostel," Rakesh said.

"But then, why wasn't a complaint made?" Mrs. Nisha asked.

"She was seen while she was leaving the hostel; so the boys who saw her decided to keep quiet about it. They didn't want her to get into trouble," Rakesh reasoned.

"What loyalty! What unity!" Punit was sarcastic.

"Shouldn't we tell all this to the director?" Mrs. Nisha asked.

"Oh, forget it! If there is an inquiry committee or something, then I will tell them," Rakesh said.

"The director should know this now! Maybe she went to meet the boy and then something happened, and after that, he took his own life," Mrs. Nisha was indignant.

"Ok, as soon as the Heads' meeting is over, I'll tell the director. Now are you satisfied?" Rakesh asked.

"Anyway, let's talk about other things. This is just too awful. I need to divert my mind," Vinita said.

Everyone was quiet. They would not admit it, but the suicide had unsettled them all.

"I was thinking of doing some shopping this weekend," she resumed.

"Shopping? How can you talk of shopping?" Mrs. Nisha was disgusted.

"Why not go today evening? Prepare for tomorrow's classes now itself, and then you will be free," ignoring her, the Physics lecturer, Punit, suggested.

"My God! You people are really something. How can you make such plans at a time like this? Really! I'm going to my department," Mrs. Nisha stomped off angrily.

"Well, she has a lot to learn about living," Rakesh said. "Life has to go on after all," he continued.

"Forget her. I too want to buy some things. Let's go to the Tibetan market," Mona said.

"What Tibetan market? There are Tibetans in Doon?" Vinita was surprised.

"Arre, the Bhotia market. Don't you know about it?" Mona asked her.

"No. I don't belong to this place, remember?" Vinita said. She was from Rishikesh and had shifted to Dehradun a couple of months back, since joining MIST.

"Right — I too want to buy a jacket; I'll come along with you," the Mechanical lecturer, Ashish, piped in.

"But what and where is this Bhotia market?" Vinita asked insistently.

"Oh God! She will not rest till she knows everything. If you had taken so much of interest in your studies, you would have completed your Ph.D by now," Punit said sarcastically.

"The Bhotia Market is in the city near the Parade Ground," Rakesh spoke. "Actually, a large number of Tibetans are settled in Dehradun and I think the government has allotted them this place where they have established this Bhotia Market. Some of these Tibetans make their living by selling stuff in this market," Rakesh could never resist showing off his knowledge of trivia.

"Oh! I really didn't know. I thought all the Tibetans in India lived only at Dharamshala in Himachal," Vinita said. "Is the market very good?" she continued.

"Of course! You get all kinds of imported stuff. But you have to do a lot of haggling," Mona said. "And that is half the fun," she added.

"It's decided then. We will go directly to the Bhotia Market after college," Ashish said.

The ladies nodded.

They reached the coffee shop. The mood inside was sombre. Everyone was discussing the suicide. Try as they might, the faculty were unable to divert themselves from the tragedy that had occurred amidst them. Most conversations veered around the possible reasons for the suicide. Some of the faculty wondered if they could have possibly helped the poor boy somehow and avoided the tragedy.

CHAPTER – 3

The canteen was packed with people. Nitish had spread word that those concerned about the state of affairs at the institute, in the wake of the unfortunate incident, should gather in the canteen at 12 noon. At the appointed time, a huge crowd of students trooped in. Some were serious; some had sauntered in thinking that it would be a good time-pass; some had come to see what the fuss was all about. A few had slunk in to carefully note all the goings-on. They intended to give this information to a few chosen faculty members in exchange for petty favours (like extra marks, extra attendance or extra out-pass from the hostel).

"Well, this meeting has been called to discuss yesterday's incident," Suresh said in a loud voice. He was keen to assert his leadership.

"Yes, we must do something about it," spoke Nitish, his staunchest supporter who was always eager to do his bidding.

A babble of voices rose in response. Some were louder than the others.

"Yeah. My God! It's awful," a boy spoke.

"It's terrible. I couldn't sleep a wink after hearing of it," a girl said.

"When did you come to know?" a senior student asked.

"Oh, right away. I was studying last night and as soon as some of the boys came to know of the incident, one of them called me up and told me," the girl said.

"Oh yes, several boys informed the girls," another boy said.

"Yes, and within minutes, everyone in the girls' hostel knew of it," a girl student concurred.

The two blocks of the girls' hostel were situated at the other end of the campus as far away from the boys' hostel as possible. Yet there was no way that the interaction or communication between the girls' and boys' hostels could be reduced to a minimum.

"The point is — what is the management doing about it?" Suresh tried to take the lead again.

"What do you mean? What are they supposed to do? It was suicide, so…," the student's voice trailed off.

Everybody was silent for a few seconds.

"Let us listen to what Suresh has to say," Nitish said.

"But has anyone wondered why he committed suicide?" a B.Tech fourth year student spoke loudly, pointedly ignoring Nitish whom he despised for being Suresh's chamcha.

"Yes, that is puzzling," another fourth year student said. "He was not the type to do this kind of thing," he continued.

"He committed suicide because of his low marks and the reason for his low marks is because the Mechanical Trio were out to get him. Remember, they threatened that they would fail him in the internals and they had done so!" Suresh raised his tone and reasserted his leadership.

It was no secret that Vipin had antagonized most of his mechanical engineering professors and lecturers. In particular, there was a group of three lecturers of mechanical who had been dubbed as the Ghastly Mechanical Trio. In time, the name was transformed to Ghastly Mechtrio (an allusion to Mechatronics, an optional mechanical engineering subject). The Trio had publicly announced that unless Vipin improved his attendance in their classes and his performance in the monthly tests, they would have no choice but to fail him in the finals. They taught three core papers in mechanical engineering, and it was essential to pass in these papers.

"Well, tell me if I'm wrong?" Suresh challenged.

A few students sitting at the next table started listening in, with interest.

"This is a clear case of harassment which has led to this suicide of one of our classmates. We should not take it lying down," Suresh's voice rose further. He fancied himself as a great leader.

"Yes, yes," Nitish chorused.

Soon, a group collected around Suresh. Everyone agreed that the Trio were obnoxious, to say the least. "But Vipin never attended any class and had written nothing in his sessional test papers," a self-effacing girl cautioned. "We simply can't say something like this," she continued.

"Yes, well, he was not able to attend many classes because he was the president of the Mechtrika club. And remember, he has been busy most of this semester in organizing the tech-fest," an architecture student said.

"And this was the case with the classes of all his subjects. But it was only the Trio who had threatened him. Something must be done about them," a girl student of Mechanical spoke.

"Yes, they are making life hell for all of us students," another student said.

"Yes, this is too much!" a girl said.

"We should complain about this to the higher authority. We

should not take things lying down. After all, one of our classmates has lost his life due to this," Suresh said.

"Yes," Nitish said.

"We should go and first ask Dean of Students' Welfare what they are doing about it. And then we should tell him about the Mechanical Trio and how they have caused this tragedy," Suresh said.

"Yes," this time a bunch of them shouted in unison with Nitish. Several students bore a grudge against the Trio. And nothing would please them more than to see action taken against the three. "Yeah, let's go!"

Everybody was in agreement.

In the director's office, an intense discussion was in progress regarding the issues related to the tragedy.

Just then, the peon announced the arrival of the deceased student's family consisting of his parents and his sister.

The Heads left.

The director asked the proctor, Professor Mrityunjaya Sharma, Col Hari Shankar and Dean of Student Welfare, Professor Bhardwaj to stay on.

"Er... you may go and see the er…the body," Professor Indresan stuttered after offering his condolences. This was too painful to bear, he thought.

The parents looked blank.

"I'll go," the sister, Vibha, said.

"Er... after that er... he can be shifted to the mortuary," Professor Indresan said.

The parents remained immobile.

Seeing their faces, Professor Indresan felt a curious hollowness in the pit of his stomach. He took a deep breath to get a grip on himself. After a pause, he resumed, "Er... if you desire,a post-mortem can be done." These were Inspector Bisht's instructions, he remembered.

The parents did not speak.

"Yes. Yes. A post-mortem must be done," the sister spoke firmly.

Professor Indresan nodded.

"There was no way my brother could have committed suicide," Vibha said loudly. She worked for Bharat Television and was widely respected for her fiery tackling of taboo issues. She was tackling her brother's death in the same manner.

"Yes. My son was no wimp," the father seemed to come to life.

The mother, still in a state of shock, simply nodded.

Professor Indresan tried his best to pacify them, but all to no avail. The parents were too distressed to say much; but the sister was particularly difficult to handle. She insisted on seeing Vipin's room also. The devastated parents decided to stay on in the director's office. The shock was too much to bear and then, to actually see their beloved son's body or the room where he had lost his life would be agonizing.

Col Hari Shankar and the proctor escorted the sister to the hostel. They waited outside the room on the ground floor where Vipin's body lay on ice. Vibha entered alone.

A while later she came out, her face ashen.

Col Hari Shankar and Professor Mritunjaya Sharma wished they could flee. This was too uncomfortable to handle.

"Take me to his room," Vibha said in a voice that was barely audible.

Wordlessly, they led her to the third floor.

Entering Vipin's room, Vibha examined every inch of it and took charge of all her brother's belongings. She was particularly interested in his cell phone and laptop. But they had been taken away by the police. Accordingly, Mr. Bisht was informed and he promised to send over the two items at the earliest after making a copy of all the data in them.

Vipin's family finally left; but not before Vibha commented darkly that she would go through everything with a fine-toothed comb and this was not the last of it. She decided to stay on in Doon for a few days in order to carry out her own investigations.

Professor Indresan graciously agreed to extend all possible help.

The Heads' meeting recommenced.

Suddenly the phone rang. The director picked it up. "What? Are you sure?" his voice rose in agitation. There was a pause while he listened. "Well then, take her to the hospital!" he spoke anxiously. His face lost some colour as he kept the receiver.

Everybody looked at him in alarm. What had startled the director? And who needed to go to the hospital? They were barely out of one crisis and now what more could have happened?

Worriedly, Professor Indresan looked at all of them. "A girl has slashed her wrists in the girls' hostel," he spoke in distress.

"Oh my God! Who is the girl?" the Computer Applications Head asked.

"Gurpreet," the director said. He paused. "Our doctor has examined her, done the dressing, and I have asked her to be sent to the hospital," he continued.

Everybody was assailed by an unknown disquiet. This was extraordinary! What was happening at MIST? they wondered.

"Apparently she did it sometime last night or in the early morning. She has lost a lot of blood and was unconscious," the director continued. Involuntarily he took hold of a slim lock of hair from behind his right ear.

"Another suicide?" Professor Girish Shukla articulated what was in everyone's mind.

"But how come she was not found earlier? Where was her roommate?" the Physics Head queried.

"What should we do now?" the director looked around somewhat helplessly.

"Sir, we should go to the girls' hostel and find out why it has happened, and also counsel the girls," Professor Shantanu spoke.

"Yes, maybe it is connected to the boy's suicide," the Head of Electrical said.

"Then is it also a suicide attempt?" the Electronics Head asked.

"Maybe the two were part of some group and it is a joint suicide pact? These kinds of things are in vogue among internet communities in Japan and USA," Professor Mrityunjaya Sharma tried to show off his half-baked knowledge.

"Yes, but in that case the entire group commits suicide. This seems to be a case of an affair gone wrong," Professor Shantanu was irritated.

"Colonel, please inform the girls' hostel that they should all assemble in the mess. The director will address them," Professor

Shantanu said to Col Hari Shankar, taking matters in his own hands.

The director looked at him blankly.

"Sir, let us go, and you please address the girls and pacify them. After that, we will inquire into the matter and get the information as to why this has happened," Professor Shantanu continued.

"Yes. That sounds appropriate," the director came back on track.

The girls' hostel was agog with news of the latest mishap. Rumours flew thick and fast. Some said it was a case of unrequited love; others said that it was a sympathetic suicide for she was allegedly the girlfriend of the deceased. A few postulated that it was merely because she was a somewhat crazy girl. Gurpreet had been studious, but somewhat odd. She was a loner and got along better with the boys rather than with the girls.

Soon the director arrived, accompanied by Dean of Research and the other professors. His address was mostly about the importance of preserving the academic environment; he talked about the dharma of a student and asked the girls to concentrate on their studies. He assured them that they were taking all possible steps to inquire into the two mishaps; and that if some corrective measures needed to be taken, they would do so immediately.

They went up to have a look at Gurpreet's room. The lady warden accompanied them. Apparently, nothing had been disturbed. A part of the bedsheet was soaked in blood. It seemed that the blood had soaked through to the mattress also. Professor Indresan felt faint. A tragedy had just been averted — the thought crossed the minds of many of them.

"Where was her roommate when this happened?" Professor Shantanu asked the lady warden.

"Sir, her roommate had been suffering from typhoid. She has taken medical leave and is staying with her local guardian," she replied.

"So that is how Gurpreet was all alone in her room," Dean of Students stated the obvious.

"So who found her?" Professor Indresan asked.

"Er... when she did not come down for breakfast, her classmate was puzzled. But then thinking that Gurpreet was asleep and also because she was getting late for the first lecture, the classmate rushed to the institute," the warden said.

"Woh kya kehte hain — who is this classmate?" Col Akash interrupted.

"Er...I don't remember the name," the lady replied tremulously at this slight lapse on her part.

"Well, go on," the director was plainly irritated at this unwarranted interruption.

"Er...yes sir," the lady warden became flustered hearing the director's abrupt tone. "Well then, during lunch, the classmate returned and decided to inform Gurpreet about the happenings of the day. It was then that she went into Gurpreet's room and discovered that she was lying in her bed, unconscious and bleeding profusely," she finished in a rush.

Back at his office, the director told Col Akash, "Inform her parents and the local guardians."

"Yes sir," Col Akash left.

"I think sir we should visit the girl in the hospital," the

Computer Engineering Head, Professor Tandon, counselled the director.

"Yes, we will go in the evening," Professor Indresan looked at him gratefully. Public image was very important for him.

"More importantly, we should determine whether the two incidents are linked," Professor Shantanu spoke.

"Yes, yes... right," Professor Indresan concurred.

"So what should we do? How should we go about it?" the director decided to let Professor Shantanu take the lead.

"I think Prof. Bhardwaj should informally talk to students and gather as much information as possible. The lady wardens can play a crucial role in this. And they should do this within a deadline," Professor Shantanu spoke firmly.

"Yes, I will call them right away and give instructions for this," Professor Indresan said.

Professor Tandon obligingly pressed the bell for him. The peon appeared a second later. "Call Professor Bhardwaj and all the lady wardens here for an urgent meeting with the director," he instructed.

Professor Shantanu left.

Professor Indresan and Professor Tandon stayed back.

"Do you think it all went off well?" Professor Indresan spoke hesitatingly.

"Sir, it was perfect," Professor Tandon reassured.

Surreptitiously the director's hand slid to the thin lock of hair, twirling tantalizingly over his right ear. The hair over the right side of his head was visibly thinner than that on the left side. Perhaps it had to do with his penchant of unconsciously playing with it whenever anxious. But everyone (including his wife) was too polite to point it out to him. More so, because Professor Indresan fancied himself a great technocrat a la the former President Abdul Kalam and believed that the similar hairstyle only endorsed this irrefutable fact.

"Sir, Infosys has confirmed the date for their pool campus," the Training and Placement Officer entered.

"Oh God, not now!" Professor Indresan muttered an expletive under his breath. But the college had to go on as usual, he thought.

"Well, sir, we were lobbying very hard for this pool and till the last minute, there was a good chance that the Shivalik Institute of Technology could have managed it at their campus. However, our efforts have paid off," the Training and Placement officer was determined to get his share of accolades, notwithstanding the situation.

"Er... yes, good job. Please get your team in order and begin the preparations," the director coiled a lock of hair around his right index finger and tried to focus. "When are they coming?"

"Next week, sir."

"O.k., prepare a draft notice assigning responsibilities etc., and make sure you get it signed by me today itself. Remember – this is a prestigious thing for us and you must ensure that it is organised without any hitch. This is completely your responsibility," Professor Indresan rapidly delegated the entire work on his able shoulders.

The Training and Placement officer left.

"Sir, don't worry, it will all be taken care of," Professor Tandon was at his sanctimonious best.

Sometimes, Professor Tandon's obsequiousness was too

much to stomach, Professor Indresan thought. But then, it had its benefits too.

Professor Bhardwaj and the two lady wardens entered. Rapidly, Professor Indresan gave instructions in line with Professor Shantanu's earlier advice. It was long past lunchtime and even his stomach had given up protesting. "Remember, I want as much information as possible by tomorrow morning," he instructed.

"Yes sir," Prof. Bhardwaj said. He left along with the wardens.

Professor Tandon summoned the peon and instructed for snacks to be brought in. He knew what the director needed at any given point of time.

Gratefully, Professor Indresan slumped back in his chair.

CHAPTER – 4

The next morning, the college campus was awash with news that the local papers carried all minute details of the suicide. One newspaper that was seemingly unbiased simply carried a small news item. But what had really got everyone talking was the news as presented in the rival paper. Somehow, this newspaper had also got hold of news of the girl student admitted in the local hospital in an attempted suicide case.

Linking the boy's death to the attempted suicide by the girl, the newspaper carried a seemingly in-depth analysis. It postulated all kinds of conjectures about the two mishaps and this was linked to the adverse academic environment and everything else that was presumably wrong with the institute. The article went on to talk about the poor security, the lack of adequate counselling facilities, lack of committed faculty, etc; there was even a paragraph about the dismal campus placement scenario.

Some mischievous student made the most of the situation and pasted photocopies of this news item on several college notice boards and on the walls of the academic block and all the hostel blocks.

Col Akash informed the director whilst giving him a copy of the offending news article -

"This is a most distressing situation. These press wallahs and these students...," distractedly the director pulled out a strand of hair from behind his right ear. He was clearly at a loss for words.

Col. Akash waited patiently.

After a while, Professor Indresan said, "I think we should call a meeting to decide how best to tackle this situation. Please ask my assistant to inform everybody for an immediate meeting. Meanwhile, I think I'll talk to the management also in this regard."

"And I hope you have given instructions for the photocopies to be removed from everywhere," he continued.

"Yes, okay," Col Akash left.

Vibha switched on her brother's laptop. There was bound to be some clue here, she was sure. She grimaced as she noted the adult content of several files. Evidently, they had been downloaded from the net. She knew Vipin was in the habit of maintaining a journal. She tried all kinds of searches, but there was no file which looked like a journal. Determined not to give up, she went through all the files she could find. There was nothing.

Then she had an idea. He had probably hidden it in an unlikely location. She tried a different search. The hard disk had been partitioned into an additional D-drive, and here she was searching only on the C-drive. There were numerous folders in the D-drive. She opened all of them. Some contained hard-core X-rated content. However, most were related to research into alternate energy sources and bio-fuels. There were several files containing details and prototypes of vehicles that ran on bio-fuels.

Evidently, Vipin was working on a project related to designing a vehicle that ran on bio-fuel. There was no way someone who was so enthusiastically working on something like this would take his own life; it was inconceivable. Tears came to her eyes. Furiously, she wiped them away. Vibha was not a weakling and neither had her brother been one.

Just then, she came across a word file entitled simply as 'ME'. Instinctively, she knew that this was his journal. Having almost forgotten what she was searching for in the first place, Vibha was elated to finally locate it. Eagerly, she clicked on it. It asked for a password. She leaned back on the chair, frustrated. Trust Vipin to make things complicated. Now what in the world could be the password? She tried everything she could think of: various combinations of his birthday, the names of his favourite stars, movies, zodiac signs, their parents' names, his favourite cartoon characters.... all to no avail.

What could it be? She re-opened the folder containing his research on bio-fuels and cars. After noting a few significant things and names, she keyed in as many combinations as she could, like jatropha etc., but none worked. What was she missing? Then, on a whim, she put in 'Fridaythe13th.' Vibha had been born on the 13th of June, on a Friday. This caused Vipin to nickname her 'the witch' and tease her unmercifully. He said that only witches were born on Friday the 13th. Miraculously, the file opened. She started crying. How much he used to fight with her, and yet, he had gone and put her day and date of birth as his password. "Oh Vipin! Why did you go away, leaving me alone?" she whispered as she brushed away her tears.

It was his journal. Entries were not made for each day, but intermittently. It seemed that Vipin wrote in it sporadically. Without pausing to read all the entries, she rapidly scrolled down. She wanted to read the most recent ones. There was nothing suspicious in the entries made in the entire month. He had written about being in love with some girl mentioned only as 'Ms. MIST'... he cribbed about some teachers named only as 'the Ghastly MechTrio'... but mostly he wrote about how exciting his project was... how happy he was to have found an excellent project partner like Deepak. There was nothing out of the ordinary.

But what these entries did indicate was that there was no way he could have taken a cowardly step as committing suicide. These indicated a boy enthusiastic about life and love, and someone ambitious about making it big. Vibha copied all the contents of the file on to a pen drive. She would show it to the director and Inspector Bisht, prove to them that her brother was not the suicidal type; and get them to investigate his death. This journal irrevocably corroborated her initial suspicion that Vipin had been murdered. She had always known beyond any measure of doubt that Vipin could never ever commit suicide.

But if it was murder, surely there could be some clue in here related to it? There had to be a motive for anyone to have gone to such an extreme as to have killed him. Had Vipin done something so terrible to someone that the person had actually gone and murdered him? Or maybe Vipin had done something unconsciously, but it had had serious repercussions? Vibha loved Vipin dearly but knew that he was completely self-centred and rather insensitive to the feelings of others, and was arrogant to boot. Or was the murderer some psychopath who didn't really need a logical reason to kill? She began reading the journal again in the hope of finding a clue to his murder.

"Cancel all my meetings," the chairman told his assistant "As soon as the police officer arrives, show him in," he continued.

G. D. Singhal rued the day that he had decided to set up this college. If it were not for his wife, he would have been content with his traditional mithai business. However, his wife's ambitions had prompted him to diversify and expand into the property business. The timing had just been right as Dehradun was expanding rapidly, and real estate was booming. Soon, he was rich beyond his wildest imagination. Then, after their son had finished school, his wife had the idea that they should do something in the education line. Soon they zeroed in on the fact that though Doon had excellent schools, it had nothing to boast of by way of higher education. Due to this fact, most students migrated to metros and other cities for pursuing higher education.

Realising the tremendous potential in this sector, the establishment of MIST was already a reality in the mind of his wife. It was just a matter of time before Gopal Das Singhal had to give in to her skilful persuasion. That was 15 years ago. And today, MIST was an acknowledged leader in the arena of technical education in the region. Admittedly, the path had not been easy, but the results had been worthwhile, more so for his wife. All her life, she had craved for respect amongst the elite of Doon's society, and MIST gave it to her.

His wife's father worked as a lowly guard at one of the numerous limestone quarries located on the outskirts of Doon. A few years down the line, environmental concerns prompted the government to order the closure of all limestone quarries. Her father lost his job and soon took to drink. He did manage to find another job as a guard-cum-handyman at a bungalow on

Rajpur Road; the owners of which came to India from USA on their yearly sojourn. But, he was never the same again. His wife was the eldest of seven children and she had to soon drop out of the government school and take care of her siblings. Her mother took up a job as a maid in a nearby school.

Life had been tough for his wife when young, but her grit and determination soon led her to reach the position she was in now. Not one to keep the accident of a wrong birth from holding back her progress, she had long ago realised the potential of Gopal Das. Gopi, as he was popularly known, helped his father in his small mithai shop located at a strategic corner of their basti. The shop did well because it was the only one in the area.

Gopi was good in his studies; but after school, he had to spend all his time at the shop instead of with his books. He had four sisters and knew very well the responsibilities that rested on his small shoulders. He had only his best friend to count on, who would later become his better half. She was the one who understood his frustration and gave him solace; and who gradually made him realise the importance of making it big in life. It was a natural progression that they should get married. And after that, their combined efforts led to his opening one mithai shop after another. Thereafter, Lord Kuber never stopped smiling down at them.

MIST had given Gopal Das Singhal tremendous prestige and clout amongst the political and government circles; but along with that had come hypertension and diabetes. This was aggravated with the establishment of their archrival SIT eight years back. An industrialist-turned-educationist from Delhi had established the Shivalik Institute of Technology (SIT). Singhal envied his rival promoter for having thought of such an apt name for his institute. Singhal wished that he had thought of it earlier. But that had been before a smart-alecky student of MIST had rechristened SIT as SHIT (ostensibly Shivalik Hills Institute of Technology). Thereafter, the acronym had stuck on.

However, in spite of it, he was perpetually on his toes to ensure that SIT did not upstage MIST. And that meant ensuring that the brightest students opted for MIST and that the best faculty too first applied to MIST. This rivalry soon percolated down to the level of the students. And whether it was a tech-fest or campus placement, there was a neck-to-neck race between the students of the two colleges as to who was able to grab the maximum accolades. It was clear to Singhal that SIT had set out to give him tough competition.

And now this. Of course, his wife could not be blamed for the current situation, which threatened to boil over into a full-fledged crisis accompanied with bad publicity. G.D. Singhal had a horror of bad publicity. An hour ago, Inspector Bisht had called him and said that there was something urgent and that he needed to meet him personally. Intuition told him that this was not going to be something good.

"Sir, Mr. Bisht has arrived," his assistant intruded into his thoughts.

"Right, send him in," Singhal felt a hint of trepidation.

Preliminaries over, Inspector Bisht announced, "The post-mortem report has come."

Singhal felt the beginnings of alarm grow within him.

"It is murder, not suicide!" Mr. Bisht announced theatrically, for maximum effect.

"Oh God! Are you sure?" Singhal was astounded. He felt his blood pressure rising.

"Of course I'm sure!" Mr. Bisht was smug. "According to the report, the victim died due to strangulation and not due to hanging!" he stated authoritatively.

Singhal was confounded. For a moment, he was unable to understand what the difference was between 'strangulation' and 'hanging'. They both meant the same thing, he thought.

"He was strangled and then hanged to make it look like suicide," seeing his confused expression, Mr. Bisht clarified. "In fact I had precisely this suspicion when I had observed the body," he emphasized on his astute powers of investigation.

Singhal's mind went blank for a moment. "This is bad, really bad," he was completely disconcerted. Such things happened in movies and not in real life, he thought. Then he quickly gained control over himself. There had been a murder and that too in his college; he had better get a grip on things! "How does the report prove it is murder?" he challenged Mr. Bisht.

"The thing is, in case of hanging, the ligature mark is high up on the throat and is in a somewhat V-shape. But here, the ligature mark is much lower, beneath the thyroid, and is transversely placed." The chairman's quick recovery impressed Inspector Bisht.

"So what? That is not enough to prove it is murder," Singhal was belligerent.

The chairman was tough, Mr. Bisht realised. "There is more in the report," he continued. "The boy was found hanging by a bedsheet, but the marks on his throat are narrow and have cut deep into the flesh. This indicates that some corded rope-like material caused the actual strangulation and death," he finished with a flourish.

There was no doubt it was murder, Singhal conceded in his mind.

"And not only this. Traces of a poison have been found in his system," Mr. Bisht declared affectedly.

"What? What do you mean?" Singhal was thoroughly mystified. This was getting more and more complicated by the minute, he thought.

"This means that first an attempt was made to poison the victim, but then he was strangled and it was made to look like suicide," Inspector Bisht explained triumphantly.

"This is bizarre," Singhal was baffled. This couldn't be happening to him, to his institution, he thought.

"Yes, it certainly is," Mr. Bisht concurred decisively. "And the poison is one that is extracted from a local plant," he added.

"So... what is to be done now?" Singhal asked. He ignored the last detail; he had heard enough; he was a man of action.

"We will have to carry out an investigation and find out who the murderer is," Mr. Bisht explained blandly.

"Oh..." Singhal fell silent. "This is not good. It will be very bad for the college," he paused. "You mean to say that the murderer must be someone from the institute?" the obvious suddenly struck him. God help me in this; he prayed inwardly.

"That is most likely," Mr. Bisht spoke gravely.

"Oh God!" Singhal almost choked. This was one shock too much! he thought.

Mr. Bisht looked at him understandingly.

"This can affect our reputation," Singhal said. "Our admission process will commence soon." He was lost in thought.

"I am aware of that, sir. That is why I have come personally to discuss the matter with you," Mr. Bisht spoke smoothly. He knew he could milk the situation for all it was worth.

Singhal nodded shrewdly. "Well, what must be done has to be done," he became brusque. Not for anything had he become the owner of such a vast empire.

"You can start with your investigation. Just ensure that it is carried out with the utmost discretion. Our academic environment should not get affected," Singhal spoke imperiously.

"Yes sir," Mr. Bisht looked at him in awe. This was one tough cookie.

"No details are to be divulged to the press under any circumstances. I will handle the press myself," Singhal continued. He flicked the intercom, "Inform the director that he should come right away." He pressed the buzzer. His peon entered, head bowed. "Why haven't you brought refreshments for Bisht saab?" Singhal admonished.

"Sorry sir," the peon retreated.

"Singhalji has himself told me not to ever bring refreshments for anyone unless he says so, and now he scolds me for it in front of the officer," he muttered to the assistant peon.

"Well, that is why you are paid more than us. To listen to these scoldings," the assistant peon smirked.

"Shut up and get on with the tea," the senior peon said, irritated.

Hurriedly, the director entered the chairman's office. "Sir, I was busy with the matter of the girls' hostel and er... the newspaper report," he said in an apologetic tone, which, at the same time, conveyed his conscientiousness in handling such a delicate matter so promptly and sensitively.

Ignoring his excuse, abruptly Singhal apprised him of the situation and instructed him to extend all possible help to the police. Indresan was to maintain the utmost discretion and confidentiality about the situation.

"Yes sir," the flabbergasted Professor Indresan managed to utter, as he felt a sharp pain in the centre of his sternum that radiated towards his back. Murder! He felt faint at the thought. He swallowed and resisted the urge to rub his back. His ulcer was acting up again. This job was ruining his health and would surely lead him to his death, he thought. "Don't worry sir; it will be taken care of," he somehow articulated.

Singhal looked at him disdainfully for a split-second, and then instantly masked his expression, but not before Mr. Bisht had made a mental note of it.

Ignoring his pain, Professor Indresan continued, "We... er... I have already formed an inquiry committee to look into the possible causes of the er... incident. I have also formed a counselling committee to counsel the students so that they should not lose their focus from academics."

Singhal gave a miniscule smile.

"The inquiry committee has already proceeded with its investigation and will be submitting its findings in about," he looked at his watch, "half an hour. I'm sure Mr. Bisht will find the report most useful," he gave a smile, which turned into a half-grimace. The pain was not letting up.

"Well, that is good," Singhal was appeased.

The peon entered with a lavish spread of refreshments. Mr. Bisht looked happy, Singhal observed.

A little later, the director sent for Ramesh Bhardwaj, Mrityunjaya Sharma and Shantanu Bose for an urgent meeting with Mr. Bisht. He hoped to God that the inquiry committee had done some inquiring, or else Mr. Bisht would surely convey the hollowness of his boast to the Chairman.

"Well, sir, we have found that Gurpreet was seen in the boys' hostel on the night the boy died," Professor Mrityunjaya Sharma spoke triumphantly.

"Who Gurpreet?" the Director was perplexed.

"She is the one who cut her veins," Professor Mrityunjaya Sharma reminded him. He then paused and looked towards Mr. Bisht, wondering whether he should continue.

"Yes, please go on, Inspector Bisht needs to be told all the details because the situation has changed dramatically. I'll soon tell you about it," the Director said.

Encouraged, Professor Mrityunjaya continued, "She was also er... allegedly involved with the boy."

"What! Oh my God!" Professor Indresan said. All these details had several ramifications. On the one hand, it indicated the girl's involvement in the murder and on the other, it indicated the weakness in their security system. It was also a pointer to their poor discipline.

Everybody was quiet.

"I will need to talk to this girl," Mr. Bisht said.

"Currently she is in the hospital. After she is discharged, she will be going to her local guardian's place," Professor Bhardwaj said.

"Then I need the local guardian's address," Mr. Bisht said.

"No problem," Professor Mrityunjaya said. He rang up Col Akash and asked for Gurpreet's local address to be sent in.

"Has something else happened?" Professor Shantanu asked what was on everyone's mind.

"It is murder, not suicide!" the director looked tormented.

"Oh my God! Are you sure?" Professor Bhardwaj was dismayed.

"Of course," Mr. Bisht looked at him scornfully.

Professor Shantanu and Professor Mrityunjaya were stunned. This was no less than a full-fledged disaster, they thought simultaneously.

"Please ensure that this information remains confidential for as long as possible," the director said. He knew that sooner or later, it would be common knowledge, but he had to follow the chairman's orders.

"Yes sir," Professor Mrityunjaya knew that this was easier said than done.

"Bisht Saab needs to start his investigation. Please see to it and extend all possible help and cooperation from our side," Professor Indresan instructed.

"Yes sir," Professor Mrityunjaya repeated; his mind had gone blank trying to assimilate the changed dynamics of the situation.

"I want to visit Vipin's hostel room again. I hope it has not been disturbed," Mr. Bisht said.

"No. It remains sealed. Let's go," Professor Mrityunjaya said, after recovering somewhat.

Professor Bhardwaj hesitated, wondering whether he should

make good his escape. He felt hopelessly overwhelmed by the latest development. But, it was too late. "You should also go," the director prompted him, knowing very well that he could not give the same instruction to Professor Shantanu who marched to his own drummer.

"Er…yes," Professor Bhardwaj blankly followed Mr. Bisht and Professor Mrityunjaya.

"Well, I'm going to my lab," Professor Shantanu said abstractedly; he seemed miles away, his expression fathomless.

His mind seemed to have already gone back to his pet project, Professor Indresan conjectured. God forbid that he should end up getting the Shanti Swarup Bhatnagar Prize or some such thing. He winced; his ulcer continued to act difficult.

CHAPTER – 5

"You know I think there is some deeper aspect in this entire business," Professor Shantanu spoke. His mind was on anything but his pet project.

He was sitting with Naresh in his Research and Development lab, ostensibly working on his Department of Science and Technology Project. But his brain was grappling with the fact of murder.

"Yes sir," Naresh responded.

Naresh was a nice, dutiful boy, a part of Professor Shantanu's brain reflected. Clearly, he had no idea what he meant, but out of a sense of respect, Naresh had simply concurred with him. That is not to say that Naresh was not intelligent or did not have a mind of his own. Professor Shantanu had had ample proof of his insightful intelligence, which had prompted him to choose Naresh as his student researcher — a position coveted by several other M.Tech students. But Naresh had beaten them to it. Apart from his keen intelligence, Professor Shantanu was impressed by Naresh's quiet demeanour. He only spoke when spoken to; and most importantly, was miles away from mindless net-surfing, smsing, drinking, partying, etc. He was a rare species — an old-world student, mostly confined to research or reading.

"Actually, I was thinking that Vipin's death is not a simple case of suicide due to a love affair gone wrong," Professor Shantanu was careful not to reveal the fact that it was murder, keeping in mind the director's instructions. And yet, he wanted to use Naresh as a sounding board. He continued, "He was not the type to commit suicide because of a girl… I mean, that does not go with his personality."

"Yes sir," Naresh was deferential.

"Don't yes-sir me all the time, my boy; tell me what your opinion is!" Professor Shantanu was mildly irritated. Too much reverence was not always a good thing. "I mean, tell me your analysis of the whole thing." Instantly he softened. Naresh should not have to bear the brunt of the uneasiness of his own mind.

"Well sir, as far as I know, Vipin was an extrovert and an outgoing boy, not really the type to commit suicide, but you never can tell," Naresh paused.

"Yes. After all, how well can one truly know a person?" Professor Shantanu became philosophical.

Naresh remained silent, waiting for the professor to continue.

After a while, he said, "Bring me Vipin's personal file and compile a list of all his friends and any other information that you can find. Did he know any one in the city? Which places did he frequent? How many times did he go out of the hostel? Tell me anything that might be of any importance."

Professor Shantanu saw the look of curiosity on Naresh's face, but the latter was too respectful to cross-question him. Clearly, he must be wondering about the need to collect such stuff when it was suicide. Ah well, he would soon know. "Well, go on, get me all this information," he prompted.

Naresh hesitated for a split-second. Then, without any further query, quietly left.

Professor Shantanu leaned forward on his office table and drummed upon it with his fingers. This was most unprecedented.

It was extremely troubling that the sanctity of the academic environment had been violated in this manner. He could not come to terms with it. And then, there was the vexing question of how and why all this had happened. It was like an unsolved cipher. And there was something innately intriguing and hypnotic about it, something mystifying.

Unwittingly, his mind flashed back to the days when he had been a faculty member at one of the IITs, where he had begun his academic career. He had been a young lecturer at the time when the campus had been rocked by the murder of a senior professor's wife. After months of investigation, the police had concluded that she had been the victim of a burglary gone wrong. The young Shantanu had been unconvinced. His penchant for research was such that anything that did not fit into a logical order prompted him to investigate it. He went about investigating the murder on his own, in a methodical manner, as though it were a technological problem — which it was, in a way. Soon enough, his astuteness led him to the real murderer — her husband. The motive was age-old; the senior professor had suspected his young wife to be involved with one of his Ph.D students.

Way back then, the police had commended him on his fantastic investigation. Shantanu himself had felt pleased on solving the murder. For quite some time thereafter, he wondered if he was in the wrong profession. Perhaps he should have joined the CBI or the famed Research and Analysis Wing, he fantasized. But then, he was soon back to his first love — technical research and teaching.

And now, once again, there was a murder so close to home. He could not sit idle. He had to take matters into his own hands and begin the investigation. He had already done so in a manner by asking Naresh to get him the preliminary information about Vipin. Was it some intuition that had prompted him to see Vipin's body first-hand on the night of the murder? Perhaps. He would inform the director and chairman in due course about his investigation; he was sure they would not have any problem with it. Who knew! History might repeat itself and he may even solve the murder – that would provide him immense satisfaction. He had better visit the scene of crime again, he thought.

Quickly he got up. Rapidly, he walked towards the boys' hostel. The assistant warden immediately let him inside the sealed room. Professor Shantanu looked around. There was nothing to indicate the violence that had occurred there not so long ago. He walked out into the balcony. Without a doubt, anyone could have jumped in from any of the two balconies of the adjacent rooms on either side. That was possible, of course, for people who had access to the hostel rooms.

What if it had been an outsider? Could someone enter the hostel hoodwinking the hostel security system? But there were guards at the gate and there was no way an outsider could have entered the hostel premises. And yet, it was inconceivable that some student could have committed such a heinous crime. It had to be an outside person. But then again, why? The question of motive too was puzzling.

Professor Shantanu went around the entire block. There was a six-foot wall encircling the entire hostel block. There was only one point of entry that was at the entrance gate manned by a guard. He looked beyond the walls. There was an uneven sort of shallow ravine all along the wall. The hostel was constructed atop an undulating land mass, part plateau and part hillock — a common topographical feature in that part of Dehradun.

As he walked along the entire periphery, he noticed that at one point, the ground outside the boundary wall rose up in such a manner that the effective outer height of the wall was a mere two feet. This was opportunely located towards the back of the hostel where it would not be easily noticed. Clearly, anyone could jump across and enter the hostel premises. This was a serious lacuna in the security. Why had nobody noticed it?

But, the four-storey hostel block had only one main door for entry which was duly locked at 11 p.m. And nobody could gain entry after that. He went around again. There was a particular apartment on the first floor, with a balcony facing just the spot where the boundary wall was low. Someone could climb up through the boundary wall and then perhaps climb to the first floor using a few jutting notches on the side of the building and jump inside the balcony. But then, how could he reach Vipin's room?

Professor Shantanu went up, and entered the said apartment on the first floor. There was a central lobby that led to the balcony. There were three rooms on either side of the central lobby, the doors of which were locked. Evidently, the students of those three rooms were attending their classes. The apartment door leading into the lobby was normally left open so that the rooms were accessible to any of the respective students living in them. Professor Shantanu went outside to the balcony. Yes indeed, this was the most easily accessible balcony for someone climbing in through the two-foot part of the boundary wall.

Would an outsider coming in through this route then walk

out of the apartment lobby and into the corridor and risk being noticed by students? And what about the six students living in this particular apartment? Any one of them could catch him. Would they be away somewhere else at that point of time? Professor Shantanu looked outside all along the long corridor. After a while, he noticed that across the corridor towards the right, there was a narrow, half-open wooden door. He looked inside. It led to a narrow airshaft that seemed to run up on all the floors. One wall of the airshaft had a built-in iron ladder.

He went into Vipin's room and entered the bathroom. The bathroom had a small window near the ceiling. He climbed on the cistern and looked through the window. As he had conjectured, it opened into an airshaft. Professor Shantanu nodded. Well, this certainly widened the scope of possibilities and of suspects. It could have been an outside job but with inside information. No outside person could venture inside unless he knew of the exact layout of the hostel architecture. He would need to know exactly which airshaft to enter in order to reach Vipin's room via the bathroom.

He went downstairs to the hostel office. Since he was already here, Professor Shantanu decided to make the most of the situation and talk to the administrative staff of the boys' hostel. If there were an outsider involved, they would know of it. Immediately, he summoned the assistant wardens, the mess-in-charge and the guards. They were insistent that no outsider had access to the hostel premises, because of the stringent security. When Professor Shantanu mentioned the airshaft, the guards looked troubled. There was a remote possibility but a decidedly distant one, they conceded. And if at all an outsider was to take the airshaft route, he would need inside information; they corroborated his own conclusion. Although curious about this line of questioning, they refrained from asking anything, out of respect for the professor.

One thing they were unanimous about, and that was that Vipin had been too arrogant. He used to behave as if he was lord of the manor and treated everyone, particularly the staff, like servants. Everyone was fed up with him but had to somehow tolerate his behaviour. They had made several complaints and Vipin had been counselled by the wardens, but all to no avail. As a last resort, Mayank, the most widely-feared warden, had threatened him too, but Vipin was scornful of all such intimidations.

But at the same time, a boy as egotistical as Vipin was not likely to have committed suicide — was the hesitant verdict of all of them. And yet, no one recalled any untoward happening on the night of the incident or on the day preceding it. As was the usual case at nights, several boys were up and about. Most of them up to no good — surfing the net, listening to loud music, and generally creating a nuisance, the assistant warden said mournfully; though some did study late into the night — he conceded as an afterthought. It was only when Mayank took one of his impromptu rounds around midnight that things quietened down.

And no one had noticed Gurpreet entering the boys' hostel. There was no way a girl could enter the hostel. It had never happened and was never likely to happen — the guards said indignantly. One of the guards looked somewhat apprehensive, with guilt written all over his countenance. It was clear they were trying to save their jobs. Professor Shantanu decided not to pursue this line of questioning for the moment.

The mess-in-charge did have some curious information. According to him, Vipin had had an altercation with a mess worker named Ramadin. It seemed that since quite a while, Vipin had antagonised Ramadin due to his supercilious attitude and treated the latter in the manner of a lowly outcaste. Somehow, the altercation had turned ugly and Ramadin had warned Vipin with calamitous consequences. This had happened a couple of days prior to Vipin's death. Professor Shantanu asked the mess-in-charge to get in touch with Ramadin and send him to his office at the earliest.

"You know, we got some great stuff from the Bhotia market," Ashish, the lecturer of Mechanical, said.

A group of faculty members were sitting in the canteen, catching up with each other over a cup of tea.

"Really?" Rakesh asked.

"Yeah. Terrific jackets, t-shirts, lots of trinkets," Mona, the Electronics lecturer, gushed.

"What about the price? Was it reasonable?" Punit asked.

"We had to really haggle a lot. But it was great fun," Vinita said.

"Whenever we quoted a really low price, they would talk amongst themselves in their own language. And then state a higher price," Ashish said.

"I was really surprised. I didn't know that they had their own language," Vinita said.

"You really are an ignoramus, aren't you? What did you think? That Tibetans spoke in Hindi?" Rakesh smirked.

"Too bad that they have to live here almost like aliens. I'm sure they wish they could go back to their country," Ashish said.

"That is, if Tibet can be called a country. You people really have no G.K.," Rakesh was sarcastic.

"Anyway we had better get back now. I have to take the next class," Mona said.

"Arre, go a bit late," suggested Rakesh.

"I wish I could do that. But you know nowadays there is constant checking of whether all the classes are being held on schedule," Mona said, suddenly serious.

"I know specially after Vipin and now Gurpreet's attempted suicide," Vinita spoke broodingly.

"I really don't know what has got into these students," Ashish was pensive.

"Yes, I think as teachers, we should do our bit, and somehow always counsel students about facing life and not thinking about taking such a cowardly escape route," Mona said remorsefully.

"They should think of their parents at least," Punit said gravely.

Everybody fell silent.

"Yeah, right. Let's go," Rakesh was contrite. The group trooped out of the canteen.

CHAPTER – 6

"Hey, you know what? Gurpreet could be involved in Vipin's death," Suresh said. He fancied himself now as not only a student leader, but also as a budding sleuth.

"What? What do you mean?" Nitish said. He had great respect for Suresh's perspicacious intelligence, and believed this was ample enough reason for taking on the role of Suresh's closest ally.

The two were having coffee sitting on the narrow parapet that ran all along the boundary wall of the academic block.

"She was awfully upset after Vipin told her that he saw her only as a friend. And then he had publicly declared that he was crazy about Ms. MIST."

"Well, who isn't crazy about Ms. MIST?" Nitish grinned. "She is the college beauty, after all."

The girl in question, actually named Kanika, had won the Ms. Thomso title two years in a row. Thomso was the name of the annual inter-college cultural festival of IIT Roorkee. This achievement led to her being stuck with the nickname Ms. MIST.

"Since then, Gurpreet has been acting strange," Suresh continued, as though Nitish had not spoken. His interest in girls was non-existent.

"Strange how?" Nitish asked dutifully.

"Well, she mentioned on her blog about wanting to take revenge…,"

Nitish was surprised. "When did you read her blog?

And how did you know that she had a blog in the first place?"

"Ever since I learnt that she was in the boys' hostel on the night of the death, I have been investigating Gurpreet," Suresh spoke loftily.

"Wow!" Nitish looked at him in admiration.

"I have concluded that she could have tried to kill him for dumping her," Suresh continued solemnly.

"What! What are you saying?" Suresh seemed to have gone into a fantasy world, Nitish thought.

"I think Vipin did not commit suicide, but was murdered," Suresh lowered his voice.

"Are you crazy?" Nitish was flabbergasted. Suresh had truly lost it now, he thought.

"You remember that day when I had gone to the hostel to get the tutorial copy in the middle of the Artificial Intelligence class?" Suresh said seriously, ignoring his dumbfounded expression.

"Yes, and you returned very late." Maybe there was a logic to this, Nitish thought and tried to be patient.

"Well, while passing Vipin's apartment, I saw that the door was open and voices could be heard from inside," Suresh said. His apartment was on the same floor as that of Vipin.

"But... but that apartment was sealed," Nitish said. "Are you sure?"

"Hear me out," Suresh said. "Well, then naturally I had to investigate. I was already thinking about Gurpreet's role in the death and now this was too suspicious."

"Go on," Nitish was excited.

"I was standing outside and trying to listen when suddenly

I heard footsteps. Quickly I turned and ran. But it was too late. Professor Mrityunjaya came out and saw me. Behind him was Professor Bhardwaj and the police officer, Mr. Bisht," Suresh paused.

"Then?" Nitish asked.

"Professor Mrityunjaya shouted at me for being in the hostel while classes were on. I tried to explain that I had come for the tutorial copy; but as usual, he was not ready to listen. And he hurled his choicest abuses at me," Suresh smiled.

Nitish chuckled.

Professor Mrityunjaya's short temper and penchant for abusing at the slightest provocation was the stuff of hostel folklore and food for much mimicry and mirth.

"Then Professor Bhardwaj trying to show that he was very nice, said that I should take care not to forget such things like tutorial copies, and told me to go back to class," Suresh continued.

"Oh… so what does it all mean?" Nitish was perplexed.

"Now I'll tell you the main thing. Before they came out, I managed to hear something," Suresh paused for effect.

"What?" Nitish was agog.

"Before they came out, I heard Mr. Bisht say that it was unfortunate that someone could commit murder in a temple of learning," Suresh spoke with a flourish.

"Are you sure? Really sure? Or did you imagine it? You are reading too many murder mysteries, you know," Nitish was unwilling to believe this.

"Of course I'm sure. I heard what I heard. What is there to be sure?" Suresh was irritated.

Nitish was quiet. He did not want to antagonise Suresh. "So, you mean?" he asked.

"So you see, it is clear that it was not suicide," Suresh said.

"Then why isn't it being reported in the papers and all?" Nitish asked.

"Arre, you know they are trying not to reveal this for as long as possible, because it will lead to bad publicity," Suresh paused. "And also, because they want to find out the killer first."

"Oh!" the word 'killer' cast a frosty pall over each cell of Nitish's body. He looked intently at Suresh. It was obvious that Suresh had more information. "You know something more, don't you?"

"Yes," Suresh displayed his superior smile.

"Tell me," Nitish entreated.

"I simply put two and two together," Suresh replied.

"Meaning?" Nitish hated riddles.

Suresh relented. "I put together the police officer's comment with Gurpreet's visit to the hostel that night, plus the contents of her blog. And well, there you have it; Gurpreet is the... the...," Suresh swallowed. Even he was not able to articulate what his brain prompted. Gurpreet was his batchmate after all. An odd girl, no doubt, but a batchmate nevertheless.

"You cannot say such a thing!" Nitish was indignant.

"If you read all the postings on her blog, you too will agree with what I am saying," Suresh spoke condescendingly.

"But then, why did she cut her veins?" Nitish knew this would stump Suresh.

"It's simple, silly! She was in love with Vipin and after she murdered him, she could not bear the pain and the guilt, and so attempted suicide," Suresh spoke as though explaining the alphabet to a child.

Could this be true? It sounded plausible enough, and of course, Gurpreet was peculiar. She could indeed do anything, Nitish thought.

"But would she have managed to actually kill Vipin?" Nitish said.

"Why?"

"Vipin was a strong boy, after all, and she is a mere girl," Nitish pointed out the obvious.

"Have you forgotten Gurpreet's size? A tall, hefty girl like her is more than a match for any boy," Suresh shivered.

The image of Gurpreet appeared in Nitish's mind.

"Remember when she had joined college? Had it not been for her thick long plait we would have taken her for a boy; a well-built boy at that," Suresh reminded him.

Nitish nodded.

They were both quiet, lost in their own thoughts. "I think we should tell all this to the authorities," Nitish suggested after a while.

"I also thought about it. But there are two things. Firstly, I want to take credit for solving this murder. And secondly, I will have to admit that I was listening outside the door of Vipin's apartment. God knows what punishment will come on my head for this."

He had a point, Nitish had to concede. "But still, we should tell someone, at least. This is a serious thing."

"You know, any teacher we talk to will ultimately lead us into trouble," Suresh said mournfully.

"How about telling the police officer?" Nitish suggested.

"Are you mad? That is worse. He might want to take some kind of statement, and want to know who and where my parents are, etc.," Suresh was scornful.

Nitish saw his point.

"I think the only safe bet is Professor Shantanu," Suresh continued.

"Oh yes! That is brilliant. He will take care of both your conditions. He is the best you know. He is just and always has the best interest of the student in mind." Most students hero-worshipped Professor Shantanu, and Nitish was no exception. The Dean of Research and Development was the youngest professor on the campus. His formidable knowledge and good-natured wisdom added further charisma to his tall, fair, lean and handsome frame.

"It's decided then, let's go to his office," Suresh said.

"I think you should go alone." Nitish was unwilling to stick out his head more than was necessary.

"Why?" Suresh asked. Nitish usually followed him everywhere.

"Professor Shantanu might not like that you have spoken about such a sensitive thing to some student. It is best that you tell him that you have not told anyone, and are only sharing this with him," Nitish improvised.

"Yes. All right, I'll go alone and tell him. But first, I'll have to see that he is free," Suresh agreed.

"Sir, the French teacher is here," Dean of Academics, Professor Girish Shukla informed the director.

"Er... right. I'll meet him. Academics must go on as usual,"

Professor Indresan sighed. "I hope he knows English," he continued.

The French national Pierre Iselin had arrived at MIST for teaching a value addition course in basic French language under an exchange programme.

"Yes sir. This is his fourth visit to India. His English is fine, though the accent is a little difficult to understand. He is working on his Ph.D, related to Buddhism or something," Professor Girish Shukla said.

Niceties over, Professor Indresan asked the painfully thin, tall, muddy-blonde Pierre to elaborate upon his Ph.D work. A French national working on Buddhism for his Ph.D was interesting, he thought.

Pleased to find an avid listener, Pierre explained about his early interest in Buddhism and later his decision to study the preservation of the Sakya lineage of Tibetan Buddhism for his Ph.D.

"I have already carried out several field studies in Nepal, Dharamshala and Varanasi. Actually, one of my guides is a professor at the Central Institute of Higher Tibetan Studies at Sarnath. So, during the semester break, I will be visiting him. I have also planned that after my daily lectures, I will visit the Tibetan colonies, temples and monasteries in and around Dehradun, and collect data related to their religious practices," he explained.

Professor Indresan was surprised to learn that there was a sizeable population of Tibetans in Dehradun.

"It's ironical," he smiled. "It takes an outsider to tell me more about the city that I am living in."

"Yes," Pierre concurred, warming to his favourite subject. "There are various monasteries around here and in fact, there is a Sakya College right next to MIST."

"Really?" in spite of himself, Professor Indresan found this fascinating.

Pierre elaborated, "It is a place of learning where students study for a minimum of seven years and receive the degree of Kahcupa or B.A. After that, they may study for two more years and gain a Lobpon equal to M.A; and a few may even go up to a total of thirteen years and be awarded the Rabjampa or Ph.D. The main purpose of this college is the preservation and dissemination of the Sakya tradition of Tibetan Buddhism."

"I see," Professor Indresan was impressed; this Pierre had done serious research work.

"Yes. These scholars, once they complete their studies, are in great demand all over the world for serving as teachers and monastic leaders," Pierre continued.

"So, how much of your thesis is complete?" Professor Indresan asked.

"Well, actually, I have done most of the literature survey and field work and written about 60 pages. I am aiming at about 300," Pierre said.

"That is good. I would like to read what you have written," ProfessorIndresan's interest was genuine.

"My thesis is in French," Pierre beamed.

"Oh," the director smiled back. This simple fact had not occurred to him.

"I think we should let him settle down first," Professor Girish Shukla interrupted; miffed that he had not been able to get in a word inbetween and besides, this was too boring anyway. At the same time, he wanted to create a good impression of himself in the eyes of visitors, especially a foreign one.

"Yes. Right, I'm sorry. You should first be at ease. We have made arrangements for you to stay in our guest house. One of our deans, Professor Shantanu, is also staying there, so you will be in good company," Professor Indresan smiled.

CHAPTER – 7

Increasingly, there were more and more reports of a ghost appearing at odd hours in the boys' hostel premises. The ghost was most often seen in Block 3 where the death had occurred; but at times, was seen wandering through the corridors of the other hostel blocks and the basketball court as well. The boys had taken to turning in early at night. There were no more late-night soirees, or group studying, or anything. An unnamed fear clutched at everyone's hearts. Even the girls started becoming terrified; conjecturing that the ghost might come to their hostel as well. There was no stopping a ghost after all, as the students unanimously concluded.

Professor Shantanu was sitting in his Research & Development lab. He too had heard about the rumours of the ghost and wondered whether he should do something about it. Just then, his eyes fell on the stuff lying on his table. There was a note from Naresh saying that he had put together as much information as possible, and would get back after his classes. Great kid, Professor Shantanu thought in approval. He picked up Vipin's personal file, and the names of his friends listed in order of their importance. There was also a copy of his academic timetable and his normal schedule. He sent for Vipin's roommate, who was listed as the first name on the list. He needed to get as much information as possible.

The roommate arrived shortly thereafter and looked as if he had not had much sleep. Upon prodding, he admitted that he was afraid to sleep, as he feared the ghost of Vipin might come and trouble him. Apparently, there had been an altercation between the two, the night before the death, and Vipin had threatened the roommate with ominous consequences. And now that he was a spirit and had unlimited powers, the roommate was convinced that Vipin would have his revenge. The squabble was about a sum of money that the roommate had borrowed but had been unable to return as promised. Professor Shantanu tried to convince the roommate as best as possible about the non-existence of ghosts. However, he was categorically told that the entire boys' hostel, particularly, the third block, resounded with authentic reports of Vipin's ghost appearing at strange hours.

This was a bad situation and something definitely needed to be done. Professor Shantanu assured him that soon they would take action on this account. He made a mental note to instruct Col Akash to get a havan organised. This was the best method to convince the student community that the sanctity and purity of the hostel was restored.

Better still, he decided to take immediate action. He rang up the director and convinced him about the importance of organising a havan. Professor Indresan was pliable and left everything to him. Next, Professor Shantanu rang up Col Akash and explained that the havan needed to be organized on a priority basis. Fifteen minutes later, Col Akash called back and informed that the Panditiji was available, and the havan would take place in the third hostel block the next morning at nine.

Pacified somewhat at this prompt action, the roommate willingly answered all his queries. Ostensibly, though Vipin did not have any foes as such, since he was so aggressive, he invariably antagonised several students. In addition, he had also been involved in ragging some juniors who could have turned into enemies; the roommate disclosed somewhat hesitantly, for ragging was banned. Professor Shantanu asked him to list the names of all such students.

There had been an innate arrogance in Vipin that came from being born with a silver spoon in his mouth and being spoilt rotten by his parents, the roommate explained. Whatever he desired was his for the asking. The one redeeming quality he had had, was his intelligence. However, this too he had denigrated almost successfully by not working hard enough and by not attending classes. As a result, his subject teachers too were perennially upset with him. More so, since he made it a point to be scornful of their abilities, and that too, in such an insolent manner in the class, that any teacher would take umbrage. Vipin also flouted all norms laid down by authoritarian figures, and that included periodically aggravating the wardens by violating hostel rules and regulations.

Would any of these teachers or wardens want to harm Vipin? Professor Shantanu suggested delicately. It was impossible, of course, but he wanted to explore all possible angles. Absolutely! the roommate was indignant; the faculty wardens hated him and were out to get him. And the subject teachers, particularly the Ghastly MechTrio, had given less marks to Vipin due to which he had failed in a few papers.

Professor Shantanu was well aware that if a student received less marks by a particular teacher (mostly deservedly so), he complained that he had failed in the overall result because of discrimination by the teacher, whereas the truth was that the student had only himself to blame. Not wanting to quibble over it, Professor Shantanu sighed deeply and asked him to list them. The roommate wrote down the names of all such teachers and faculty wardens and handed over the list.

Professor Shantanu looked at the two lists — one — of the students and the other — of the faculty — all of whom actively disliked Vipin; perhaps even hated him. This was not a happy situation. This gave several people sufficient motive. But would anyone have gone to such lengths as to actually commit murder?

No, it had to be an outside job, Professor Shantanu was convinced. The roommate did not know of anyone outside the campus with whom Vipin had any contact. Vipin belonged to Delhi and so confined himself to only the campus while in Dehradun; and at the slightest opportunity of even a day's holiday, made it a point to escape to Delhi.

"Was Vipin romantically involved with someone?" the professor asked delicately.

"Er... well, he was," the roommate paused.

"Who?" Professor Shantanu encouraged benignly.

"Ms. MIST," the roommate said.

The professor was surprised. "I thought he was involved with Gurpreet," he said.

"No — not at all," the roommate was emphatic.

"But there seems to be an involvement of Gurpreet in some way," the Professor persisted.

"Well sir, you see, Gurpreet was just his friend," the roommate paused.

"And?" the Professor prompted.

"Er... Gurpreet loved Vipin but he loved Ms. MIST, Kanika,"

the roommate explained. Ah! a love triangle, the professor thought to himself.

There was nothing else of substance that the roommate could tell him. He gave him a final list of all of Vipin's friends, and left. Professor Shantanu tallied the friends list with that left by Naresh. Most of the names were common, though the roommate's list was longer.

One by one, Professor Shantanu called all the students listed as being a part of Vipin's clique. A couple of them were on leave, and he decided to talk to them later. The ones who came, merely corroborated what the roommate had already revealed. A few of them did point out that Mayank, the hostel warden, had warned Vipin on numerous occasions that he would come to a bad end.

Mayank was enigmatic and somewhat of an oddball, according to all students. He wore the same t-shirt and jeans everyday — no one knew whether he ever washed them. And even if it snowed in Mussoorie (which was practically next-door), his attire did not change. No one had ever seen him wearing any woollens. There was no doubt about his eccentricities; everyone, including the management, knew of it. But they thought that most of his peculiarities were harmless. And since he did an excellent job of keeping the hostellers in control, everyone ignored his minor peccadilloes.

It was rumoured that Mayank never slept; for he could be found taking rounds of the hostel and campus at all times of the night and day. His sole purpose in life was to catch students flouting some rule or regulation. And once he caught such a student, Mayank was in his element — using all forms of interrogation till he achieved his objective of prising out a confession from the culprit student. Thereafter, he ensured that the Disciplinary Committee awarded the maximum possible punishment to the culprit. The unspoken conclusion amongst the students and several faculty members was that Mayank was a sadist at heart.

And yet, Mayank had cultivated a band of faithful students in the hostel who were his eyes and ears; constantly spying on the other students and keeping him informed of all that went on in the boys' as well as the girls' hostel. No doubt, Mayank was a veritable encyclopaedia of everything that happened in the institute and he even knew of the history and predilections of most of the hostel students.

Despite all this, Mayank being implicated by the students in this particular instance was a serious allegation. Would a faculty warden do something like this? Professor Shantanu had to concede that he too was somewhat uncomfortable about Mayank. He decided to call all the wardens and find out their views.

All the other wardens including the ladies corroborated the students' verdict. One of the lady wardens went so far as to say that Mayank was more interested in the goings-on in the girls' hostel than in the boys' hostel, and that he was often lurking around the girls' hostel in order to catch any late-coming girl and penalise her. There was no doubt in her mind that he needed psychiatric treatment.

Professor Shantanu leaned back on his table after the wardens had left. It seemed that he had opened a Pandora's box.

Of course, Mayank's academic credentials were impeccable. He had a B.Tech from NIT Warangal and M.Tech from IIT

Kharagpur; but he never taught much. His perennial excuse was that he was busy taking care of some hostel indiscipline case or the other. His shortcomings in class were mostly overlooked by the director and the management as long as the hostel was taken care of.

Some time back, there were rumours that he had been in love with a female colleague. Apparently, she spurned his advances. The affair ended with Mayank's failed attempt to jump off from the roof of the academic block building. Admittedly, the lady was to be blamed for leading him on, so to speak. She belonged to Saharanpur and soon after joining, had latched on to Mayank, who became her Man Friday. Whether it was finding accommodation for her, or helping her to get study material for her subject, he was constantly at her beck and call. A year later, her engagement took place with someone else, and she left soon after.

Mayank was never the same after that. His misdemeanours increased and he seemed to vent all his frustrations on the hapless students; particularly, the girls, even though they were not under his jurisdiction. The management often thought of letting him go before he did any more harm.

Had that time come? Professor Shantanu wondered. Could it be possible that Mayank had a role to play in this heinous crime? If so, what could be the motive? Or had Mayank metamorphosed into a psychopath as most students and several faculty members alleged? The professor shook his head. This situation was really getting to him; now he too was entertaining bizarre thoughts akin to the students. And then, what about the lacunae in the hostel security which indicated that it could just as easily have been an outsider? An outsider with inside information, though. This was getting too complex. He decided to take a walk to clear his head.

Professor Mrityunjaya and the Chief Warden Col. Hari Shankar entered the director's office.

"Last night I got several calls from the boys' hostel saying that there was a ghost roaming about," Professor Mrityunjaya commented. "In fact, I'm being disturbed by such calls about a ghost over the last several days and nights," he was angry. "Why do they call me when we have so many wardens, a chief warden, and a registrar?" the irritation in his tone was palpable.

"I too have been getting these calls, and in fact, I had come to the hostel last night as well; in order to pacify the students," Col. Hari Shankar defended himself.

"Anyway, Professor Shantanu has already made arrangements for a havan to be held in the hostel and hopefully, this problem will not be encountered anymore," Professor Indresan spoke. The last thing he needed was an altercation among his senior faculty.

"It was murder," a third year B. Tech Electronics student said to his girlfriend in a whisper while they were working in the Digital Signal Processing lab.

"My God! Are you sure? How do you know?" the girl asked.

"Have you ever known me to be wrong?" the boy was smug.

The girl knew he was right. He had his sources even among the faculty members, and so was always in the know of whatever was happening in the college. "So, who do you think has done it?" she asked.

"Mayank sir, of course. Who else?" her boyfriend whispered back.

The girl was stunned. She opened her mouth to speak, but nothing came out.

"You know, Mayank sir was out to get him," the boy reminded her.

Everybody had been aware of the ongoing feud between Vipin and Mayank. The root cause was Vipin's continued and adamant refusal to follow hostel rules and regulations. Mayank had recommended his ouster from the hostel on several occasions, but the management had overridden it due to one reason or the other. A few weeks before this incident, Mayank had openly threatened Vipin of dire consequences.

"But Mayank sir is out to get so many students. That does not make him a...," the girl stopped. The idea was simply preposterous, she thought.

"But you must agree that he is a weirdo of the highest order," the boy pointed out.

Mayank sir's oddities were the stuff of hostel legend. It was widely accepted that he never slept, at least not at night when it was time for ordinary mortals to do so. No matter in which part of the boys' hostel there was some mischief, at whichever hour of the night, Mayank would promptly reach there like a jinn and put a spanner in the works. No one had as yet figured out how he did it; but most conjectured that it was courtesy his vast student spy-network.

"Yes. He is certainly peculiar," the girl had to concede.

"Both of you please see me in my office after the practical,"

Professor Shantanu spoke blandly, startling them. They had no idea when he had come up behind them or how much he had heard.

Professor Shantanu was back in his lab, more troubled now than he had been before going for his walk. Naresh was seated on a chair beside him. Could there be some truth in what he had just overheard about the involvement of Mayank in the murder? And how did that boy know about the murder? These students were far too clever for their own good, he thought. No matter how confidential some news was, they managed to ferret it out like chipmunks on a trail of nuts.

He wondered whether to discuss it with Naresh. How much should he reveal to him? He was sorely tempted to tell him the truth, for he wanted to discuss aspects of the case that were troubling him. Maybe Naresh already knew the truth. And Professor Shantanu really needed to get some student input, particularly regarding the complicity of Mayank.

He decided to approach the topic from a tangent. "I suppose you must have read the newspaper report criticizing MIST?" he asked.

"Yes," Naresh replied.

"Well then, what do you make of this entire business now?" the professor asked.

"I think sir that somehow the Shivalik Institute has prompted the newspaper to carry such adverse news about us. Otherwise, it is a simple case of suicide and the matter should be laid to rest," Naresh spoke blandly.

"I see." There did not seem to be any scope for further discussion unless he revealed what he knew to Naresh, Professor

Shantanu concluded.

"And with due respect, sir, if I may speak my mind...," Naresh paused delicately.

"Yes, yes, my boy, by all means. You know I encourage everyone to think for themselves," Professor Shantanu egged him on.

"I think sir that you don't really need to talk to so many students and look into the matter so thoroughly. Human nature being what it is, you never know when a person, especially a young student, may be prompted to take such a step. Who knows what was actually going on in Vipin's mind at that time or what had transpired moments or days before he took this step?" Naresh said. His guileless eyes looked earnestly at the professor through his rather thick spectacles.

Professor Shantanu looked back at him; he was about to say something. But just then, the director's peon entered. "Sir, you need to attend a meeting," he said.

Professor Shantanu followed reluctantly. Would he ever get any work done with the number of meetings that were conducted in this place? he thought.

"You know the latest?" the Electronics Head, Professor Mishra, said to the Electrical Head, Professor Dinkar, over the phone.

"What?" Professor Dinkar was sitting in his office cabin and getting bored. He had no classes that day. Although it felt great, it did cause a certain emptiness, not having to teach for a whole day.

"It wasn't suicide!" Professor Mishra spoke in a forceful whisper.

"What? Oh my God! What do you mean?" Professor Dinkar could not bring himself to say the word aloud.

"Yes. The post-mortem has revealed that it was murder," Professor Mishra said.

There was silence.

"I remember, Professor Shantanu was telling me that Inspector Bisht said that there was something not quite right about the ligature marks on the neck of the boy," Professor Dinkar said.

"There you have it."

"This is terrible. Nothing like this has ever happened here," Professor Dinkar said.

"Yes. There has never even been a suicide in the campus and murder is something unthinkable," Professor Mishra concurred.

"But are you sure?" Professor Dinkar was sceptical.

"Of course. Apparently this being such a sensitive matter, Mr. Bisht came and met the chairman as soon as he learnt of the post-mortem results."

There was silence.

"Singhalji must be really upset. This will lead to the very thing that he was trying to avoid," Professor Mishra continued.

"Yes, there will be considerable bad press, and it will probably impact our admissions this year," Professor Dinkar said.

"Yes, in fact the police should find the culprit…er…the murderer," Professor Mishra's voice lowered to a whisper. "And they should find him as soon as possible, so that there is a satisfactory end to the matter and we can put up a justified front to the press."

"But who could have done it and why?" Professor Dinkar said.

"Yes, that is what I have been wondering."

"I'm disconnecting the call; the director's peon is here. Maybe there will be a meeting," Professor Dinkar said.

"O.k. then, see you there," Professor Mishra said.

CHAPTER – 8

"The post-mortem report has revealed that Vipin did not commit suicide but was murdered!" Professor Indresan's tense tone mirrored the anxiousness writ all over his face.

There was shocked stillness as all the heads tried to assimilate the ghastly news.

"Needless to say, this does not augur well for the institute at all," the director continued. "Now we have to decide how to handle the situation. On the one hand, there will be an investigation by the police. On the other, there will be bad press and then there is the question of whether we should allow this news to reach the students."

"Sir, if this news gets in the papers, then automatically the students will learn of it," Professor Girish Shukla being the first to recover, pointed out the obvious.

"Er... yes, you are right. Then what do we do? It could have a very bad effect upon the students," Professor Indresan looked confused.

"We should expand the counselling team that we had constituted the other day, and also employ a professional counsellor who can be available for the students in the evening," Professor Shantanu said.

"Yes sir. *Woh kya kehte hain,* that is a good idea," Col. Akash gathered his wits and said.

"Fine then, there is the question of the press and the police investigation," the director continued.

"Sir, we have to also determine how the news is to be

conveyed to the students," Professor Mrityunjaya reminded him.

"Ah! Yes." For a moment, a look of helplessness passed over the countenance of the director. He had certainly been better off at IIT. What in the world had prompted him to take up this ghastly job? Firmly, banishing the thought from his mind, he decided to focus on the matter at hand.

Exercising his authority, he said, "Professor Bhardwaj, you can be in charge of informing the students. Also, please expand the counselling team and work out the counselling schedule and inform me about it by today evening."

"But sir, why will anybody listen to me for being in the counselling team?" Professor Bhardwaj swallowed, distressed at being put in a spot like that.

"You are just being asked to constitute the team and the schedule on paper. Then you bring it to me and I will bring out the order from the director's office," Professor Indresan was happy that no one had the kind of power that he was able to brandish with such ease.

"Right, sir," Professor Bhardwaj hoped that no one would come to know that he was the one to propose the names of the faculty members who would have to counsel the students. "Well, that is done," the director was pleased. "Now about the press. What do we do? Our main concern is that the institute should not get any bad publicity."

Everybody knew that he was actually worried about G.D. Singhal's explicit dictum that MIST should remain untouched by adverse news, no matter what.

There was silence. No one spoke.

Unconsciously Professor Indresan's fingers rose to his right ear. He was about to pull out a lock of hair, but checked himself in time. Quickly, he brought down his hand and kept it behind his back.

Professor Tandon took note of it and thought that normally the director never toyed with his curls in a meeting; today he was really stressed. Taking pity on him, he said, "Sir, I think perhaps our management has some links with the press and they should prevail upon them to present the institute in an unbiased light."

"Yes sir," Col Akash seconded his opinion.

"Ah well," Professor Indresan continued. "I have spoken to the management and they will certainly do their part. But as director of the institute, I should also release a formal statement."

It was clear that the management had instructed the director to do this, and they may already have taken steps to keep bad publicity to a minimum.

"Actually, the major concern is that the Shivalik Institute of Technology might take advantage of the situation and show us in a bad light," Professor Indresan continued.

Everybody knew that the Shivalik Institute of Technology (SIT) located at the other end of the city was their rival in every sense of the term. It was common knowledge that there was a perennial game of one-upmanship between the two institutes. And it was alleged that the Shivalik Institute did not baulk at underhand activities to achieve its ends. After all, hundreds of crores were at stake.

Now he had come to the crux of the matter, the Dean of Students thought. This was probably G.D. Singhal's major apprehension.

"Yes, well, we cannot do much about that," Professor Girish Shukla said, his cleft lip quivering with unease.

"I think, sir, we should limit ourselves to issuing a matter-of-fact press release and deal with Shivalik as and when the occasion arises." Professor Shantanu said. If he did not offer solutions, this meeting would go on forever.

"Yes sir," everybody quickly agreed and the meeting ended.

The next day, all the local papers carried a sombre news report about the death being murder and not suicide. There was a matter-of-fact line mentioning that the police were carrying on their investigations.

Professor Shantanu was sitting in his lab with Naresh. "So now you know why I was speaking about this death being peculiar," he said.

"Yes sir," Naresh said dutifully.

"I cannot believe that it could be an inside job," Professor Shantanu spoke absently. Evidently his brain was working at top-speed.

"Why sir?"

"Well, you see, I have found a way in which an outside person could have reached Vipin's room," Professor Shantanu shared his findings. He knew he could implicitly trust Naresh.

"In that case, the person should have had inside help also," Naresh said the very thing that was troubling Professor Shantanu.

"Yes," he concurred.

They fell silent.

"Sir, the director has called you to his office," the director's peon intruded into his thoughts.

"I'll be back soon," Professor Shantanu followed the peon.

The director was alone in his office. He was absently twirling a lock of hair around his right index finger.

Professor Shantanu sat down quietly.

"Oh, good — you are here," Professor Indresan said. After a while he continued, "I understand you are looking into the matter."

Evidently, the director must have learnt of Professor Shantanu's visit to the boys' hostel and his extensive talks with students, faculty members, wardens etc. connected with Vipin.

"Yes. I could not sit idle in the face of such a horrendous situation," Professor Shantanu paused. Briefly, he explained about investigating the murder while at IIT. "So I decided to investigate this murder too and was planning to inform you at the first available opportunity," he finished.

"This is a good decision," Professor Indresan looked relieved. "I think we will let Inspector Bisht carry on with his enquiry, but you also go ahead and do your own investigation. Feel free to talk to anyone who you suspect has any information or knows anything about the murder. These are dire circumstances and I will feel better if you are directly involved in the problem," he elaborated. "Please keep me informed of your progress," he said after a pause.

"Yes; don't worry. As soon as I learn anything, I'll inform you immediately," Professor Shantanu assured him.

Gratefully, the director nodded. "In fact, I will tell Singhalji also about your investigation. I'm sure he will also be reassured to know that you are looking into it because you will have the best interest of MIST in mind," he said.

Professor Shantanu nodded.

"Meanwhile, Vibha is here almost everyday, wanting to know about the progress. She says she will not rest till her brother's murderer is brought to book," Professor Indresan looked troubled again.

"Yes, well, that is natural. But then, I hope you have explained to her that there is not much we can do and that it is for the police to do the needful," Professor Shantanu paused. "Which they are doing, I suppose," he continued.

"Yes. I have. She has also left a soft copy of Vipin's e-journal and some other files which reassert that it cannot possibly be suicide," Professor Indresan sighed.

"Right. I think one copy can be given to Mr. Bisht and I too will like to have a copy," Professor Shantanu said.

"Sure," Professor Indresan was only too glad to get the so-called evidence off his hands.

Professor Shantanu left.

"Vipin had it coming to him since a long time," said Mohit to his roommate. The two second-year B.Tech students were sitting in their hostel room and copying the maths tutorial questions and answers from the tutorial copies of one of their classmates. The tutorial assignments had to be submitted the next day.

"Yes. Why do these teachers give us these tutorials, when they know very well that we just simply copy from each other?" the roommate asked.

"Arre they just want us to build our hand muscles. That's why AICTE (All India Council of Technical Education) has included these tutorial classes so that if we do not get any employment, we can at least carry bricks!" Mohit guffawed.

The classmate chuckled. All the while, his fingers wrote rapidly, "You are right, though. Vipin had it coming."

"Yes, in fact, I would have loved to kill him myself," Mohit said.

"Wh...what are you saying?" the roommate stopped writing.

"Why, have you forgotten how badly he treated us last year? I have never experienced such humiliation in my entire life," Mohit was bitter.

"Yes. He did go a bit far with you," the roommate concurred.

"I can never forget it as long as I live!" Mohit's voice rose.

"Hey c'mon, it's over. Now leave it. Forget about it. Remember — these same seniors are now helping us with notes and books like they had promised!" the roommate tried to pacify Mohit.

"So that gives them the right to treat us badly?" he paused. "And remember, Vipin had never helped us."

"Well, Vipin himself never studied, and he never jotted down any notes.. So how could he have helped us in anything?" the roommate said.

"Well, two weeks back I had gone to him for help related to my attendance. Actually, as you know, I was debarred from appearing for the sessional exams due to my short attendance and as a last resort, I went to Vipin."

"What could he have done in this context?" the roommate interrupted.

"Just listen. I told Vipin to include me as a member of his Mechtrika club and to tell the Dean of Students that I was involved in organising the tech-fest. You know that all the guys involved in the techfest got 10% extra attendance. And you know what? He refused. Point blank. Just like that," Mohit's voice was one that clearly expressed pain. "At that moment, I could have gladly killed him," his face twisted with hate.

The roommate looked into Mohit's frosty eyes. A shiver of fear went through his spine. Was it possible? No — no way. He had known Mohit since the past one and half years. They had met during hostel allocation; been allotted the same room and had been roommates and best friends ever since. But how well could one really know a person? He had better be careful. He had not seen this side of Mohit before. Should he tell someone? No — it was probably nothing... and yet...

Professor Shantanu's phone rang.

It was the mess-in-charge calling. "Sir, as you wanted, I'm sending the mess worker Ramadin to meet you."

"Who?" Professor Shantanu asked, puzzled for a moment.

"Ramadin was the mess worker who had an argument with Vipin, just before his death," the mess-in-charge explained.

"Ah yes. I remember. Please send him in," Professor Shantanu said.

A little later, Ramadin entered Professor Shantanu's office.

"What were you doing that night in the boys' hostel?" Professor Shantanu came directly to the matter at hand.

"Er...," Ramadin was taken aback and clearly not expecting this attack.

"Well, go on, tell me," Professor Shantanu was stern.

"I was not there," Ramadin mumbled.

"Which night were you not there?"

"Er... the night of the er... death!"

"How did you know I was talking of that particular night?" Professor Shantanu raised his voice.

"Er... because everybody is talking about that night," Ramadin was out of his depth now.

"And why would I call you to ask about it? You timings are till 8.30 p.m. only, isn't it?"

Ramadin was quiet.

"And you could have told me that in any case you are supposed to be in the hostel till 8.30 p.m. So, technically, I am questioning you about something which is normal for you," the professor paused. "Instead, you are giving unnecessary explanations."

Ramadin did not say anything. His face crumbled.

"Should I call the police and hand you over?" Professor Shantanu shouted. He rang the bell. The peon entered. "Call the security officer! I want him to call the police officer saab!" he spoke grimly.

"No, wait, saab, I have small children. Have mercy on me," Ramadin appeared close to tears.

Professor Shantanu waved the peon away. "Well then, tell me the truth and everything that happened."

"Sir, I was at fault for going to the hostel that night, I admit, but you see, that boy was terrible. He was so rude and treated me so badly. Saab, I'm also a human being. I'm poor and just a servant in all your eyes, but I have feelings," Ramadin spoke earnestly.

Professor Shantanu waited. He knew that he had to give Ramadin a patient hearing, only then the complete truth would come out. "Tell me what happened that night."

"Sir, please believe me. Sir, I only wanted to scare the boy. I had no other intention. I was angry, so very angry. Since the past three years, that boy had tortured me. I had had enough. Please believe me," Ramadin's eyes filled with tears.

"Go on," Professor Shantanu's tone softened.

"Well sir, I got drunk to give myself courage and then, then I went up to the boy's room. I had thought to threaten him. But he, he was already dead... hanging," Ramadin spoke falteringly.

"What time was this?"

"About 2 a.m. I did not do anything, saab."

"How did you enter the hostel at that time of the night?"

"I'm sorry sir. Please forgive me. But you see, I had become mad. I was not in my right mind," Ramadin paused.

Professor Shantanu waited patiently.

"I know I should not have done this... but you see, at the back of the hostel, at one place the boundary wall is very low. I simply jumped over it, climbed on to the balcony of a room. I knew that at night the boys of that room were always in the next apartment doing something on their computers. And then I climbed through the air-shaft and entered Vipin's room," he paused. "I'm sorry saab. I know I should not have done such a thing."

Professor Shantanu nodded, "Then?"

"When I saw the boy hanging, I was petrified and hurried back through the same way out of the hostel as fast as I could."

"Why didn't you tell all this to someone?" Professor

Shantanu admonished him, even though he knew full well the answer to his question.

"Saab, I didn't want to lose my job. Now saab, only you can save me. Please, I beg you," tears poured freely down his pock-marked cheeks. "I'm ready for any punishment. But not at the cost of my job. Because truly, sir I didn't do anything," he pleaded.

After dismissing Ramadin, Professor Shantanu walked outside the academic block. Should he believe him? What type of boy was this Vipin to have aroused so much anger in a simple mess-worker? Of their own volition, his steps turned towards block three of the boys' hostel. He walked up to the infamous apartment. The hostel warden let him in without question.

He went into the bathroom and looked at the entry point of the airshaft. He would have to rule that out if he believed Ramadin, he thought. Well, at least his hunch was correct. There had been an entry thought the airshaft, after all. But had it led to the murder? There was also the presence of poison in his system. Had the killer first tried to poison Vipin and after he was sufficiently weakened by the poison, strangled him?

Then there was the question of Gurpreet. The matter remained as complicated as ever, he thought. Ramadin, Mayank and Gurpreet; all three seemed to be involved in some way or the other. But their involvement seemed merely circumstantial. He needed concrete information. For that, he needed to investigate further. But where should he start? He decided to review all the information he had. Mayank's involvement was indicated mostly by the students. They had ample reason to indicate his collusion; but it all seemed subjective actually. He needed to analyse things systematically, beginning with Gurpreet.

It was indeed a queer coincidence that Gurpreet had visited the boys' hostel that night. It clearly indicated her connection to the death. Had she gone there to meet Vipin? To what purpose? To kill him? Why would she do that? Was it true that she was involved with Vipin as some of the students had confided to him earlier? And if so, would she have been able to overpower a strong boy like Vipin? No, that was not plausible, he thought. Although Gurpreet was a strapping girl and she seemed strong enough, yet...

He needed to speak to her. That would surely lead him somewhere. Making the decision, Professor Shantanu strode to Col Akash's office. He would take her local guardian's number and address and pay her a visit. But before that, he needed to get as much background information about her as possible.

Returning to his lab, he sent for the girls' hostel warden and Gurpreet's roommate. They had nothing much to offer except to corroborate what he already knew about Gurpreet being a loner.

The roommate was a final year Pharmacy student. This was not the usual living arrangement. Usually girls of a similar branch were assigned the same room. If that was not possible at all times, then at least they were from the same course. And by that logic, the roommate should have at least been from some branch of B.Tech, if not from B.Tech Mechanical.

Since both were from Gurdaspur, so, as a special request, they had been assigned the same room, even though Gurpreet was one year junior; the girls' hostel warden explained.

"Gurpreet is a wonderful girl," the roommate was tearful.

"Yes. But why did she do this? Cut her veins like this?" Professor Shantanu asked encouragingly.

"I don't know," the roommate answered blankly.

Looking at her lips firmly pursed together, it was clear to him that it would be difficult to extract any kind of information related to Gurpreet's relationship with Vipin. "Tell me about your friendship," the professor tried another track.

"Oh, she is great. Do you know, she helps me in everything! Whether it is shopping or completing my assignments, she is always there for me," the roommate smiled.

"But how can she help you in assignments, when she is from Mechanical?"

"Well now! She knows more about Pharmacy than I do!" the roommate smiled wistfully. "She often says that she should have taken Pharmacy instead of Mechanical."

Professor Shantanu smiled and nodded gently.

"Why only recently she went with me on a field trip to Chamoli for my project related to the verification of the medicinal usages of a few of the plants of this region," the roommate was in earnest. "In fact, she did all the work on it."

"What kind of work?"

"Well, you know, she had detailed talks with the local population and based upon their inputs, listed the various uses of the plants of the region, their medicinal values, if any, etc. etc.," the roommate explained. "And only after this preliminary finding did I get down to the actual lab work about verifying the claims made by these hill people."

"I see," the Professor said.

"Actually, I am doing a study of the pharmacological

efficacies of endemic plants of the Chamoli region." Evidently, the roommate was passionate about her project.

"Do you know — our ancient texts, particularly those of Shushruta, give a list of plants with medicinal properties. We collect these plants, get it verified by a taxonomist, and only then go on for the lab study to determine the medicinal properties," the roommate was in earnest.

"Good. I'm glad to see how ardent you are about your work. You will go far," the professor genuinely meant the praise.

The roommate smiled happily.

"Well, if there is anything you might like to tell me, please feel free to get in touch," Professor Shantanu knew there was not much more that he was likely to learn from her about Gurpreet.

"Are you always this serious?" Pierre asked Professor Shantanu.

The two were having dinner at the guesthouse. Living together in adjacent quarters, they often found themselves together during mealtimes.

"No, no. I'm sorry," Professor Shantanu smiled. "Its just that I'm a little preoccupied these days."

"You mean, because of the murder?" Pierre asked.

"Yes. I cannot rest till I get to the bottom of it," Professor Shantanu said.

"Do you suspect someone?" Pierre asked.

"Yes," Professor Shantanu paused, "but I'm not sure ..."

"Give it some time. Perhaps then you will be able to come to some conclusion," Pierre suggested.

"I suppose you are right." Professor Shantanu decided to

change the topic, "Tell me how you like the college?"

"Oh it's very nice," Pierre smiled.

"And how is your research coming along?"

"Oh, very well," Pierre paused. "Though I do feel very bad that so many Tibetans are forced to stay here almost like refugees," he continued.

"But I believe they are quite well-off," Professor Shantanu said.

"Yes; but it is not the same as being able to live in your own country," Pierre was emphatic.

"Yes, I suppose you are right," Professor Shantanu concurred. Dinner was almost over and there was no need to stretch the point.

CHAPTER – 9

"Hey, you know what, the Chinese Premier along with top officials will be visiting Dehradun!" Suresh announced.

"So?" Nitish asked.

The two were on their usual early morning swim at the hostel pool. Suresh was the state swimming champion and never neglected his early morning practice. On most days, he practised during the evening slots as well. Nitish accompanied him whenever possible, though he was not too fond of swimming himself.

"So, isn't it exciting? For the first time, the Chinese Premier is visiting Dehradun," Suresh said.

"But why would he want to visit Dehradun? Don't these guys visit only Delhi and then they are off to wherever they come from?" Nitish said.

"Yes. You are right. They've already had their meetings in Delhi. But this time I think it is because joint military exercises are scheduled between the Indian Army and the People's Liberation Army of China."

"So?" Nitish was bored.

"So, isn't it exciting that all the Chinese military top brass would also be visiting?" Suresh said.

"But I still cannot understand why they are coming here."

"Arre, these joint exercises will be held somewhere near Chakrata and they will finalise it with the Army officials at Indian Military Academy," Suresh explained.

"Why?" Nitish was least concerned.

"Actually, an MOU was signed in 2006 between the two countries for increased cooperation and exchange in the field of defence," Suresh paused.

"The first Sino-Indian Joint Training Exercise was conducted at Kunming, South-West China in 2007," Suresh continued.

"Ok," Nitish said.

"Then in December 2008, joint military exercises were held in Karnataka where the Belgaum Army Commando School hosted a 147-member Chinese Army contingent."

"Oh," Nitish said.

"In fact, some years ago, the Chinese Premier had visited the Indian Space Research Organisation and agreed on a plan for increased collaboration in applications of space technology," Suresh was in full flow.

Nitish was quiet. He could not be bothered to respond.

"Now they are coming here to discuss the next phase of the future military sharing and exercises. They are also planning for increased collaborations in science and technology. So maybe they will visit the Defence Research and Development Organisation etc. also," Suresh elaborated.

Nitish nodded half-heartedly.

"So now I think security is being beefed up at the Military Academy and in the areas surrounding it and the Defence Organization," Suresh said.

"Well, how do you know so much about it?" Nitish asked.

"Duffer, some of us are just better informed than the others," Suresh preened.

"Oh c'mon," Nitish said.

"Arre, you know that I'm preparing for the Civil Services and

I keep reading up about everything," Suresh had aspirations of becoming an IAS officer, which was the ultimate dream of many young students from Bihar. He had started preparations in right earnest and planned to appear for the exams immediately after his B.Tech. Every afternoon saw him in the library religiously digesting at least three newspapers.

"Well, anyway, what do we have to do with it?" Nitish was fed up with all the information.

"Nothing, really. I was simply updating your G.K. so that you become less of a moron than you already are," Suresh laughed.

Nitish smiled gamely.

"You know — actually I am not being able to study. This thing about Gurpreet and Vipin keeps going on and on in my head," Suresh said on a serious note.

"Why haven't you talked about it to Professor Shantanu as yet?" Nitish said.

"Yes, I will. Right away after the swim," Suresh said.

There was a timid knock on Professor Shantanu's door. It was Ms. MIST, Kanika. This was a surprise. She had never come to him for anything and as far as he knew, she had never approached any teacher for any academic matter. Perhaps there was something serious that she wanted to talk about. As she sat down, Professor Shantanu noted that her usually perky demeanour was considerably diminished; and there was a hint of dark circles around her rather large eyes.

"Yes beta, what can I do for you?" he asked softly.

"Er... sir, I want to tell you something...," she spoke softly.

"Yes. Yes, go on," Professor Shantanu spoke encouragingly.

"It's nothing really, it is probably very silly," she paused.

Professor Shantanu waited patiently.

"Well, you see, Vipin's best friend was Deepak. And Deepak is missing," Kanika's anxious voice was barely above a whisper.

"Missing? What do you mean?" Professor Shantanu was perplexed. Would another body be found now? The terrifying thought flashed through his mind. He shut his mind against the thought.

"Sir, you know how important attendance is. And yet, Deepak has not been coming to college since the past one month," she explained her concern.

"Perhaps he is ill," Professor Shantanu suggested.

"No sir, we have tried to get in touch with him, but he is not responding to our phone calls, or mails or anything," she looked troubled.

"How is that possible?"

"Well sir, his mobile says that this number does not exist; and as for our e-mails, there is simply no response."

"And how could he leave the hostel for such an extended period without permission?" Professor Shantanu asked.

"He is a day scholar," she paused. "Actually he and Vipin were working on a project about which they were really crazy. And then for him to suddenly vanish...," Kanika's voice trailed away.

Just then, Professor Shantanu recalled that Deepak's name was in the list that Vipin's roommate had given him. But since the name was in the 'friends' category and he was on leave, the Professor had not really bothered to pursue it. Clearly, this was an oversight on his part.

"Ok, now confirm the facts for me. This Deepak is a day scholar and a classmate-cum-bestfriend-cum-project-partner of Vipin and is on leave since the last one month, right?" Professor Shantanu said.

"Yes sir. You please find out. I have a feeling that there is something strange going on," she pleaded.

"Right, don't worry. I'll find out everything."

The professor hesitated for a split -second and then asked, "Were you involved with Vipin?"

"Er... sir, I don't know what you mean," the girl tried to collect herself in the face of the unexpected question.

"You can tell me, beta," the professor spoke softly.

Kanika hesitated.

Professor Shantanu looked at her understandingly.

"Er... well... Vipin used to like me very much," she paused. "And I liked him very much too."

The professor decided to leave it at that.

After she left, Professor Shantanu sent for Deepak's personal file and the faculty coordinator of his class. How had he overlooked this? He fished out the lists that Vipin's roommate and Naresh had compiled for him. Deepak's name figured near the top of the roommate's list with an asterisk saying he was absent. This explained why he had ignored his name. But he had better look into the details of this boy. His name was not present in Naresh's list. But then probably Naresh did not know about all of Vipin's friends.

The faculty coordinator arrived. He knew nothing about Deepak being absent. Apparently, neither the Department Head nor Professor Girish Shukla nor Col Akash knew about Deepak having taken such a long leave. He was simply being marked absent. Maybe it was all unrelated; but recalling Kanika's grim face, Professor Shantanu made a mental note about checking up further on Deepak.

But first, he needed to verify the extent of Gurpreet's involvement. He had to go about it in a systematic manner, otherwise he would end up in circles. Before proceeding further, he decided to find out about Mr. Bisht's progress. The director would probably have information about it.

"Has Inspector Bisht found anything?" Professor Shantanu asked the director.

"No. On the other hand, if he has, he is only telling the chairman. But if he had told something of significance to the chairman, then surely I would have also been informed," he paused. "Time and again, he turns up in the campus, wanting to talk to some student or the other, or to visit the hostel. But what progress he has made, he only knows," Professor Indresan sighed.

"I suppose he will inform us or the chairman, once he comes to some concrete conclusion," Professor Shantanu said.

"Yes. In the meantime, we must get on with as much semblance of normalcy as we can," Professor Indresan said.

"Well, I am going to visit Gurpreet and see what I can gather from her," Professor Shantanu said.

At the home of Gurpreet's local guardian, Professor Shantanu found her parents rather reluctant to let him meet her. Apparently, the visit by the police officer had left her disturbed. And in any case, she would be going back to the hostel in a couple of days. He could just as easily have waited and talked to her when she was back at MIST, they pointed out. He apologised and explained that it was imperative that he talk to her at the earliest. They led him to her room and left.

Gurpreet was listlessly looking out of the window.

After a little small talk, Professor Shantanu came to the point, "Beta, were you involved with Vipin?"

She looked pained, but kept quiet.

"See beta, I know you were involved with him. Everyone knows it. There's no point denying it," he was matter-of-fact in his approach.

Gurpreet gave an imperceptible nod.

"Why did you slash your wrist?" he asked.

She remained immobile.

"Were you attempting suicide?" the professor persisted.

Tears welled up in her eyes, but she did not speak.

"Beta, I know this is distressing. But you must speak up. I want to help you!" he spoke insistently.

"No one can help me! Vipin is dead and nothing matters now," her voice held extreme despair.

"No beta, life must go on," he felt aggrieved seeing her state.

Tears poured from her eyes.

Steeling himself, he asked, "After Vipin died, why did you attempt suicide? Did you do it because you did not want to live without him? Or was it something more?"

She looked at him in anguish through her tears.

"It was something more, wasn't it? For Vipin never loved you, did he? So in any case you would have to live without him, wouldn't you?" The professor knew he was being cruel, but it had to be done. There was no other way he could get her to speak.

"You didn't attempt suicide because of Vipin's death, you did it because of some thing else, isn't it?" he spoke forcefully.

Her eyes widened in surprise.

"Yes, I know. I know you had gone there that night to kill him!" he announced forcefully.

"No!" she shouted, her tears forgotten. "I didn't, didn't...," she covered her face with her hands.

"Yes you did!" the professor shouted. "You poisoned him and when that did not lead to his death, you strangled him and then hanged him to make it look like suicide. You are a terribly wicked young lady, yes you are!" he bellowed.

She looked at him in anger. "What proof do you have? From where could I get the poison and then manage to hang him and escape unseen?" she challenged.

Professor Shantanu felt a flicker of admiration for her spunk. "You were seen leaving the boys' hostel that night!" he spoke severely.

She looked taken aback. "So? That does not prove anything!" she countered aggressively.

"The post-mortem report said the poison was one extracted from a local plant," he paused. He decided to go with his gut feeling. "The same one which you took while helping your roommate in her pharmacy project that documents the medicinal uses of local plants!" he declared triumphantly.

Gurpreet looked defeated. All her bluster vanished. "I'm sorry, really sorry. But I didn't kill him," she spoke in desolation. "You must believe me," she entreated.

"Tell me everything," Professor Shantanu was firm.

"Sir, I loved him. I truly loved him. I went there that night to reason with him," she paused.

"Yes. Go on," he said.

"But even before going to meet him, I knew that he would not see things my way. That Kanika had cast a spell on him," her voice was bitter.

"So I took some coffee and added a bit of poison, just in case. I put in a very little amount, just enough to cause a stomach upset. It certainly wasn't enough to cause death!" she spoke convincingly.

"Then?" he asked.

"I took the coffee with me in a flask, along with some pastry. And when he did not listen to me, then I offered him the coffee and pastry," her eyes took on a vindictive hue.

"I told him that it was a peace offering so that we may remain friends forever," she continued, her voice lifeless.

Professor Shantanu nodded. "Then what did you do?"

"Sir, I never wanted to actually harm him. I just wanted to teach him a lesson," she pleaded. "And after he finished the coffee and pastry, I left. He was absolutely fine when I left him. I knew it would be a while before the poison would take effect," she said.

He waited for her to continue.

"Then when I heard that he had died, I... I assumed that I had put in too much poison and it had led to the death. I never bothered to ask anyone how he had died. I just assumed that I had caused his death," she was distraught. "Then in a fit of remorse, I decided to take my own life," she spoke plaintively.

"Are you sure you know nothing about the hanging?" Professor Shantanu spoke harshly.

"Sir, I swear to God I know nothing about the hanging. I

have told you the absolute truth," she implored.

"Then who strangled him?" he asked grimly.

"Sir, since the time I regained consciousness, there is only one thought in my mind. Who would have wanted to kill him? I knew right away that he would not have committed suicide. I knew someone had murdered him. But who?" she looked bewildered.

"He was not liked by many people," Professor Shantanu stated.

"Yes. But I don't think anyone would go to the extent of killing him," she said.

"Except someone who loved him and then had the love turned to hate," he goaded her. He was not entirely convinced of her innocence.

"Love-hate, I don't know what I feel for him or felt for him. But truly sir, I did not have anything to do with his hanging. The poison, I admit I administered, but it was such a small amount. It was only intended to make him fall ill for a day or two," her voice remained emotionless.

Professor Shantanu looked into her eyes. She looked back unblinkingly.

"Would Gurpreet do this sort of thing? Would she commit murder for unrequited love?" Professor Shantanu asked Naresh rhetorically. He was back in his lab after having visited Gurpreet.

"Love can lead one to do all kinds of things!" Naresh said emphatically. "There is no greater passion than love," there was a faraway look on his face.

Professor Shantanu looked at him askance. This was the first time that Naresh had said something with so much feeling. And that too, about love. As far as he knew, Naresh had only one passion in life; and that was research. Perhaps he was mistaken. Perchance there was more to him than just work. But love? From what he had observed till date, Naresh seemed to have no interest in girls. But then, Professor Shantanu was himself unobservant about the numerous so-called romantic liaisons going on in the campus, he reflected wryly.

"But it would require great strength to strangle a brawny boy like Vipin," he came back to the topic at hand.

"Well, come to think of it, Gurpreet can be a match for anyone," Naresh pointed out.

He was right, reflected Professor Shantanu. Gurpreet was certainly well-built. "But it seems impossible," he said instead; unwilling to believe her connivance in this dastardly act. Girls were soft, kind-hearted creatures hardly liable to indulge in such cruel acts. This was a somewhat gender-biased opinion though, he thought.

"Sir, let's look at the facts," Naresh seemed intent on his line of logic. "All the evidence points to her. She was seen at the boys' hostel. She has herself admitted to poisoning him and she is as strong as any boy her age," he paused.

"Everybody who knows her confirms that she is somewhat of a kook. And above all, she had the motive. The strongest motive of all. Unrequited love!" Naresh finished with a flourish.

Stated this way, Professor Shantanu had to concede that it seemed to make sense. But somehow, he was still not completely convinced that this was a simple case of a girl killing a boy as a result of being scorned in love. And besides, there was something niggling at the back of his mind — something he could not quite put a finger on ...

There was a knock on the lab door. "See who it is," Professor Shantanu said. "And tell him to come later."

"Sir, it is Suresh, a third year Computer Science student," Naresh re-entered and said.

"I hope you have sent him away."

"I tried sir, but he says that he wants to tell you something very important related to the murder."

"Ok, send him in."

Suresh entered.

"Well, tell me what is the important information you have?" Professor Shantanu came right to the point.

Suresh looked pointedly at Naresh.

Professor Shantanu waved at Naresh, prompting him to leave.

After being assured of complete confidentiality and of being given credit when it was due, Suresh sat down and related all that he knew. He disclosed everything related to his conclusions about Gurpreet's complicity, including the contents of her blog.

Professor Shantanu leaned back after Suresh had left. Could there be some truth to what he said? He began reading Gurpreet's blog which Suresh had obligingly opened at his request. This was one troubled and highly complex girl, Professor Shantanu concluded. Or, were all kids of this generation like this? he wondered. Then he came to the particular entries referred to by Suresh.

Several statements talked of the gloriousness of love and

the entries dated a few weeks later talked about the nobility of revenge. All kinds of examples from Lord Rama to the Pandavas were given to prove the point that revenge was righteous, holy, and even condoned by the scriptures and mythology. My God! this certainly aroused suspicion towards her. However, Professor Shantanu had to be sure. All this was pure conjecture. There were several loose threads; until they were tied, he could not draw any firm conclusion.

He decided to take a look at the soft copy of Vipin's e-journal and other files that his sister had handed over to the director. He also needed to check out the facts related to Deepak as brought to his notice by Kanika. The fact that Deepak, bestfriend-cum-project-partner of Vipin had not been attending college since the past one month, indicated something amiss somewhere. The college laid great emphasis upon attendance and for a student to not turn up for a month was certainly unusual. Perhaps Deepak knew something about Vipin's death.

Sure enough, Vipin's journal entries and other files clearly indicated that the duo were inseparable, as far as the project was concerned. They seemed to be passionate about their engine design and elements of some sort of bio-fuel. They had apparently also visited the Uttarakhand Renewable Energy Development Agency in order to gain information about the availability of fuel that was extracted from the Jatropha plant. Clearly, Deepak was obsessed with the project and was the driving force behind it. Without his constant prodding, Vipin could not proceed an inch.

Then there was an abrupt break in his journal regarding any mention of their project or proposed engine design or any such thing. It coincided with Deepak having taken long leave from the college. Oddly enough, Vipin too seemed to have no prior knowledge of it. There were journal entries about sending several plaintive mails to Deepak, seeking a response. Apparently, the mails had had no effect. Considering that Deepak had been so close to Vipin, this was mysterious and worth exploring, Professor Shantanu thought.

The last entry was dated three days prior to Vipin's death. It mentioned receiving a terse mail from Deepak saying that he was busy with something and so was not coming to college but would be back eventually after which they could resume their project. Vipin had apparently sent several mails in response to this last communication from Deepak, seeking his phone number and querying about his whereabouts; but there had been no response. This was unusual. Since these kids were perpetually online, Deepak should have responded to Vipin. This needed some looking into. Professor Shantanu decided to visit Deepak's home and find out the reason for his absence.

CHAPTER – 10

Saransh looked at himself in the mirror and grimaced. He wished for the umpteenth time that he was fair, well — if not fair, at least wheatish. He hated his skin, his features and everything about his physical appearance. God had truly been unkind to him. He was short, stocky, with the beginnings of a paunch; dyed hair that looked an unnatural shade of ebony; and to top it all, he had very dark skin colour.

All his life, Saransh had had to fight discrimination, which was at times covert, but mostly overt. For one, his appearance was repulsive and for the other, he was saddled with the SC (Scheduled Caste) tag. He had got admission in engineering, thanks to reservation. And no matter how hard he worked, neither his fellow students nor his professors acknowledged that he had any merit in him.

And now this job, where he had to teach these privileged kids; a majority of whom were good-looking(fair-skinned) as well. They had never faced any kind of discrimination in their entire fortunate lives. They all needed to be taught a lesson. The way they sneered at his pronunciation! Their supercilious air as if they knew more about engineering than he did was most irritating. Well, he would show them all. And that Vipin had already faced the music. That bastard who led the pack of brats who had made fun of him in his very first class... Saransh could never forget the humiliation in all his life.

The problem was that Saransh was unable to correctly pronounce certain letters of the alphabet; particularly 's' for which his articulation was 'sh' and 'p' which he pronounced as 'ph'. On that day when he entered the class for the first time, all the students stood up as a mark of respect. Pleased, Saransh smiled affably and greeted them with a cheery good morning and then without thinking about his pronunciation, said, "Everybody please shit down!" There were hoots of laughter and after that, there was no way he could live it down. During every class in this particular section, there was either some nasty comment scribbled on the whiteboard, or some barely audible murmurings, which he was sure, were dreadfully offensive.

And then Vipin had learnt of his background. Thereafter he and his cronies came armed with twisted questions, intent on discomfiting and shaming him publicly. Class after class Vipin and his group posed complex queries, which Saransh was somehow never able to answer satisfactorily; and the students soon classified him as a nincompoop. He knew they had nicknamed him 'quota-wallah-kaalu'. Quota being a reference to his SC status and kaalu, of course, for his skin colour.

Saransh was simply biding his time until there was a faculty vacancy in some government engineering college. There was sure to be some vacancy for the reserved class and now he had decided to go all out with a vengeance and encash his SC status. And why not? But not before he had taught these kids a lesson that they badly needed. Vipin was out; there were a few more to go and then he would be free of the demons that plagued him constantly.

Professor Shantanu knocked on Brigadier Kalra's door. Naresh accompanied him. Deepak's father, Brigadier Kalra, was a senior Army officer posted at the Indian Military Academy. He lived within the Academy premises, which was located a good 20 kms from MIST.

Preliminaries over, Professor Shantanu came directly to the point and asked why his son was not attending college. Brigadier Kalra replied that there was nothing wrong. It was necessitated in the middle of the college semester due to some urgent family matter, which he was not at liberty to discuss with anyone outside the family. He explained everything tersely in a tone that encouraged no questions or comments.

Throughout this exchange, Mrs. Kalra sat immobile. Professor Shantanu knew instinctively that she wanted to say something but was unable to do so. There was definitely something not quite right here.

"Well then, can I have his current phone number as I would like to speak to him about a project that he has been working on?" Professor Shantanu tried a different trajectory.

"I'm sorry he does not have a phone number since he is in Singapore, and it would have turned out to be expensive," Brigadier Kalra returned after a miniscule pause.

"Singapore?" Professor Shantanu was puzzled.

"His grandmother lives in Singapore," Brigadier Kalra said.

"Well then, how about his grandmother's number?" Professor Shantanu asked.

"I'm sorry that would not be possible. She is an old lady and I do not wish for her to be disturbed unnecessarily," Brigadier Kalra's voice was steely. Yet his eyes seemed sad somehow.

"Your queries will have to wait till Deepak returns," he spoke louder than was necessary. Mrs. Kalra suddenly got up jerkily and disappeared inside; but not before Professor Shantanu noted her eyes misting.

They took their leave. Professor Shantanu walked ahead; but as soon as the door closed, he motioned Naresh to wait, and quickly doubled back.

He went round to the window adjacent to the drawing room. This was the room that Mrs. Kalra had disappeared into, he reasoned. His actions were soon justified. He could hear raised voices. He leaned closer to decipher the words. There were heavy drapes on the closed windows.

He heard snatches. ‘“Please get him back,” this was Mrs. Kalra. "I’m doing the best I can,” this was her husband. Professor Shantanu had heard enough. He walked away quietly before ~~he~~ they could catch him snooping. As they headed back to MIST, Professor Shantanu asked Naresh what he made of the day’s incident. Naresh’s response surprised him.

“Sir, I think it is a family matter. Deepak must have indulged in some mischief due to which he may have been sent away. It has nothing to do with Vipin,” Naresh said.

Had he been wrong about Naresh’s intelligence after all? Professor Shantanu wondered. Naresh knew all the aspects about the closeness between Vipin and Deepak and yet, why was he saying this?

Further, Deepak’s record at MIST over the past three years had been impeccable. In fact, he was diametrically opposite to Vipin. He was an exemplary student; disciplined, polite and courteous. Naresh knew this as well. So, how could such a boy indulge in something mischievous at home? Something prompted Professor Shantanu to keep these thoughts to himself.

Ordinarily, he would have argued the point with Naresh.

"You know, the Electrical Head shouted at me in class today, because I did not appear for the first sessional test and did not submit any assignment either," a third year Electrical student said.

"Oh God, don't you know that he is very particular about such things?" her classmate responded.

A bunch of students were sitting on the benches scattered around the Nescafe stall located within the campus. The conversation veered around the fact that most of the teachers were very strict about the students appearing for sessional tests, submitting assignments, regular attendance and following all institute rules and regulations. Students who didn't bow down to these norms were always reprimanded by the teachers.

"These teachers are too harsh with us, you know!" Nitish said.

"Yeah. And the wardens are even more so," a boy concurred gloomily.

"Yeah. Particularly Mayank sir. He makes sure we toe the line in following the hostel rules," a boy said.

"And he often goes to an extreme as far as the hostel is concerned," a third year student said angrily.

"True! In fact, Mayank sir is somewhat crazy!" The Electrical student spoke agitatedly.

"Yeah. I'm sure he is a psycho!" a girl said.

"Yeah, he sends shivers down my spine," Nitish said.

"You know, I think there is something peculiar about Saransh sir also. And... I feel he too had it for Vipin," a third year Mechanical student said.

"What makes you say that?" Nitish said.

"Well, you know how much Vipin and his group have troubled Saransh sir," the boy responded.

"Who Saransh sir?" a girl asked.

"Arre that Quota-wallah-kalu who says shit for sit,' a boy smirked.

A few students tittered whilst others smiled.

"Anyway, what I was saying was that Vipin was very wicked to Saransh sir," the third year Mechanical boy repeated.

"Yes, that is true. But Vipin has been nasty to almost every teacher since he joined MIST. That does not mean every teacher is out to get him," a girl said.

"Yes, but you all will agree he was relentless in torturing Saransh sir. And it was a bit mean of him to make fun of a person's god-given appearance. And besides, it is not sir's fault that he comes from a particular background," the third year Mechanical boy elaborated.

"And remember the look of hatred on Saransh sir's face that day when Vipin had gone too far?" he continued. "I'm sure he could have killed Vipin that day," the boy spoke somewhat forcefully.

"You really think so?" Nitish said.

"Yes," the boy said.

"Then maybe we should tell someone," Suresh who was quiet until now, suddenly spoke up.

"I think I was Asian in my previous birth," Pierre said.

"Why do you think so?" Professor Shantanu smiled. "And more importantly, do you believe in rebirth?" He was eager to divert his mind from the complex conundrum that was of late constantly weighing upon his mind.

It was Sunday morning and after a leisurely breakfast, the two were sitting in the lawn in front of the guesthouse, gazing at the Mussoorie hills and sharing a cup of coffee. It was a much-needed respite for Professor Shantanu.

Pierre Iselin and Professor Shantanu had developed a tenuous friendship over the days, after being thrown together at the guesthouse.

"I felt at home the first time I came to Asia. Whether it is Nepal or India, I feel as if I belong here. Now I have to just somehow manage to go to Tibet. That is the final frontier," he said in the manner of the refrain of the old television series Star Trek.

"How did you get interested in this whole Tibet thing?" Professor Shantanu asked.

"Actually, my step-father is a professor of Buddhist Philosophy, Ethics and Non-violence, in the School of Philosophy at the University of Tasmania; and somehow, I just picked it up from there," Pierre said.

"And how did your mother meet him?"

"Well, she had gone as a visiting professor to the University of Tasmania, and the rest was destiny," Pierre smiled.

"He must have been a rather nice father to you for you to follow in his footsteps," Professor Shantanu smiled back.

"Of course. I never really knew my real father. He left when I was six," Pierre's tone became edgy.

"So, you were telling me about your being an Asian in your previous birth," Professor Shantanu hastily changed the subject.

"Yes. Everything I discover as a part of my research feels oddly familiar as if I already know it; and that I am simply evoking it. In fact, most of the places I visit give me a great sense of déjà vu. When I visited the Sakya Temple near Clement Town today, I swear I felt as though I had already been there earlier."

"Really?" the professor paused, somewhat surprised.

"But the temple is really beautiful, isn't it?" he continued. This French fellow seemed a bit soft in the head, Professor Shantanu thought.

"Yes, it is. There is a great sense of peace about the place. I think I will plan to settle somewhere here for the rest of my life," Pierre said with a faraway look in his eyes.

"Actually, I saw that student of yours at the Tibetan colony up on Rajpur the other day," Pierre said after a while.

"My student? Who?" Professor Shantanu asked.

"The one who keeps coming to the guest house and who is always with you," Pierre said.

"You mean Naresh? He is the one who is most frequently with me," Professor Shantanu said.

"Yes. I don't know his name, but recognised him by his face," Pierre said.

"But what could he be doing there?" Professor Shantanu was puzzled.

"I don't know. He was with some Tibetan chap. In fact, I called out to him as well. But he probably did not hear me," Pierre said.

"Really? Are you sure it was him?"

"Yes. I guess so," Pierre said.

Professor Shantanu was sure that Pierre was mistaken; but

decided not to push the point. It was of no consequence in any case.

They sipped their coffee in silence.

"But I really wish this stalemate would come to an end. These Chinese atrocities on the Tibetans should be condemned vociferously everywhere. But no country seems willing to support the Tibetan cause. Even the Indian Government has washed its hands off the issue," Pierre's voice was bitter.

"Well, what can you expect?" the professor said.

"I was truly hoping that during the last Olympics at Beijing, there would be some massive world backlash which would bring the predicament of the Tibetans to the forefront so that something positive could have happened regarding the granting of autonomy to Tibet," Pierre intoned as though speaking from an oft-repeated script.

"Yes, you are right of course! But politics is politics and business is business. China is a rapidly-growing power and a great market. No country wants to lose out on a potential market," Professor Shantanu pointed out.

"True. That is why the poor Tibetans are now resorting to extreme measures," Pierre looked troubled.

"What extreme measures?" the professor asked.

"Some time back a Tibetan attempted a self-immolation in front of the Chinese Embassy in Delhi." Pierre was distressed.

"Oh yes, I remember the news. But what can be done? This is a complex issue." Professor Shantanu said, trying to put things in perspective.

"Yes. But still I wish I could do something for the Tibetan cause," Pierre said.

"I hope you are not planning anything," Professor Shantanu was somewhat apprehensive.

"I'm not. But let me tell you — certain Tibetan groups are definitely planning violent things. They are no longer content to let things slide nor are they buying the Dalai Lama's policy of non-violence," Pierre became serious.

"I suppose the young generation is impetuous."

"And they should be. Enough is enough," Pierre said harshly.

Professor Shantanu was surprised at Pierre's passion for the Tibetan cause.

"I'm thinking of floating a website for free Tibet," Pierre said.

"I don't think that would be wise. And I would strongly advice you against it," Professor Shantanu said. This had better be nipped in the bud. MIST had enough problems on its head without creating another one.

Pierre was non-committal and simply stared at the mountains with a determined expression.

He had better keep an eye on Pierre and ensure that things did not get out of hand, Professor Shantanu thought. This seemingly innocuous fellow could get entangled into something unsavoury; and by association, MIST would be embroiled as well.

Later Professor Shantanu asked Naresh whether he had visited the Tibetan Colony.

"Tibetan Colony?" Naresh looked puzzled.

"Yes, the Tibetan Colony located up on Rajpur," Professor Shantanu explained.

"No. Why would I go there?" Naresh was mystified.

Professor Shantanu's earlier inference had been right. Pierre was possibly mistaken. Being a foreigner, he was in all probability not able to distinguish Indian faces very well and had most likely seen someone else, Professor Shantanu thought.

"Did I tell you that Vipin was working on some engine design which would run on bio-fuel extracted from Jatropha?" he changed the topic.

"No. But it is unlikely. A boy like Vipin would not be into research, I think," Naresh said.

"I thought so myself. But contrary to our belief, he was not so frivolous after all. He, along with Deepak, was very seriously working on this project," Professor Shantanu said. "It is admirable."

"Well, sir, if you say so, that must be the case," Naresh was taciturn.

"And the strange thing is that it seems Deepak is missing," the professor continued as though talking to himself. "Now why would a boy suddenly stop coming in the middle of the semester particularly without applying for leave or even bothering to be in touch with his friends?"

"Sir, who knows why these young boys behave the way they do?" Naresh asked. He could not understand why his hitherto research-inclined guide was taking so much interest in something so inane. His concern about Vipin was fine; but to now get into the details of Deepak's absence from college was unwarranted. Maybe the professor was getting on in years!

"Besides we have already found out that Deepak has gone to his grandmother's place," Naresh continued.

"My boy, I'm not completely convinced about that," Professor Shantanu said.

"Sir, I think we should not encroach upon the personal life of the students or intrude upon their families," Naresh said.

"Ordinarily, I would agree with you, but the circumstances now are very different," Professor Shantanu could not understand Naresh's way of thinking. Perhaps the latter was concerned about wasting time and energy in things unrelated to their research project.

"Yes, but that is for the police to investigate — we should not get involved in this; our priorities are different," Naresh echoed Professor Shantanu's thoughts. "In any case, it seems quite clear that Gurpreet is the culprit. So why should you bother about Deepak?"

"Well, maybe you are right," Professor Shantanu said, though unconvinced.

"And since Gurpreet is back at the hostel, maybe some action can be taken against her," Naresh said.

"But there is no direct evidence," the professor said.

"Then let the police do their work and let us get back to our research," Naresh said, now a trifle annoyed.

"Right," Professor Shantanu decided there was no point in discussing the matter any further.

But the first thing to do next morning was to have another chat with Gurpreet. There were several things that she needed to explain — her blog being one of them. Moreover, she probably knew something about the circumstances leading to Deepak taking this unprecedented long leave, Professor Shantanu thought.

CHAPTER – 11

"Gurpreet is dead!" Professor Indresan announced, looking panic-stricken.

"What? My God! How?" Professor Shantanu was astounded.

"It is either an accident or... or... a murder," Professor Indresan's distressed voice became hushed. He pulled at the lock of hair from behind his right ear.

Professor Shantanu, shocked beyond words, could only stare at him.

"She... er... the body was found in the ravine behind the girls' hostel. She fell or was pushed from the roof," the director shook his head, deeply tormented.

"Why do you say pushed?" Professor Shantanu tried to gain control over himself. Poor girl... he thought sorrowfully. Could he have done something to prevent this? he wondered.

It could very easily have been an accident," Professor Shantanu paused. Had she been taking a walk on the roof and accidently fallen over? he mused.

"Or... or maybe it was suicide, given her last attempt," he continued. Though there was no reason for Gurpreet to commit suicide, he thought. But then, she had been terribly depressed when he had met her. And, she was sort of unpredictable — different from the run-of-the-mill girl. So maybe...

"Yes. You may be right. But my nerves are shot. With all these unwarranted happenings..." Professor Indresan reached for a glass of water.

Professor Shantanu was quiet as he tried to marshal his thoughts.

"Inspector Bisht has come and is doing the needful," Professor Indresan paused. "Now how do I manage all this?" he continued plaintively.

"Don't worry. I'll go and take care of it. First, her parents need to be informed," Professor Shantanu recovered somewhat.

"Of course, the management will manage the press," he added as an afterthought.

The director seemed lost as he stared into his glass of water.

Walking away from the director's office, Professor Shantanu was filled with remorse. He should have had that talk with Gurpreet much earlier. Maybe, just maybe, he would have learnt something that could have saved her life. Some instinct told him that Professor Indresan was right; the death was no accident but murder.

"You know, it's great that these deaths have occurred," Mohit said smugly.

His roommate looked at him askance. "Wh... what are you saying?"

"You know...," Mohit had an unfathomable expression on his face.

"All I know is that one death has occurred — that of Vipin, which is rather unfortunate. Why do you say it is great?" his roommate paused. "And why do you say deaths in plural?" he continued.

"Well, someone else has died too," Mohit said mysteriously.

"What? What are you saying? Have you gone mad?" the

roommate was astounded. Was Mohit losing his mind? He did appear rather crazy nowadays.

"Well, you know Gurpreet?" Mohit said.

The roommate nodded.

"Yeah well, she has been done away with," Mohit announced with a flourish.

"Done away with? What do you mean?" the roommate was perplexed.

"Murdered!" Mohit's tone was frosty.

For a full minute, his roommate was unable to speak. Seeing Mohit's set expression, there was no doubt that he spoke the truth. In any case, why would someone lie or even joke about such a thing!

"How do you know?" the roommate's voice emerged in a whisper as his brain tried to grapple with this shocking news.

"I have my sources," Mohit again looked secretive.

The roommate looked at Mohit apprehensively. He had perhaps befriended the wrong person, he thought. He did not know this Mohit at all. "When and how did it happen?" he managed to articulate instead.

"In the girls' hostel last night, or early morning," Mohit said.

"How do you know it is murder?" the roommate asked after a pause as he absorbed the dreadful information.

"I just do," Mohit gave a wicked smile.

"But if it is so...,"

"Of course it is so, I'm telling you, am I not? Are you doubting my words?" Mohit cut him in mid-sentence and spoke vehemently.

Taken aback, the roommate continued hesitatingly, “But... but, this is terrible! Think of the poor parents, and besides,... it is not good for the institute.”

“Who cares! It serves the Institute right! The way they harass us students, all for nothing... Now they will know what it feels like to be harassed and troubled. The media will give them bad press, and there will be a lot of shocking publicity. It will be great,” Mohit spoke gleefully.

The roommate stared at Mohit in fear.

“I just remembered. I have to submit an assignment to the Head. I'll soon be back,” the roommate escaped, panic-stricken.

He had better tell all this to Suresh. Suresh would know what to do with this information. And should he also try to get his room changed? A shiver went down his spine. He was genuinely afraid to be near Mohit now.

Back in his lab, Professor Shantanu looked through Gurpreet's personal file. She belonged to Gurdaspur and her father was a businessman. There was nothing unusual in the file.

He opened her blog again on his laptop. He had already gone through it earlier but now the situation was ominous — he had to look closer. Perhaps he had missed something. He began reading carefully. It was all the same. The only thing he noted was the mention of her *Facebook* profile. There was no harm in checking her *Facebook* account, he thought. He was literally clutching at straws; but then what else did he have to go on with?

He knew that the students were crazy about *Facebook* and most of them spent a considerable amount of time on it; networking, as they said in their parlance. Whenever Professor Shantanu was on a round of the Learning Resource Centre where students had the facility to access online technical journals and various subject-related software, he found that most of the students were logged on to *Facebook* instead. In the last Heads' meeting, he had proposed that the site should be banned from the college server. Everyone was convinced, particularly after he mentioned that *Facebook* was banned at one of the IITs.

Professor Shantanu summoned the System Manager. Since *Facebook* was banned, he would need help accessing it. The System Manager informed him that the students had found an alternate pathway to open *Facebook*. As a result, they all still managed to open *Facebook* through some proxy server. Currently, he was trying to block all such alternate pathways. Why couldn't these students use such innovative thinking for worthwhile purposes, was a question that often troubled Professor Shantanu.

Soon *Facebook* was open. He then asked whether there was any way of finding out the password for opening Gurpreet's account. The System Manager had no idea. Neither did he know of any student who could help. The System Manager was standoffish and kept a distance from the students lest they pester him for troubleshooting. Professor Shantanu was aware of this.

Letting him go, Professor Shantanu sent for Suresh.

Suresh was curious at the professor's request; but did not dare ask any questions. Instead, he got busy in trying to open Gurpreet's account.

Within minutes, Gurpreet's account was open.

"How did you manage this?" Professor Shantanu was amazed.

"I just did," Suresh smiled. He was proud of his prowess as a hacker.

Professor Shantanu decided to let the matter be for the moment. There were more urgent matters at hand.

Suresh left.

With a cup of coffee, Professor Shantanu began going through everything in the account.

There was not much. But she did have a large circle of virtual friends unlike in real life. Professor Shantanu opened some of the mails that she had sent to some of these friends. They seemed ordinary enough.

Then he noticed that more and more mails were exchanged with someone named 'Enigma'. Gurpreet seemed to have developed some sort of closeness with this person with whom she shared her feelings on the futility of love and the nobility of revenge. This 'Enigma' seemed to be a close confidante of Gurpreet. She had also revealed several personal details to 'Enigma'.

Rapidly, Professor Shantanu began reading all the mails that the two had exchanged. A few of the mails talked about strange goings-on in the college; then there were a few in which Gurpreet talked about being fearful, not feeling safe, and that she would rather kill herself than face an agonizing death. Professor Shantanu was startled. What did this mean? Why was she fearful?

While he was at it, he decided to try and find something which could give him a clue about Deepak.

Professor Shantanu searched all over for some mention of Deepak, but there was nothing. It seemed Gurpreet was only concerned about herself and Vipin. Nothing else in the world existed for her. Probably that accounted for her somewhat lopsided view of life... and which, in some way, had perhaps led to her demise, he thought.

"Oh God. Just look at him," a third year Computer Engineering girl commented.

"Yeah, he is gorgeous," her classmate replied.

They were seated in the computer lab, ostensibly working on their minor project, whereas actually artfully gazing at the new Computer Engineering lecturer. This lecturer had joined the Computer Science Engineering Department a few months back; and almost immediately the entire female student community was smitten by him. Not only was he devastatingly handsome, he was knowledgeable as well. And his sonorous voice made his classes a veritable treat.

"Aww girls, come off it!" Nitish commented.

"Why don't you mind your own business? He is the best eye-candy the college has to offer. I could just look at him the whole day," the third year Computer Engineering girl sighed.

"Yes," another girl concurred. "Let's go and ask him to explain this program."

"But this program is so simple," Nitish pointed out.

The girls ignored him. "At least we can interact with him," the third year Computer Engineering girl was dreamy-eyed.

"Sheesh! You girls are disgusting," Nitish turned away. This was too much even for him.

"Hey! There has been another death," suddenly a boy announced.

"What!" a group of students spoke in unison.

"Yeah. I just got an sms from my friend in Mechanical," he

said.

"Oh God!" Everybody looked frightened. What in the world was happening? Was this for real? they all thought simulataneously...

Just then the bell rang. Instantly, the group rushed out to get more news.

"Sir, may I come in?" It was Suresh.

Professor Shantanu waved him in.

Naresh took one look at him and turned back to his research.

"Er... I wanted to tell you something," Suresh said. He looked pointedly at Naresh.

"Beta, go ahead. Naresh knows everything in any case. And now the situation has changed dramatically," Professor Shantanu said.

"Well sir, there is this boy in the second year, Mohit. He was treated very badly by Vipin. So he, er... he could be involved in this entire business in some way," Suresh paused.

Professor Shantanu was surprised.

"I have learnt from my sources that there was an incident a couple of weeks prior to Vipin's death which could have made Mohit angry enough to harm Vipin," he continued.

"Oh," the Professor muttered. "But earlier you were of the firm belief that Gurpreet was the culprit?"

"Yes sir. But now Gurpreet is no more," there was a catch in his voice. "It is all very confusing. I still don't know what to think. But since I came to know of this, I thought... I thought that I must tell you," Suresh spoke falteringly.

"It is good that you have told me," the professor spoke

soothingly. "Well, all right, I will keep it in mind."

Suresh turned to go. He hesitated and then turned back again. "Sir, there is something else. I don't know whether I should say this or not. But you see — since all these things have happened, I can't help but keep thinking about who all could be involved."

"Yes. Go on," Professor Shantanu said encouragingly.

"Well sir, Saransh sir could..., could also have something to do in all this," Suresh spoke diffidently.

"What do you mean?" Professor Shantanu was startled.

"Well sir, Vipin was always trying to humiliate Saransh sir in the class. Actually in almost every lecture, Vipin and his group tried to prove that Saransh sir was academically incompetent."

"So?" Professor Shantanu was unconvinced. What kind of boy had this Vipin been? he thought yet again.

"Well, sir, there is a limit to tolerance and Saransh sir had reached it. We...er...I am sure of it," Suresh explained in a rush.

"All this has to do with Vipin's death. Where does Gurpreet's death fit into all this?" Professor Shantanu said, ruminating almost to himself.

Suresh was quiet.

"Actually, Gurpreet's death has left me flummoxed. And so — so I thought I must share everything I know. Perhaps you will be able to connect it all together," Suresh looked deeply troubled.

Professor Shantanu decided to try another question.

"Tell me what you know about Deepak." Professor Shantanu was sure that Suresh could help him to arrive at a satisfactory explanation for Deepak's absence.

"What about Deepak, sir?" Suresh was perplexed at this change of subject. It was totally unrelated to what they had been discussing, he thought.

"Well, you know Deepak, Vipin's project partner?"

"Yes sir."

"He has not been coming to college since the past one month."

"Really? I don't know anything about it. Maybe he is not well...," Suresh's voice trailed away.

"You don't know anything about him?" Professor Shantanu was disappointed.

Suresh shook his head.

"And do you know of anyone named 'Enigma'?" the professor asked.

Suresh looked at the professor askance. What was wrong with the professor? he wondered. "No sir," he said instead. "In any case, we should think about Vipin and Gurpreet, and that is why I have come to tell you whatever I know about people who could, could have... er... something to do with it." Was he right in having come to the Professor for help? Suresh wondered.

"Well, my boy, it is a good thing that you have shared all this with me. If you think of anything else or come to know of anything else, please come to me immediately," Professor Shantanu sent him away.

"What do you make of all this?" Professor Shantanu asked Naresh.

"Maybe there is something to it," Naresh was vague. "But we should leave all this well alone."

"Maybe," Professor Shantanu said, though he knew he could

not rest until this matter was resolved. He wished he had thought of talking to Gurpreet earlier. But now it was too late.

And with Suresh mentioning Mohit and Saransh, the matter seemed hopelessly bewildering. Perhaps he had better talk to these two — before — before anything untoward happened yet again.

There was no getting away from the adverse publicity now. Gopal Das Singhal was at his wits' end, although owing to his clout, the damage was not as bad as it could have been. Most news reports merely reported the second death. It was only the Shivalik Times that had a field day. It linked the two deaths together, relating it to the falling academic standards and deplorable conditions at MIST. There was no doubt that their arch-enemy, the Shivalik Institute, had instigated this particular news item.

Gopal Das could only hope that the investigation would bring out the real culprit in a satisfactory manner and result in his institute regaining its immaculate reputation. The paper further alleged that this would adversely impact the city also. Dehradun was a quiet little town and had seldom seen such a case where a single institution had two seemingly related deaths within a fortnight of each other. This was a first in the history of this peaceful city. And trust it to happen in his college. Singhal sighed. He did not know what to do.

And to top it, that damn police officer seemed to be no good. He was hardly any nearer to determining the first murderer... and now this second death! Was he capable enough? Or was he simply feeding a toothless tiger? Gopal Das began to have doubts. It was a good thing Professor Shantanu was also investigating the murder and interrogating the suspects, he thought. He had great respect for the Dean of Research and was confident that the Professor would somehow ensure that everything turned out right for MIST in the end.

"I had gone for the Tibetan rally," Pierre took recourse to his favourite subject in an attempt to divert the Professor's mind, as well as his own. "It was held near Gandhi Park," he added.

The two happened to be taking lunch together at the guesthouse.

"I see," Professor Shantanu smiled softly. It was sweet the way Pierre was trying to take his mind off from MIST, he thought.

"What was the reason for the rally?" he asked.

"It was held to commemorate the anniversary of the March 1959 uprising when Tibetans protested against Chinese atrocities in Lhasa after which their exodus took place," Pierre was animated.

"In fact in 2008, around the anniversary, there were demonstrations and rioting in Lhasa, which did succeed in focussing world attention on Tibet," he paused.

"This led to the Chinese crackdown after which several Tibetans tried to cross over into India across the mountain border," Pierre continued.

"I see," Professor Shantanu said.

"During that crackdown, a few Tibetan monks were convicted of bombing a government building. The Chinese government also claimed to have recovered an immense cache of arms and ammunition from several Tibetan monasteries," Pierre added.

"Really? I thought that these monks were by and large

peaceful," the Professor said.

"God alone knows how much truth there is in these reports and how much is pure Chinese propaganda," Pierre shook his head.

"You may be right," Professor Shantanu concurred.

"Beijing claimed that the rioting was engineered by the Dalai Lama and that he had also planned to sabotage the Beijing Olympics," Pierre continued.

"I think you should not worry too much about all this," Professor Shantanu counselled.

"I guess you are right," Pierre paused.

"But I think that certain groups of Tibetans in India feel quite strongly about all this,' he continued.

"Yeah, well, it's natural for them to feel this way, I suppose," Professor Shantanu said.

"In fact, I'm quite sure that a few of them are itching to get back at the Chinese Government," Pierre said.

"I hardly think that is possible given the might of the Chinese. And anyway, we should really not get too involved in it," Professor Shantanu said. This Pierre was getting unnecessarily fanciful ideas, he thought.

"Hey, let's go and talk to Miss Meenal," a first year Electronics student said.

A few students were sitting in the internet lab. The server was down and not being able to access the net, the students were getting bored and wondering what to do. Working on practicals, studying, or going to the library were passé, of course.

"Yeah, that's a good idea," his friend agreed eagerly.

"You know, I heard that she had received several modelling offers but had taken up teaching instead, due to pressure from her conservative family," another first year student spoke.

"Yeah, all to our good luck!" a boy smirked.

Ms. Meenal was a young lecturer in the Physics Department and taught the first year students. Most of the boys were her ardent fans, owing mostly to her charming countenance and demeanour.

Ms. Meenal was sitting in her tiny cubicle in the Physics lab, absently toying with her pen. Seeing a group of boys approach, she perked up.

"Yes?" she looked up and smiled.

"Ma'am, we need some advice," the first year Electronics student said. "Yes, tell me. Only I'm not much older than you so I don't know whether I would be the right person to give you advice," Ms. Meenal smiled.

"Yes ma'am, in fact when we saw you the first time, we thought that you were some student," the first year Electronics student said, forgetting about the advice he wanted.

"Yes, I know. Many students tell me this," she smiled happily.

"In fact, ma'am, you know, you are in the wrong profession. You should have been a model," another first year student said.

"Yes ma'am, we all feel this," the other students chorused. Happily, Ms. Meenal related her oft-repeated story of wanting to be a model but being forced to study Physics by her overbearing mother. These students were really very nice, she thought.

Soon the conversation veered towards the recent tragedy. Everybody agreed that it was a dastardly act.

"Two murders is too much," a boy said.

"How can you say that the second was murder?" Ms. Meenal asked.

"Well, it's obvious," another first year student stated.

"But she did try to commit suicide earlier," Ms. Meenal pointed out.

"Even so. Ma'am, just look at the facts. If she wanted to commit suicide, she would have again cut her veins or taken poison. Why resort to a terrifying and uncertain way of jumping off from the roof?" the first year boy explained.

Everyone was quiet.

"But who could have done it?" Ms. Meenal broke the silence.

"It must have been an outside person," she said after a pause.

"No ma'am, it has to be an inside person," the first year Electronics student said.

"Why?" she was surprised.

"Because no one can enter the campus, much less the hostels, so easily," a boy pointed the obvious.

Everybody was quiet. The mood turned sombre.

"But who would want to kill these innocent students?" Ms. Meenal was perplexed.

"Mayank sir," the first year Electronics student burst out.

Everybody looked at him.

Ms. Meenal was aghast. Agreed that Mayank was a weirdo, but he was a colleague, after all!

"Don't talk nonsense!" she admonished.

"Ma'am, you don't know him. He hates students and he is a

bad person," the first year Electronics student paused. "He is so bad that his own family has disowned him," he revealed.

"What? What do you mean?" Ms. Meenal was shocked. What were these students up to, and from where did they gather such information? she wondered.

"My close friend studies in Ghaziabad in the same college where Mayank sir worked before coming here. He told me that he used to harass students there too and for this reason, his service was terminated there," the first year Electronics student said.

"But how is that related to his family?" she asked.

"There he had harassed a girl particularly and her parents had come to the college, complained to the management, and made a big issue about it. The management simply asked Mayank sir to leave, and said that they could do nothing more," the first year Electronics student said, all in one breath.

"Oh," Ms. Meenal was taken aback.

"Then the girls' family found out his home address in Ahmedabad and visited his house there. And Mayank's parents said that they had disowned him several years ago due to something he had done. But they were not willing to reveal what exactly he had done due to which they had disowned their own son," the first year Electronics student revealed.

Everybody looked at him in surprise.

"But it must have been something really bad. Maybe he had murdered someone. Maybe he is a serial killer!" the first year Electronics student spoke in a rush. Evidently this was in his mind since a long time and he needed to get it off his chest.

There was absolute silence.

After a while, Ms. Meenal spoke. "I think you all should think about your studies and not about such things. Now all of you go to your classes," she asserted her authority.

After the students left, she got up. This information needed to be conveyed to Professor Shantanu. He would know what to do with it. If she told any other professor, they would simply make a joke of the issue.

The whole thing sounded implausible, of course, but that first year Electronics student was earnest and clearly believed what he had said was true. And she should do her duty and convey it to at least someone. What if there was some bit of truth in it?

"Sir, the girl's parents are here," the Director's assistant announced.

"Send them in," Professor Indresan sighed. Where were Professors Mrityunjaya, Bhardwaj, Girish Shukla and Tandon, when he needed them? Would he have to deal with the parents on his own? he wondered.

A portly man walked in, followed by a pretty, diminutive lady. Professor Indresan expressed his condolences after which there was absolute silence.

After a while, the father said, "I never wanted to send her to study engineering. And that too, so far away in a hostel."

Nobody said anything. There was nothing to be said.

Professor Indresan wondered how not to prolong this meeting. It was too painful by far.

A little later, the father asked, "But how did this happen? My child was too sensible to do something like this. There has to be foul play involved."

"Er... the investigations are going on. We will let you know as soon as something concrete comes up," Professor Indresan mumbled whilst fiddling with a lock of hair.

"During her last call, she seemed particularly upset," the mother sniffed.

"Then why didn't you ask her to come back?" the father almost shouted. "I could have got the best of the best family to take her as their bahu," he paused.

"But no—you had to put the nonsense of being a career woman in her head and now look what has happened! You didn't want her to end up like yourself. And she hasn't, has she? She is dead!" the father's voice broke.

Professor Indresan shifted uncomfortably in his chair. He didn't know what to say or do. He pressed the intercom and asked the p.a. to send some of the deans to take care of the parents.

"She was disturbed; no, she was scared," the mother continued as though she had not heard any part of her husband's ranting. Evidently, this was not the first time she had heard these words from him.

"Scared about what?" Professor Indresan asked. He hoped it was nothing that would show the institute in bad light.

"I don't know. Since the time she had cut her veins, she seemed strange," the mother said.

"She was always strange," the father spoke wearily.

"No, this was different. She hinted that people were not what they appeared to be. She said something like, let me recall ... evil has come to root in this campus ... or something like this," the mother spoke haltingly.

"Shush! Woman ... you are talking rubbish," the father admonished his wife.

"No, I'm telling you, this is what she said," the mother was adamant.

Professor Mrityunjaya and Professor Ramesh Bhardwaj entered.

The director sighed in relief. He let go of his lock of hair.

The parents barely noticed them and continued in their own vein.

"Well, what else can be expected! Being close to you, she was bound to develop such fanciful ideas which have no basis in reality," the father scoffed.

"Sir, I'm telling the truth; please pay heed to what I am saying," the mother turned towards Professor Indresan and pleaded.

"Well ma'am, I'll convey all this to the investigating officer, and if required, I will put him in touch with you. This might help in the investigation," the director said, as he was keen to get out of this difficult situation, though he was inclined to agree with the father. Evil had come to root? What a load of bosh!

"What is the point? We have lost our daughter. Nothing matters now," the father's voice was barely audible.

"Of course it matters! The murderer had better be caught and brought to justice! I will not rest till my beloved daughter gets justice, and neither will her soul!" the mother's voice rose in agitation.

After a good ten minutes of more such altercations, somehow Professor Indresan with the help of Professor Bhardwaj and Professor Mrityunjaya was able to end the meeting. He saw them off, after promising to keep them posted about all the developments related to the investigation.

CHAPTER – 12

The post-mortem report of Gurpreet confirmed everyone's suspicions. It was indeed murder.

"She was hit on the back of the head with a heavy object and then pushed or thrown off from the girls' hostel roof," Professor Indresan said tensely to Professor Shantanu.

"Could the blow have come from hitting her head on some sharp rock or something, after having jumped?" Professor Shantanu asked, trying hard to conjecture that she had committed suicide.

"No. The report says that the nature of the blow and the angle of the fall are at variance with each other. Also, remember, the area at the back of the hostel was cleaned just after the rainy season. At that time, our over-zealous administrative officer had ensured that all jutting boulders were also removed," Professor Indresan explained.

The administrative officer was a retired junior commissioned officer from the Indian Army and always did more than was expected of him.

"Further, bits of crumbling plaster of the parapet have been found embedded in some of her nails," Professor Indresan looked pale.

"Evidently she tried to save herself by clawing at the parapet that lines the edge of the boundary wall of the roof. So, it is a clear case of murder," Professor Indresan restated the obvious, feeling sick to the core of his heart.

Somehow, Professor Shantanu had already known that

Gurpreet's death was murder, but he was unwilling to accept it. Two murders within a span of a fortnight were too much to stomach.

"So this means that we will have to chalk out a fresh strategy to deal with the students, staff and the press. The session is in full swing and it cannot be allowed to be disrupted," Professor Shantanu said, trying to gain a semblance of structure in his mind.

"So what do you suggest?" the director looked lost.

"The Dean of Academics should ensure that there is no slackness whatsoever, as far as academics is concerned. He should call a general faculty meeting and convey this. Subsequently, all the Heads should also ensure that academics does not suffer," Professor Shantanu said.

"Er... yes." Absently, Professor Indresan pulled out a lock of hair.

"And the counselling of students is needed and for this the faculty coordinators will have to be sensitised under the leadership of Professor Bhardwaj," Professor Shantanu continued.

"Yes," the director nodded disconsolately.

"Also, the management would have to look into the matter of appointing a proper, professionally-trained counsellor," Professor Shantanu was firm.

Professor Indresan smiled tremulously, "Yes, you see, this is why I have called you," he said gratefully. He paused, "In fact, I would appreciate it if you would do all that is necessary to ensure that the college goes on as usual."

Professor Shantanu nodded.

"Yes, well, I think I will also do all that you have suggested.

Meanwhile, you take care of things in your own way. Do continue with your investigation and interrogate all those who could in any way be related with these dastardly murders." He summoned the peon. "Send for the Dean of Academics and Dean of Students." Firmly, he pushed back the lock of hair behind his right ear. The director was back in control.

Professor Shantanu needed to clear his head. He walked out into the garden. Restlessly, he paced across the narrow pathway surrounding the lawn. The myriad, brightly-coloured flowers were in full bloom in the neat beds on both sides of the pathway. But the professor scarcely noticed. It seemed impossible to make sense of all the conflicting inputs. There were too many people who had the opportunity and motive to do away with Vipin. It really was impossible that a boy so young had infuriated so many people; and apparently, someone's aggravation was so great that it had led to murder.

Then again, there were the set of circumstances related to Ramadin and Mayank... could they be involved?

Moreover, there was the peculiar indication about the complicity of Saransh and that second year student... what's his name? Ah yes, Mohit.

And now there was the puzzle of Gurpreet's murder. The post-mortem report proved beyond doubt what he had known all along; but had refused to acknowledge. It was indeed murder. Obviously, the two murders were connected. This gave the entire set of events a new perspective.

There was no doubt that the matter was more serious than it appeared. It was not a simple case of an affair gone wrong. Or if it was, then there was perhaps another girl or boy involved whose identity was not yet clear. And could there be the possibility of that person, 'Enigma', mentioned in Gurpreet's *Facebook* account knowing something about this ghastly turn of events?

And where did Deepak fit into this complex picture? Maybe there was no connection. But something prompted Professor Shantanu to compulsively look for any clue related to Deepak's unexplained absence. Maybe he was unnecessarily diverting his mind from the main issue at hand. But then, that had always been his psyche; anything that did not neatly fit into its designated slot left him with a feeling of niggling discomfort. And he simply could not rest till the cause of the disquiet was taken care of. Rapidly, he walked back, intent on action.

Back in his lab, Professor Shantanu sent for Saransh and Mohit.

"Well, Saransh, tell me, did you have anything to do with Vipin's death?" Professor Shantanu did not believe in beating about the bush.

"Sir, I would be lying if I said that I have not wished on numerous occasions for something bad to happen to Vipin. But I would never actually do something, least of all, commit er... murder," Saransh was in earnest.

"But Vipin was a horrible, nasty boy. And he made it a point to torture you in every class. He truly deserved what he got," the professor spoke provokingly.

"Yes. He was the wickedest boy I have ever come across," Saransh's face twisted with hate.

"And it is right to teach such boys a lesson," Professor Shantanu instigated him.

"Yes," a brief smile began at the corners of Saransh's mouth.

Immediately he masked it. Suddenly, he realised what the professor was doing. "No sir," he said blandly.

"No what?" Professor Shantanu challenged him.

"I mean, sir, you are right in everything you say. But I did not have anything to do with Vipin's death," Saransh paused. "No matter how much I hated him," he added.

"Are you sure? Do you know the repercussions of lying?" Professor Shantanu issued a veiled threat.

"Sir, I'm an honest person," resolutely Saransh looked back at him.

"Where were you on the night of the murder?" the professor asked.

"I was at home," Saransh said.

"Can anyone swear to it?"

"Well, no, sir. I live alone and so you will have to take my word for it," Saransh spoke evenly.

"What do you know about Gurpreet's death?" the professor asked.

"Well, not much. Just what is commonly known," Saransh spoke blandly.

"You didn't like her too, isn't it?" the professor goaded.

"Well, to be frank, I don't like any of these students," Saransh stated matter-of-factly.

"And where were you on the night of her murder?" Professor Shantanu asked.

"At home, alone," Saransh smiled.

Professor Shantanu sighed. There was nothing more to be gained from this conversation, he realised. "Well Saransh, if there is anything you know or can think of related to this matter, please let me know."

Saransh nodded and left.

Mohit entered.

"You know why I have called you?" Professor Shantanu decided to take the soft approach.

"Not exactly, sir," Mohit said.

"Do you know anything about these deaths?" the Professor asked.

"No sir," Mohit replied.

"Tell me something — I have heard that you did not particularly like Vipin. Is that right?" the professor decided to prompt him into making some kind of admission.

"So?" Mohit's tone became insolent.

Professor Shantanu was taken aback. For a moment, he did not know what to say. "Well then, is it possible that you would have wished to harm Vipin?" he said, after a pause.

"Nobody really liked Vipin, and all of them would have wished to harm him. So why pick on me?" Mohit countered.

"You are right. But I understand that a couple of weeks prior to his death, you had gone to Vipin for help. But he had refused," Professor Shantanu said.

"So? That does not make me a murderer." He would find the guy who leaked this information and beat him up, Mohit thought.

Professor Shantanu watched the play of emotions on his face. This was one tough nut to crack, he thought. "So you had nothing to do with this entire thing?" he decided to ask for one last time.

"Even if I had something to do with Vipin's death, how do

you explain Gurpreet?" Mohit was belligerent.

He did have a point there, thought Professor Shantanu.

"May I go now?" Mohit said.

Professor Shantanu was only too glad to send him away.

Later during dinner with Pierre, Professor Shantanu shared his concern, "I really don't know what is happening in this campus."

"Yes sir. I too am appalled. Two murders!" Pierre concurred.

"I really hope we are able to arrive at the identity of the culprit soon," Professor Shantanu pushed the vegetables around on his plate.

"But surely the police must have made some headway by now," Pierre said.

"God knows what they have found out. All this is very bad for the academic atmosphere and even worse for the reputation of MIST," the professor was morose.

"Yes, and it is not good for the psyche of the students too," Pierre said.

"Yes. But you know how the youth are. They are very resilient. I'm sure they are taking it in their stride and coping rather well, all things considered," Professor Shantanu said. He was still trying to come to terms with Mohit's audacious attitude about the murders.

"Anyway, let's change the topic. Tell me how your Ph.D is coming along," the Professor asked.

"Oh, just great. I have managed to gather a great deal of information from the Tibetan Colony here, and from the Sakya

College," Pierre smiled happily.

"But how are you managing to get the information so easily?"

"Well, you see, I know the Tibetan language and so it becomes very easy for me to strike up a conversation with these Tibetans. And they are only too happy to discuss stuff with a foreigner." Pierre paused. "They are a neglected lot. And when they have someone taking interest in them, they are all too ready to talk," Pierre warmed to his favourite subject.

"I see," Professor Shantanu said.

"Your student also has a friend in the Tibetan colony," Pierre said.

"My student?" the professor was surprised.

"I told you the last time I was there that I had seen him at the Tibetan colony? What is his name? Yes! Naresh," Pierre said.

"I think you must have mistaken someone else for him," Professor Shantanu said.

"Er... maybe, but I do think it was mentioned that someone from MIST visits the Tibetan Colony. So maybe I just assumed it," Pierre's voice trailed away.

"Maybe you are confused about what you have heard. Why would anyone from MIST be visiting their colony?" Professor Shantanu said.

"Yes, perhaps you are right," Pierre acquiesced.

"I hope you have given up your idea of the free Tibet website etc.," Professor Shantanu smiled.

"Aah...yes. It was just a thought. You know — sometimes I do get carried away thinking of their strife. But it is for them to work it out. I'm afraid I really can't do much in this regard. I know that perfectly well," Pierre said.

"Good," the professor was relieved.

"In any case, my area of interest is Tibetan Buddhism and I should stick to it. If I fritter my energies elsewhere, I'll never be able to finish my Ph.D in a million years," Pierre spoke solemnly.

"Yes," Professor Shantanu nodded.

"But some of these Tibetan guys are up to something, I think," Pierre seemed to be speaking to himself.

"Mm," Professor Shantanu kept his reserve.

"In fact, I do believe that some Indians could be helping them too in some way," Pierre said.

"Helping them? For what?" Professor Shantanu asked perplexed.

"Helping them in furthering their cause for free Tibet or something," Pierre said.

"Really? The whole idea seems far-fetched. I don't think Indians could really be bothered with what Tibetans are up to," Professor Shantanu said.

"Maybe you are right. It's just something I heard the other day which gave me this idea," Pierre paused.

"As long as you are not helping them, its ok," the professor smiled.

"Yes," Pierre smiled back.

"Well, anyway, I'm glad you are being able to accomplish what you came here for," the professor said.

"Yes," Pierre smiled.

"And how is your experience teaching our students?" the professor asked.

"Oh, great. These students are really eager to learn. They soak up everything like a sponge." Pierre was enthusiastic.

"Good. I'm glad everything is going right with you," Professor Shantanu said. At least some things were as they should be, he thought.

Saransh looked at himself in the mirror. He was compelled to undertake this repulsive task inspite of himself. He hated his appearance and yet he spent most of his free time examining his looks. What could he do to look good? he wondered for the billionth time. Had he the resources of Michael Jackson, perhaps he could have had some form of skin lightening surgery done. But then MJ had claimed that his skin colour changed because of some rare disease. What was it? Yes, vitiligo. Or had he mislead the media? Who knows? In any case, it was something Saransh had no access to. And even if he could lighten his skin colour, what could he do about his physique? No matter how hard he exercised, his paunch refused to budge. Then of course, the final blow — his short height and a stocky body...

Oh, God! Why did you do this to me? he cried inwardly. Being around physically beautiful people made the pain of ugliness more acute.

Ah! but then, finally justice was taking place. That bloody Vipin was dead. How he must have suffered in the moment of death... finally having to pay for his supercilious attitude, wicked deeds and his lean, good looks... And that Gurpreet too. Perhaps she did not need to die, but then she too was guilty by association. To love a boy as degenerate as Vipin, she had to be immoral too.

Who must have suffered more? Justice dictated that Vipin

should have endured more, but Gurpreet's death must have been painful as well. To fall from that height...was she killed instantly? In that case, she may not have suffered much. Vipin's strangling must have been unbearable — the slow choking, the final moments of breathlessness... until life was gradually and agonizingly snuffed out.... Yes, Vipin's death must have been excruciating...and that is how it should have been.

Saransh smiled lopsidedly at the man in the mirror. For a moment, the man in the mirror looked almost handsome, he noted idly.

The next morning, Professor Shantanu sat in his lab, absently doodling on his writing pad. This had turned into a most vexing matter. It seemed certain that the same person was involved in both the cases. Was this person alone or did he have an accomplice?

And if it was a man, how did he enter the girls' hostel without being detected? But all the same, what had Gurpreet been doing on the roof? Clearly, she must have willingly gone up to the roof. And if so, why? And then, had the killer known of it and lay in wait for her?

The time of her death was around 4 a.m. So perhaps even if it were a man, it was quite possible for him to enter the hostel. Not too many people would be about at such an unearthly hour. Hence, the killer may have snuck in quietly and remained unobserved by anyone.

Professor Shantanu decided to examine the scene of the crime closely.

Soon, he was on the roof of the girls' hostel. It was a steep fall below into the gorge and no one could possibly survive it.

Yet the killer had decided not to take any chances and had hit her first on the head, and then thrown her off the roof.

Had the killer come and hid on the roof some time in the middle of the night and not in the morning? In that case, he must have known that Gurpreet would come up to the roof around 4 a.m. There were five huge black boilers located on the roof next to the five water tanks. He could have easily hid behind any of these. However, there was only one staircase leading to the roof and this could be accessed only from inside the girls' hostel.

There was no way a man could have entered the hostel, and then climbed all the way through the four floors to the roof and remained undetected. He had probably climbed from the outside wall holding on to the jutting pipes, parapets, and the convenient balconies on the outside of each room. But there was a minute probability that the murderer was female; in which case, she had easy access from inside the girls' hostel.

Perhaps someone had seen something. He decided to talk to the girls' hostel wardens and the other hostel staff. He went down to the girls' hostel office located adjacent to the lobby on the ground floor. The warden reported that she had seen nothing suspicious on the night of the death.

"Though Mayank sir did come over on one of his rounds," the assistant warden said.

"Mayank?" Professor Shantanu was puzzled. "But he is only supposed to be in charge of the boys' hostel, isn't it? Why does he come here?"

"Er...," the assistant warden paused. She knew that she had given out a vital piece of information, judging from Professor Shantanu's tone. What if Mayank came to know? He was crazy, after all, she thought.

"Well, I don't know who has permitted him, but he often comes and checks the girls' attendance register in the office and the outpass register maintained in the guards' room at the hostel gate," the warden explained. She hated the fact that Mayank was able to encroach upon her territory.

"Does he come inside the girls' hostel?" the professor asked.

"Well, he comes up to the lobby. Men are not permitted beyond that," the warden said.

"And he came that night as well?" the professor asked.

"Yes," she concurred.

Professor Shantanu then quizzed the guards, cook, mess workers and other helpers. They were not able to tell him anything more of importance.

"Are you sure none of you saw anyone who normally does not come here?" Professor Shantanu asked one last time.

"Er...well, I did see Ramadin," one of the guards said.

"But Ramadin is assigned to the boys' hostel. Why would he come here?" the professor asked.

"Actually, he is the uncle of one of the mess helpers. Maybe he had come to meet him," the mess-in-charge said.

"Where is that helper?" the professor asked.

"He is on leave," the mess-in-charge said.

"I see. But why did Ramadin come only on that particular night?" Professor Shantanu asked nobody in particular.

Everybody remained silent.

Back at his office, Professor Shantanu found the young Physics lecturer waiting for him.

"Sir, there is something you should know," Ms. Meenal spoke in a rush.

Professor Shantanu did not really want to waste time talking to her, but decided to humour her. "Yes, tell me," he said.

Rapidly, the lecturer related everything that the students had told her about Mayank's history and their suspicions about him.

Professor Shantanu decided to revise his opinion of this young lecturer. Clearly, she was not as superficial as her appearance indicated. "Thank you for telling me all this. If you learn anything else, please let me know," he said gratefully.

The physics lecturer left. She was glad that she had told Professor Shantanu rather than Professor Mrityunjaya, or worse, Professor Girish Shukla. They would simply have scoffed at her. Professor Shantanu, on the contrary, was so gracious, sophisticated and unbelievably good-looking, too. Admittedly, the last bit had nothing to do with sharing information with him; but then it didn't hurt either.

Professor Shantanu sent for Ramadin and Mayank.

"Why did you go to the girls' hostel?" The professor asked Ramadin as soon as he entered.

Taken aback at this unexpected attack, Ramadin stuttered, "Er... er, I don't remember."

"On the night of Gurpreet's murder, you had gone to the girls' hostel — where you were not supposed to go — why?" Professor Shantanu said.

"Er...yes, my nephew is a mess helper there, and he was not well. And so I went to see him. And I told him to take leave and get some rest," Ramadin was in earnest.

His reason sounded plausible enough, Professor Shantanu thought, and it tied up with his prior information as well. He let Ramadin leave, asking him to inform him in case he recalled anything related to Gurpreet.

Mayank entered.

"Mayank, why did you go to the girls' hostel on the night of Gurpreet's murder?" Professor Shantanu asked.

"Well, sir, it is my habit to make surprise checks in all the hostel blocks. So it was a matter of routine," Mayank spoke blandly.

"But you are not supposed to go to the girls' hostel," Professor Shantanu pointed out.

"Yes sir, but you see, I'm being paid so much by the management and I take my role very seriously. In fact, I hardly sleep. I am always concerned about student discipline and do not differentiate among the boys and girls," Mayank spoke conscientiously.

"And where were you at the time of both the murders?" the professor asked.

"Probably taking a round at some part of the campus," Mayank smiled.

This was getting them nowhere. Professor Shantanu decided to try another line of questioning.

"Tell me, you know everything that goes on here, so then why haven't you managed to find out how and why these murders have been committed?"

"Yes. You are right, sir. I do have some clues, and I am working upon them. As soon as I am able to arrive at the answers, you will be the first to know," Mayank said.

"So why not share these clues with me?" the professor persuaded.

"They are rather flimsy clues and not really worth sharing. As soon as I come to know something big, I will tell you," Mayank said.

Professor Shantanu was quiet.

"May I go now?" Mayank asked.

Professor Shantanu waved him away.

CHAPTER – 13

"Sheesh! I really have not been able to stick to my time-table," Suresh got up from his table with a jerk. A look of frustration marred his usual calm countenance.

"What's wrong?" Nitish was concerned.

"Since Vipin's murder, I have not been able to study, and now, after Gurpreet, whenever I sit down to study, all I can think of is the fact of their murders," he paused.

"You just try and study!" Nitish said. He knew how important it was for Suresh to make it big in life. Not only his family, but his entire village had high hopes from him.

"No yaar, till this thing is resolved, I cannot study peacefully," Suresh said in a distressed tone.

Nitish looked at him in alarm.

"Actually there is one thing which is really troubling me," Suresh said, looking upset.

"What?" Nitish asked.

"There is no doubt now that there is some serial killer amongst us," Suresh declared distraught.

"How can you say this?" Nitish was aghast.

"Arre yaar, just consider the evidence. We have one murder that was made to look like suicide and then we have another murder made to look like an accident or suicide," Suresh said, getting back to his usual logical self.

Nitish nodded.

"And to top it, these are two people who were also somewhat involved with each other." Suresh paused. "So what does that tell you?"

"What?" Nitish had no idea what Suresh was getting at.

"*Arre* stupid, it indicates that the murderer is firstly a person who is very devious, clever, with perhaps a technical bent of mind. And secondly, he/she is a conservative person who does not like boys and girls mixing with each other. And thirdly, this person is nuts," Suresh finished with a flourish, impressed with his own powers of deduction.

"Yes. You are right I guess," Nitish concurred.

"And who do you think fits this profile?" Suresh asked.

Only one figure face danced in front of Nitish's eyes. "Mayank sir," his voice was barely audible.

"Right!" Suresh was triumphant. "Now what we must do is gather evidence against him."

"What? Are you mad?" Nitish was genuinely horrified. He did not want to get on the wrong side of Mayank sir even in his wildest nightmares.

"See here buddy, this Inspector Bisht is not a very capable man. And Shantanu sir is brilliant, but only in his research. He will not be able to do what we can do," Suresh was excited.

Seeing the gleam in Suresh's eyes, Nitish knew it was pointless to argue with him. "But it could be dangerous. If you are right, this is a ... a ... killer we are dealing with."

"If I am right? What do you mean?" Suresh was affronted.

"No. Of course, you are right. I just meant, meant that ...," Nitish fumbled for words to pacify him.

"Shut up! I know what you meant. Now listen to what I am saying. This is what we will do. First, we will hack into his system and download everything that is there on his laptop," Suresh

said.

"Er... right," Nitish did not like the direction in which this was going. "Then?"

"Then… then, I'll tell you later," Suresh was himself unsure of the next step. "The contents of his laptop will give us a clue about what we should do next," he ad-libbed.

Nitish nodded gloomily. He did not know how he could get out of this without jeopardising his friendship. But he was getting into dangerous territory; he would have to back out now. He had better think of something before things got out of hand. Suresh was a great guy, but somewhat headstrong and reckless.

"But you told Professor Shantanu that Saransh sir and Mohit too could be involved," Nitish made a last attempt.

"Yes. So? I can change my mind, can't I?" Suresh paused. "Actually the more I think of it, the more convinced I am about Mayank sir. But yes, I will have to rule out Saransh sir and Mohit too… mmm…," Suresh was quiet.

Nitish knew there was no point saying anything. Suresh would very much do as he pleased.

There was an uneasy silence.

After some time, Suresh said, "You know, I was also wondering why Professor Shantanu mentioned Deepak. Perhaps there is some mystery about this too."

"Really Suresh, you should not get into all this. Your studies are suffering, as it is," Nitish cautioned yet again.

"I know. But I can't help it. Everything about Vipin and Gurpreet keeps going on and on in my mind. And since the time Professor Shantanu brought up the issue of Deepak, I'm forced to think that there really is something very strange in his taking such a long leave without giving a proper application or informing anyone," Suresh paused.

Nitish was quiet. He wished fervently that Suresh would somehow give up investigation.

"You know Deepak could lose an entire semester, maybe the complete year this way... His attendance has fallen short. He has not appeared for the first two sessional tests. And it is likely that he will not be allowed for the third unless he turns up soon enough," Suresh continued.

"There must be some reason. Why should we bother?" Nitish said.

"Arre, for a boy as regular and as academically sincere as Deepak, such a thing is unthinkable. There has to be something behind it. And then the fact that Professor Shantanu also mentioned it just proves that there is something amiss here," Suresh paused.

"Well, ok, if you say so," Nitish said gloomily. He knew it was futile to try and divert Suresh's mind from something once he had set his mind to it.

"And the professor mentioned some 'Enigma' too. Now who could that be?" Suresh seemed to be speaking to himself.

Nitish looked blank.

"I'm going to get at the bottom of this. Until I find a logical explanation for Deepak's absence, and who this 'Enigma' is, I will not be able to relax. But first I have to find evidence against Mayank sir," Suresh looked unseeingly at the faraway trees.

Nitish knew that Suresh's mind had already reached somewhere else.

Vipin really deserved to die, Mayank reflected as he sipped his black sugar-free coffee whilst strolling on the roof of the third block of the boys' hostel. He looked around. The Shivalik range on which Mussoorie was located seemed so near that he felt that he had to merely reach out and he would touch it. The air, the environment, the clouds brushing the mountaintops — it was all pristine; seemingly untouched by the polluting hands of man.

But no — this purity was already being defiled, defiled by these students. Well, Vipin was gone and so was Gurpreet. Their deaths would serve as a lesson for the others to fall in line. What these students were up to, was horrendous. And if no one cared enough to stop them, then well, he surely would. Perhaps more students needed to go before the purity of the campus was restored.

The girls nowadays were worse than the boys, he reflected. They were more westernised than the westerners themselves were. Their clothes, their behaviour, their moral values — in fact they were the ones to instigate boys to bunk classes and indulge in all kinds of indecent activities. He knew all about what these students surfed for on the net. He knew what they were up to when they bunked classes. And he certainly knew what went on in the abandoned sheds at the back of the campus.

Involuntarily, his one and only love came to his mind. She was never far from his thoughts ever. How much he had loved her! And she had seemed to love him too. After all, why else would she have spent all her free time with him? He had helped her to adjust at MIST when she had joined as a lecturer; helped her to get a suitable PG accommodation. She had been pure at first, the perfect girl.

But then, she too had turned out just like all the others. The episode of seeing her kissing another man had scarred him forever. A searing pain stung his heart at the memory. Later, he had learnt that the man was her boyfriend from the previous college where she had worked. Then he knew for sure that womankind was not to be trusted. They were witches incarnate.

He had always known that women were evil, of course, but his beloved had lulled him into a state of complacency. But he was soon back to being wary of all women. And why not? When his own mother had never loved him but had instead rejected him, how could he blame other women?

Admittedly, no one could condone what he had done many years earlier. But for his own family to disown him! Family members always stuck to each other, didn't they? Every family had a skeleton to hide. Then why had his family made such a hue and cry over his misdemeanour — which of course was not very pardonable...

Although it was nothing really... well perhaps it was... but then it was not wholly his fault. After all who knew Ruchi would not respond to his advances? After all they had been friends for a good two years. Of course she was just 14 then... but then he was certain she loved him exactly the way he loved her. Then why rebuff his lovemaking? And then to go and commit suicide like that? That was stupid... and most importantly how could he be held responsible for it?

Ok, perhaps the family could not stomach it. Of course the ensuing social scandal and police inquiry had been unrelentingly horrendous. But his mother? She too did not shield him, protect him, and take him into her fold... Surely she could have stood up for him, taken his side, begged for forgiveness on his behalf from the family... What were mothers for, if not to protect their children? But no — not his mother. She was made of stone...

Suddenly, he heard a sound. From his vantage point, he looked towards it. A group of boys had collected in a corner of the second floor corridor. It seemed that an argument was taking place. Rapidly, Mayank bounded down the stairs, two at a time, eager to catch the erring students and bring them to book.

Far away, near the basketball court, Professor Shantanu stood watching the entire tableau unfold. Mayank's behaviour certainly appeared somewhat crazy. He recalled the words of the Physics lecturer. Could he be a psychopath?

"Hey, you know what? Remember I was telling you about the visit of the Chinese Premier?" Suresh said, whilst trying to hack into Mayank's system. The two were sitting in their hostel room and Suresh was intent on finding his way around the security system of the institute server via his laptop.

"Huh," Nitish only half-listened. He was too anxious with the way Suresh's hacking was going. He prayed fervently that Suresh would not be able to make any headway.

"Well, you know, they will be visiting the Indian Military Academy and security all along the Chakrata road has been beefed up," Suresh spoke while his fingers moved rapidly on the laptop keys.

"So?" Nitish couldn't care less.

"Well, this is quite exciting," Suresh said.

"How do you know all this?" Nitish asked.

"Arre, I read the local Hindi paper too, you know," Suresh

explained. "And since I had read about this in the Times of India, it seemed natural to follow it up in the Doon paper also."

Nitish nodded. He knew that Suresh was fanatical about keeping his general knowledge updated, particularly about events that caught his interest. It was all ostensibly for his preparations for the impending Civil Services exam next year. But Nitish knew that it was more than that. Suresh was simply interested in too may things.

"Particularly, the small housing colonies and slums around the Military Academy have been combed thoroughly by the security forces," Suresh continued, all the while intent on his laptop.

"Let's go and get some coffee," Nitish tried to divert Suresh from his task.

"Later. I'm about to achieve a breakthrough," Suresh said absently. "The visiting Chinese delegation will also visit the Defence Research and Development Organization," he continued.

"Mmm ... you already told me this earlier," Nitish fell quiet, anxiously observing Suresh's machinations on the Institute wi-fi network.

"Eureka! I'm in!" Suresh shouted, startling him.

Sitting idly in his lab, ruminating over everything, Professor Shantanu decided to put everything down on paper. That might help him make some headway. He fished out his writing pad and made three columns. In the first, he wrote suspects, in the next, he put down motive, and in the last — evidence. Methodically, he listed Mayank, Ramadin, Mohit, and Saransh as suspects.

Clearly all of them had the motive for murdering Vipin. But apart from the motive which was mostly circumstantial, given their nasty history with Vipin, there was no real evidence against them.

And then came the question of Gurpreet's death. Only Mayank seemed to have a motive for doing away with her, based upon his own warped and convoluted thought-process. Was it possible that Ramadin, Saransh and Mohit too could have had a motive to kill Gurpreet? He had no answer to this question. There was no evidence to link them to Gurpreet's death either... but at the same time, Mayank and Ramadin both had been seen in the girls' hostel on the night of the murder... Was it just a coincidence?

And why was he thinking that both the murders were committed by the same person? Was it possible that there were two murderers? The thought was too ghastly to contemplate. Two murderers and both from MIST? But Gurpreet had never antagonized anyone. Who would want to kill her? Oh God! He was going around in circles...

If it was the same person, then only Mayank with his biased sensibility might have some twisted reason to take such an extreme step. So then, should he clear the other three? Professor Shantanu was unable to make up his mind. He decided to leave it for the moment.

In the next page, he began listing unresolved questions. The first point was the reason for Gurpreet going to the terrace. There was no sane rationale for a person to go to the terrace at that unearthly hour. Once he had the answer to this question, he would be very near to the identity of her murderer. He needed to find the details of her cell phone record from the police officer. There had to be a clue there somewhere.

Immediately, Professor Shantanu made a call to Inspector Bisht. The latter responded with the information that Gurpreet's fall had damaged her cell phone beyond repair. However, he was in the process of getting details of her call records from the service provider.

He had done the same in the case of Vipin too, Inspector Bisht added helpfully. He had also determined the names of the people whose numbers were listed on Vipin's call record on the day of the death. Oh great, Professor Shantanu was excited. There seemed to be some progress. Most of the names were those of his classmates, Mr. Bisht said. There were also a couple of numbers, which apparently no longer existed, he added. He had tried to trace the ownership of these non-existent numbers, but the numbers had presumably been procured under some false id, the police officer said. He promised to fax the details of the call record for Vipin's cell phone.

What about the data from the laptops of Vipin and Gurpreet? Professor Shantanu queried. Inspector Bisht was quiet. After a while, he responded in a weary tone that he could not find anything worthwhile in either of them. There seemed to be a surfeit of pictures, songs, movies and unmentionable objectionable stuff; but nothing that would give a clue to their murders, the police officer explained. Professor Shantanu concurred that he too had gone through Vipin's journal and other files, but found nothing conclusive.

A few minutes later, Professor Shantanu had the details for the calls made and received from Vipin's cell phone on the day of the murder. They were too many. It would be a tedious task to check out all of them. Perhaps he would ask Naresh to call each of the names listed, and determine whether there was anything suspicious. He put an asterisk on the list and wrote a note for Naresh to take care of it. Well, that was done! Professor Shantanu was sure that Naresh, in his usual meticulous and diligent manner, would look into it immediately and report to him in case there was anything amiss.

He would do the same as soon as he received details of Gurpreet's call list, the professor decided. Then he would be able to perhaps get a clue as to why Gurpreet had gone to the terrace.

Next on his list, he put down the question of Enigma's identity. 'Enigma' seemed to be the only person closest to Gurpreet as evidenced from her mails to him/her through her *Facebook* account. Perhaps 'Enigma' was of no consequence; and yet the fact that Gurpreet had confided so much into the person called for his/her identity to be determined. He was sure that Gurpreet's call record would reveal that several calls were made and received from this 'Enigma' and that would easily help him determine the truth about 'Enigma'. And later, a talk with the real 'Enigma' would, in all probability, provide some important leads.

Now, the other unresolved matter was Deepak's absence from MIST. Admittedly, there seemed to be nothing to connect Deepak with the murders. Still, it was a peculiar and bothersome fact. It was like a piece that did not fit into the expected picture. And, he was not entirely convinced about Brigadier Kalra's explanation for Deepak's long leave.

Repeatedly, he went through all that he had put down. The first thing he had to do was to determine whether it was the same person who was involved in both the murders. And if it was, what was the motive?

But before that, he really was not sure of the motive for Vipin's murder either. Was it a murder committed due to hatred towards Vipin? In which case all his suspects were equally guilty. But... Professor Shantanu was not entirely convinced that it was done out of hate alone. Surely, there had to be a deeper underlying motive? The motives of Ramadin, Mohit, Saransh and Mayank did not seem strong enough to lead to murder.

Professor Shantanu shook his head in frustration. He was back to square one. And if he were to go by Suresh's hypothesis of a serial killer, it implicated Mayank, and to some extent, Saransh too. And of course, a serial killer did not need a concrete motive. The serial killer was a crazy person and a subject of study for psychiatrists...

Suddenly he remembered a quote of Woody Allen that he had come across a long time back. It went something like 'My education was dismal. I went to a series of schools for mentally disturbed teachers.' The professor smiled wryly. There was no doubt, a kernel of truth in it somewhere. The mentally disturbed bit certainly fit the bill in case of Mayank and Saransh... and no doubt there were a few other borderline cases as well.

Perhaps there was some other angle. There was something right there on the surface, which he was probably overlooking, the thought occurred to Professor Shantanu.

Perhaps he should pay another visit to Brigadier Kalra. That would be a good diversion. It would give his brain time to reboot and also settle the matter of Deepak's inexplicable absence.

Pierre entered the lab. Professor Shantanu was glad at the intrusion. He had started looking forward to his chats with Pierre. The latter always had something interesting to say.

"You know, I have been concentrating on my Ph.D since quite some time now. And in the course of my research, I have just learnt that China has virtually hijacked Tibetan Buddhism," Pierre sounded disillusioned.

"Come on! How is that possible?" Professor Shantanu was perplexed.

"Actually, you are so caught up in MIST that you don't know half the things that are happening in the world," Pierre said.

The professor looked surprised.

"Sorry, I didn't mean it the way it sounded," Pierre was contrite.

"No, you are probably right. So, do enlighten me," the professor smiled. He was beginning to like Pierre's earnestness and passion towards his subject. If only more Ph.D students in India were as passionate, there would be a whole lot of patents being filed and numerous R&D projects originating in the country.

"Well, like I had told you earlier, Beijing is busy undermining the influence of the Dalai Lama. And now, they are striking at the very root, and that is Tibetan Buddhism."

"Really? How?"

"They began by organising the first World Buddhist Forum in 2006 in which they gave a global profile to their own nominated Panchen Lama. The second Buddhist Forum was also successfully concluded recently."

"So?" The professor was puzzled.

"So you see, they have diluted Dalai Lama's position and prestige within the Tibetan Buddhist hierarchy. And their official endorsement of Buddhism will provide them legitimacy to recognise the next Dalai Lama," Pierre explained.

"Oh, I see. That is not nice," Professor Shantanu could see Pierre's point now.

"Yes, it is a very clever strategy. They have reduced the Lama's influence among Tibetans in China and also restricted his international support base," Pierre paused.

He continued gloomily, "No one in the world really cares one way or another, least of all, India. Trade is growing rapidly. Britain declared some time back that it unconditionally recognises China's absolute authority over Tibet. This is a big blow. Britain was the only western nation to have had official dealings with Tibet. But seeing where the wind is blowing... France has also been coerced into not recognising Tibet as an independent country."

"After all, economics overrides everything," Professor Shantanu concurred.

"In fact, Beijing also sent a delegation of Tibetan Buddhists led by a so-called 'living Buddha' to USA to explain to the Congress what they are all about," Pierre said.

"I see." Pierre was really keeping up to date with world affairs in this regard, Professor Shantanu reflected.

"Once the Dalai Lama is no more, the Chinese believe that the Tibetan cause will die out by itself. Currently, all the various groups of Tibetans are united by the Dalai Lama. Once he is no more, these groups will break away into many splintered factions and all free Tibetan movements will die out on their own," Pierre paused.

Professor Shantanu had truly no idea about all these ramifications.

"The Chinese are simply buying time and waiting for the Dalai Lama to pass away. That is why they fob off every Tibetan delegation that tries to discuss a solution with them," he paused.

"The Dalai Lama is unable to understand this. The very fact that the Dalai Lama seeks partial autonomy within the Chinese constitution and not complete independence, points to his weakness," Pierre was indignant.

"Hey, are you criticizing the Dalai Lama?" the professor believed that the Nobel peace laureate was above criticism.

"Of course. Dalai Lama is going senile. He is 76 after all. Can you imagine when there were talks of a successor, he declared that it could be a girl in all probability? Can you imagine such nonsense? This will never be accepted," Pierre's voice rose a notch.

"Maybe he wants to declare his heir in his lifetime, so that the Chinese are unable to install their own candidate as the next Dalai Lama after his death. But this is sheer stupidity!" Pierre was impassioned.

"Oh!" Professor Shantanu had no idea about all this.

Naresh entered the lab and went to his designated desk.

Pierre continued, oblivious to the intrusion. "Every Tibetan wants freedom, but at the same time they regard the Dalai Lama as the living Buddha, so they are torn between freedom and God. But nevertheless, Tibetans want total independence now.

They are no longer content with the Dalai Lama's stand of mere autonomy."

"Well, what can they do?" the professor said.

"Nothing much, he sighed. "And the Chinese are banking on the hope that as far as the younger generation of Tibetans is concerned — that is those born in India — they will either get assimilated into the Indian mainstream and lose their Tibetan identity, or else become marginalised and be considered a liability by the Indian government and society. So, they are simply biding their time," Pierre was morose.

"This seems to be a clever strategy," Professor Shantanu conceded.

"Yes. They are also filling Tibet with Chinese people. Very soon, there won't be a separate identifiable Tibetan-only-area left to fight for," Pierre's voice was low.

"That is bad." The professor shook his head.

"This is why there have been a series of self-immolations in Tibet to protest against all these atrocities by the Chinese." Pierre looked pained.

Professor Shantanu nodded, "Yes I did read that there have been around twenty self-immolations by Tibetans."

"I really wish I could do something — anything!" Pierre looked deeply distressed.

It seemed that Pierre was taking things too much to heart. "Well, things are the way they are. You have to just take it easy. This is how the world is," Professor Shantanu counselled.

"Yes. I should not get so emotional about it," Pierre grimaced deprecatingly. "Anyway, I should get going," he strode out of the lab.

"This Pierre is a rather endearing chap," Professor Shantanu smiled at Naresh.

"Mm," Naresh replied, his nose buried in a file.

"Though he does get a bit too worked-up about this Tibetan business."

"Well, yes, it is something to get worked-up about. After all, these poor Tibetans have to live like refugees. It is really bad," Naresh looked up and said.

The professor was surprised. He had no idea that Naresh would agree with Pierre's stand.

"And Pierre is right. Tibetans do want total independence. But they should do something about it soon, before the Chinese successfully implement their clever strategy of complete dominance over Tibetans and Tibet," Naresh spoke in a rush.

"I didn't know you were interested in the Tibetan plight," the professor said.

"Not really. Just caught the last bit of what Pierre was saying and am just elaborating upon it. Bad habit... this eavesdropping," Naresh smiled sheepishly.

"Well, I've kept the details of Vipin's call record on the day of the murder, for you to follow up. In case you find anything suspicious after talking to all those listed in the record, let me know," Professor Shantanu instructed.

"Right," Naresh looked unhappily at the rather long list.

"And I will soon have the details of Gurpreet's call records and expect you to do the same with it as well," Professor Shantanu said.

Naresh nodded. He had no choice but to follow his guide's explicit instructions.

Later, at Brigadier Kalra's home, Professor Shantanu found that the army officer was less belligerent than the last time they had met. In fact, he seemed to have aged overnight. The silver on his head seemed to have increased considerably; there were deep lines etched on the corners of his mouth, and the huge dark circles around his eyes spoke of sleepless nights. This was one troubled man!

Professor Shantanu wondered aloud why this was so.

"It's just office tension," Brigadier Kalra mumbled.

Mrs. Kalra seemed to sleep-walk through the motions of offering tea etc. She looked nothing short of a holocaust survivor!

What had happened here? This was one dysfunctional family! The parents looked extremely disturbed, thought Professor Shantanu. Was the brigadier going to lose his job?

Hesitatingly, the professor brought up the topic that he had come about. "When is Deepak likely to join back?"

The husband and wife duo looked blankly back at him.

Professor Shantanu repeated the question.

"Er... there is some serious problem with his grandmother and I think I will be putting up an application at MIST so that Deepak may be provided long leave of absence for about er... a couple of months," the Brigadier spoke hesitatingly. All his army bluster had vanished.

"I see," Professor Shantanu paused. "But you see, in this way, he would lose an entire academic year," he continued.

There was silence.

"A boy as brilliant as Deepak should have every opportunity to develop himself, and we should not allow anything to come in the way of his academics," Professor Shantanu made another attempt.

"We know what we are doing. Please leave it at that. No one can be more concerned about our son than us," Brigadier Kalra spoke fervently.

Mrs. Kalra nodded.

There was a hint of a tear in the Brigadier's eyes.

Driving away from the Kalra residence, Professor Shantanu wondered what to make of the entire episode. Apparently, they were going through some personal and professional crisis. And of course, he had no right to intrude into their personal affairs. And yet, Professor Shantanu could not make up his mind to leave the matter of Deepak well alone. But perhaps he should put it on the back-burner for the moment, he decided.

"There are too many suspicions being cast upon Mayank," Gopal Das Singhal had summoned the director to discuss this vexing problem.

Professor Indresan was surprised that Singhal was aware of this. But then, not for anything was he the chairman. He knew everything that went on in the college

"Er... yes sir," the director did not know what else to say.

"Should his services be terminated?" Singhal asked, irritated at Professor Indresan's lack of input. Normally, he would have taken this sort of decision on his own. But, in case of Mayank, he wanted to be absolutely sure. Since the time Mayank had taken over as hostel warden, the discipline in the hostel had improved dramatically. Earlier, there were at least a couple of expulsions from the boys' hostel every month, but now this was no longer the case.

"Well sir, he is very useful as the warden," Professor Indresan echoed the chairman's thoughts. "No one has been able to control the hostel as well as he has," he paused.

"Yes, but do we have a substitute for him for the hostel?" Singhal asked.

"No sir, we don't," the director said. In fact, no one was willing to take on the responsibility of being the warden due to the heavy 24-hour work it involved.

"Well, in that case, suggest to Mayank that he should take two weeks' leave," Singhal made the decision.

"Sir, this is the perfect solution," Professor Indresan genuinely meant the praise.

"Sir, I would like to show you something," it was Suresh at the lab door.

Professor Shantanu waved him inside.

"But I want only you to see it," Suresh looked around the lab to ensure that there was no one present.

"Don't worry. I'm alone," the professor said.

For a change, Naresh was away, out of the campus for some work he had. This was somewhat unusual, for apparently Naresh's entire life revolved around the lab. But thinking that Naresh too had a right to some semblance of normalcy, Professor Shantanu had not given it another thought.

"Yes, what do you want to show me?" the professor asked.

"Just a minute, sir," Suresh rapidly opened the laptop he had brought.

Professor Shantanu waited patiently.

Quickly, one by one, Suresh opened several files. They contained net-downloaded material revolving around murders, murder weapons, suicides, and murders made to look like suicides.

"Are you planning the next?" Professor Shantanu commented understatedly after glancing through everything. Some of the content like strangulation had been highlighted, he noted.

"Actually, sir, all these files have been copied from Mayank sir's laptop," Suresh said with a flourish.

"What?" the professor sat up straighter, shocked beyond words.

"And not only this, there is more...," with a look of pride on his face on getting the rapt attention of the professor, Suresh rapidly double-clicked on a few more files.

Professor Shantanu grimaced as he noted the contents. They were mostly in the realm of sado-masochism. "I get the idea. Close them," he looked away in disgust.

Hurriedly, Suresh did his bidding.

After a long pause, he said, "How did you manage to get all these details?" Professor Shantanu was honestly impressed.

Suresh hesitated, but only for a moment. "Well, I hacked into Mayank sir's system, er... his laptop," he admitted sheepishly. He knew he could trust the professor.

"And how did you manage that?"

"Well, sir, our entire campus is networked, as well as wi-fi enabled; and all the PCs or laptops that access the net do so via the internal server. It is very easy. One has to just know the IP address of a particular PC and one can hack into it," Suresh's explanation seemed simple enough.

"Even finding the IP address is a matter of permutation, combination," Suresh added.

"I see," the professor said, even though he did not see very well.

Suresh continued, "The only thing is that at the time of hacking, the other person's computer should be switched on."

"What about anti-virus, firewalls etc. on the particular system that is being hacked into?" Professor Shantanu asked.

"Oh, I can get around them," Suresh's tone held a note of scorn.

"And what about passwords that protect individual logins?" The professor asked.

"That is easy too," Suresh smiled.

This boy would go places, Professor Shantanu thought. Maybe in future, if the boy was interested in research, he could take him under his wing.

Meanwhile there were more pressing matters at hand. Mayank needed to be thoroughly interrogated.

"So you think it is Mayank?" Professor Shantanu asked.

Suresh nodded.

"But what about Saransh and Mohit as you mentioned last time?" the professor reminded him.

"Yes, well, I am looking into that angle as well; and exploring it through all the sources that I have," Suresh paused. "In fact, since you mentioned Deepak and 'Enigma', I am also trying to determine their relation with the murders," Suresh continued.

"Oh. I think you should concentrate on your studies," Professor Shantanu felt a touch of concern. Suresh was obviously neglecting his studies.

"Don't worry, sir. You know I am the university topper. I can always make up for lost time," Suresh smiled.

The professor smiled back.

"As soon as I learn more things, I will bring them to you," Suresh promised.

"Thank you, Suresh. You have done a great job. Now let me look into this. You may go now," Professor Shantanu said.

Suresh left.

CHAPTER – 14

"There has been another death!" Professor Indresan announced in a bewildered voice, looking stunned.

Professor Shantanu was horrified. "What? How?" he asked.

"Early morning the sports officer found a boy in the swimming pool. He seems to have drowned," Professor Indresan spoke nervously.

"Oh!" Professor Shantanu tried to gather his wits about himself.

"It could be possible that the boy had gone swimming early in the morning and drowned accidently," the director continued.

"Who is the boy?" Professor Shantanu asked.

"Suresh of third year Computer Science," Professor Indresan said dejectedly.

"Oh! No! That can't be possible!" Professor Shantanu was staggered.

"Do you know the boy?" Professor Indresan asked.

"Yes, I did know him," Professor Shantanu looked anguished.

"The sports officer took the help of Mayank and brought the boy…er…the body to the infirmary. The night-duty doctor confirmed that death was due to drowning. And now we are waiting for Inspector Bisht," Professor Indresan narrated agitatedly.

"What were the sports officer and Mayank doing, up so early in the morning?" Professor Shantanu was suspicious.

"The sports officer had gone for his usual early-morning

swim at 6.30 a.m. before the first student slot started at 7a.m… and Mayank, as you know, never sleeps and happened to be prowling around the first hostel block, which is near the pool. When the sports officer went looking around for help, he fortunately ran into Mayank," Professor Indresan said.

"Wait a minute! Wasn't Mayank supposed to have gone on leave?" Professor Shantanu was disturbed.

"Oh yes. I forgot about that. He was to have gone two days back." Professor Indresan looked distressed.

"We had better find out why he did not leave; or whether he came back after leaving," Professor Shantanu said.

Mr. Bisht entered. After hearing everything, he immediately proceeded to the infirmary.

Professor Shantanu left after suggesting that the director should inform the management, address the students, and subsequently release a statement for the press.

"Someone squealed to Professor Shantanu that I was angry with Vipin — angry enough to want to take revenge," Mohit pronounced angrily to his roommate.

"Any person who goes against me comes to a bad end, you mark my words," he continued ominously.

His roommate looked apprehensive, "Wh... what are you saying?"

"Well, you know, after Gurpreet's murder, Professor Shantanu called me and questioned me about both Vipin and Gurpreet. He was somehow trying to prove that I had something to do with the murders," Mohit explained indignantly.

"Oh, that is bad," the roommate was sympathetic.

"But obviously the professor could get nothing out of me. I

am too smart for him," Mohit was smug.

"Yes," the roommate smiled in feigned awe.

"And now, of course, the professor and the institute authorities are in even bigger trouble," Mohit seemed satisfied.

"What do you mean?" the roommate felt a frisson of fear in his heart.

"I mean that there has been another murder," there was a peculiar look in Mohit's eyes.

The roommate felt as though his blood had turned to ice. He opened his mouth to speak, but no words were forthcoming. He could only stare at Mohit in helpless trepidation.

Rapidly, Professor Shantanu walked towards his lab, all the while mulling over the possibility that Suresh's death was no accident, but murder. He was doing too much of snooping and this had probably led to his death. But what had he found out?

Now there was no doubt that the murderer was some diabolical person within the campus. Who could it be? All the evidence pointed to Mayank. Admittedly, the evidence was incidental at best. There was nothing that actually incriminated Mayank beyond any shadow of doubt. But then, Mayank had been asked to go on a long leave. So what had he been doing in the hostel premises that morning?

Grimly, he sent for Mayank. It was time for a serious talk with him.

"What were you doing near the swimming pool so early in the morning?" Professor Shantanu challenged Mayank.

"Sir, it is my usual practice to take an early morning walk around the entire hostel block," Mayank spoke tonelessly.

"But you were supposed to be on two weeks' leave!" The professor was incensed.

"Yes sir. But you see, right when I was to proceed, the other hostel warden took ill and had to be hospitalised. So Col Akash asked me to defer my leave by three days, till the warden returned," Mayank was matter-of-fact.

"I see," the professor was pacified somewhat.

But still, there was too much controversy around Mayank. "Tell me why the students are so afraid of you," he tried a different track of questioning.

"Sir, anyone who advocates discipline is hated by students. You know how this current generation is," Mayank spoke earnestly.

"But didn't you threaten Vipin at one time that you would see to it that he came to a bad end?" the professor paused. "And he has!"

"Sir, I have threatened scores of students in the same manner. It is the only way to make them toe the line. Otherwise, there will be complete mayhem in the hostel," Mayank smiled grimly.

"And you have too much interest in the goings-on of the girls' hostel even though you have no jurisdiction over it," the professor probed.

"Sir, let me tell you — these girls are worse than the boys and they are equally responsible in encouraging indiscipline — and what not — among the boys. And as hostel warden, it is my duty to keep my eyes and ears wide open so that I may know of everything that is going on. That is the only way to prevent any untoward thing from happening," Mayank paused.

"If I did not do this, god knows how many scandalous things

would mar the academic atmosphere of MIST," he said sternly.

He certainly takes his job seriously, thought Professor Shantanu.

"Sir, I cannot even tell you the horrible things these boys and girls are up to, nowadays," Mayank continued.

"So, that means, you do not like girls?" Professor Shantanu spoke softly.

"It's not that, sir, although girls are nasty creatures by nature. They lure a boy into all kinds of evil and then when the boy is trapped, they coolly walk away," Mayank was bitter.

"Was Gurpreet one such girl and was that why you hated her so much?" the professor spoke mildly.

Mayank looked shocked. "Sir, what are you saying?" he paused. "Gurpreet, in fact, was not such a bad girl at all, though it was love that made her somewhat unstable. To come to Vipin's room in the middle of the night...," Mayank shook his head.

"Is that why you decided to punish her?" Professor Shantanu goaded him.

Mayank stared back.

"And when Suresh found out the truth about you, you eliminated him too?" the professor was relentless.

"Sir, I think this is too much. Such allegations are unwarranted and completely unacceptable. I don't have anything to say now," Mayank's lower lip quivered in indignation.

"So, are you saying you had nothing to do with the deaths of any of these students?" Professor Shantanu raised his voice.

"Sir, I have said what I had to say. You may choose to believe me or not to believe me. I don't care. I don't care about what anyone thinks of me. I stopped caring years ago when my own

own mother…," Mayank checked himself.

"Sir, I'd like to be excused now. If there is really any evidence against me, then it is a separate matter; but for now, I would like to go," his face resolute, he stared far away beyond Professor Shantanu's head at the mountains outside the window.

Professor Shantanu motioned for him to leave.

He knew Mayank would not be forthcoming about anything now. As he had rightly pointed out, evidence was needed first. Professor Shantanu leaned back in his chair; he had had a purpose for antagonising Mayank so much. He was sure that soon Mayank would do something hasty, something thoughtless; and thereby establish his culpability in the act.

All that the professor had was anecdotal evidence. Admittedly, the stuff from Mayank's laptop was highly suspicious. But then again, it was not the clinching evidence required to nail him.

A part of him had thought of confronting Mayank with the files downloaded from his laptop; but thinking the better of it, Professor Shantanu had desisted. After all, he had better keep a few aces up his sleeve. He just might need them at a later date. And besides, challenging Mayank in his current mood would serve no purpose. Mayank would simply brazen it out.

The next day was a holiday on account of Buddha Purnima. Professor Shantanu was flipping through the newspaper after a leisurely breakfast at the guesthouse. This was a much-needed respite from the institute.

Pierre looked at him and smiled, "This is a good break, is it not?"

"Yes," the professor nodded. "What are your plans for the

day? Will you be going to some Tibetan colony or something?"

"I don't know... actually I had thought of going, thinking that today will be a big day for Tibetans. But later I learnt that their calendar is different."

"Different? What do you mean?"

"Well, you see, as per their calendar, Buddha Purnima falls a month later than it does in the Hindu calendar," Pierre explained.

"Really?" To Professor Shantanu this was news. "I didn't know that."

"Yes, well, so I will try and be a part of their celebrations which will commence after a month and will go on for fifteen days."

"Right," the professor said.

"I got in touch with a few members of the Tibetan Women's Association and they told me that there will be elaborate rituals at the Buddha Temple in Clement Town. This would include the chanting of one lakh special mantras everyday. It is considered a most holy occasion by all Tibetans."

"I see. Any particular member of the women's association?" there was a twinkle in the professor's eyes.

"I only wish ...," Pierre smiled mischievously.

Naresh approached.

"Your student is really conscientious, isn't he? He's here working on a holiday also," Pierre commented.

The professor smiled.

"Well, I'll get going and leave you to discuss your research," Pierre said.

"Hardly. Not much research work is getting done since all

these murders," Professor Shantanu spoke wryly.

Pierre nodded and left.

"Sir, I came to tell you that I have thoroughly checked the call records of Vipin and found nothing," Naresh said.

"Oh," Professor Shantanu was disappointed. He had really hoped to find something, some little fact that would give him some sort of lead.

Naresh handed back the call record list to the professor.

"Inspector Bisht has faxed the details of Gurpreet's call record as well. Why don't you pick it up from my table at the lab and check that too?" Professor Shantanu said. He hoped against hope that it would lead to something.

"Sure thing," Naresh walked towards the academic block.

In his office, Professor Indresan was facing distraught parents yet again. But this time, he had taken no chances. Professor Mrityunjaya and Professor Tandon were with him.

"Saab, he was our only hope," Suresh's father, a simple rustic man, dressed in off-white dhoti and kurta spoke.

His wife sat still; her sari-covered head bowed low.

They had started from their village near the small town of Bhabua in Bihar as soon as the news reached them.

Scrimping and saving from their meagre earnings, they had somehow managed to get their son admitted to MIST. The entire village had hopes that Suresh would be their saviour. Even if he did not do much to uplift their lot, his becoming an engineer was like a ray of hope for everyone in the village.

And now, this crushing tragedy.

Professor Indresan felt a pang of sorrow go through him,

and he felt tears pricking at the corner of his eyes.

"Hmm...," he cleared his throat. It would not do for him to become emotional.

But Professor Indresan could not help being moved by the sorrow of this elderly couple. His own father had been a farmer in a small village near Belur and had sacrificed tremendously to ensure that his son became someone big. It was almost as if a member of Professor Indresan's own family had been murdered.

"Come, I will take you to his room," Professor Tandon came to Professor Indresan's rescue.

The parents left.

Professor Indresan decided to meet the chairman. Some action was necessary.

After he explained the entire situation, Gopal Das was readily convinced about adopting a humane approach; after all, he had risen from the ranks himself.

Immediately, he issued an order whereby the younger brother of Suresh would be given admission to MIST in whichever branch of engineering he desired, and all his fees would be paid by the management.

There was a timid knock on Professor Shantanu's door at the guesthouse. It was late evening. Who could it be at this hour? the professor wondered.

It was Nitish.

Professor Shantanu waited for him to speak. He knew that Suresh had been a close friend of Nitish.

"Sir, I have been waiting for a long time to see you," Nitish looked scared.

"Then, you should have come earlier. My doors are open for everyone at all hours; you know that," the professor spoke kindly.

"Yes sir, I know that," a tremulous half-smile appeared at one corner of his mouth.

Professor Shantanu waited patiently.

"Actually sir, I was waiting for you to be alone...er, particularly, I didn't want Mayank sir to come to know that I have met you," the boy continued.

"Yes beta," the professor said encouragingly.

"Sir, Mayank sir is a serial killer and he killed Suresh because Suresh learnt the truth about him," Nitish spoke in a rush.

"What makes you say this?" Professor Shantanu was inclined to agree with him. But then, he wanted to know the basis of Nitish's conclusion.

Rapidly, Nitish explained about Suresh's hypothesis about Mayank being a serial killer and about hacking into his system and trying to find evidence against him.

"Yes, I know; Suresh showed me all the things that he had downloaded from Mayank's laptop," the professor said.

"Well then, sir, you know everything! Please inform the police. They should immediately arrest and hang this — this murderer!" Nitish's voice rose in agitation.

"Yes beta. I can understand your emotions; but the police will go by evidence only. And all that Suresh showed me was indirect evidence," the professor pointed out.

"Sir, please do something," Nitish's voice crumbled. "I'm so afraid, he will surely kill me next."

"Calm down. Nothing of the sort will happen," Professor

Shantanu tried to pacify him.

"No sir. You don't know Mayank sir. He is mad. Truly mad. He murdered Vipin and Gurpreet and then, because Suresh found out that he is the culprit, murdered him too. And now that I — I also know the truth, and Mayank sir knows it very well, he... he will kill me," Nitish spoke frantically looking panic-stricken.

"No beta, nothing will happen to you," Professor Shantanu wondered how he could pacify the petrified boy.

"Please save me," a sob escaped from Nitish.

Professor Shantanu got up, went around, and put his arms around Nitish's shoulders. Maybe he should schedule an exclusive session for Nitish with the counsellor, and then get him special leave so that he may go and stay with his local guardian.

The professor was not entirely sure whether he would be doing this for Nitish or for his own peace of mind; for he was inclined to agree with Nitish's hypothesis.

"What has Inspector Bisht concluded about Suresh's death?" Professor Shantanu knew the answer even before he articulated the question; but he just needed to know the track that the police were following.

"He says that all evidence points to murder; and the time of death is around five in the morning," Gopal Das Singhal said.

Professor Shantanu had taken to directly conferring with the chairman since the time Professor Indresan had given him the go-ahead to proceed with his own investigation and interrogtions.

"Did they find some clue as to who actually did it? Anything left behind by the killer? Fingerprints or something?" Professor Shantanu queried.

"I don't know," Singhal paused. "But if they had found some evidence, Bisht would have definitely told me."

"Mmm... so the killer is really careful. He probably wore gloves ," Professor Shantanu paused.

"Of course, it was obvious all along that it was murder," the professor continued.

"How?" Singhal asked.

"Suresh was the state swimming champion. There was no way he could have drowned," the professor explained.

"Yes. The post-mortem has further revealed signs of a scuffle. There is considerable bruising on the shoulders, upper arms and the wrists. This makes it clear that Suresh struggled," Singhal paused.

Professor Shantanu grimaced. What a way to die!

"Yes. Bisht said that it seems that his head was held forcibly under water until he drowned," Singhal said.

"But I suppose you have already surmised all this," the chairman had great respect for Professor Shantanu's mental prowess.

"Yes. But I have not managed to figure out why these three deaths have happened," Professor Shantanu's voice betrayed his frustration.

"It's okay. The police are also not able to make much headway." It was unlike Singhal to take such a conciliatory stand with one of his employees.

But then, the chairman never considered Professor Shantanu as a member of the staff. Rather, he felt somewhat fortunate that the professor had chosen to work at MIST. It only enhanced the prestige of his institute.

"Yes, well, the press has been briefed, and surprisingly, even the Shivalik Institute is taking it easy now," Professor Shantanu said.

"Yes. It is quite understandable. Something like this has never happened before and it is but natural that the matter will be handled delicately by all concerned," Singhal concurred.

"And we are trying our best to take care of the concerns of the students. The counsellors are on call 24 hours to take care of all possible psychological needs of the students," Professor Shantanu stated.

All faculty, deans and heads are personally addressing students from time to time and are ensuring that the academic atmosphere is maintained as well as possible," the professor continued.

Professor Shantanu had made it a priority that academics took precedence over all other matters at MIST and studies went on as usual. He had personally convened extended meetings with the deans, heads, faculty, and counsellors.

The director had only been too grateful for all the proactive steps taken by Professor Shantanu.

"Good. I know I don't have anything to worry about as long as you are here." Gopal Das Singhal wished yet again that Professor Shantanu was the director instead of the current incumbent. But he knew Professor Shantanu's interest lay in his outstanding research, though he was an equally brilliant administrator.

Saransh stood in front of his mirror applying gel to his hair. Maybe the latest gelled look would add something to his appearance, he hoped. He had noted that most of the boys had adopted a gelled and somewhat spiked hairstyle. And he was not much older than them, so why not try it himself? Saransh surmised.

After trying various versions of spikes, he finalised one where chunks of hair were artfully arranged on his scalp in contrived disarray. Not bad, he smiled at the man in the mirror.

Perhaps there was hope for him, after all. He was getting to be one up on the students now, he reflected. He had become smarter and had put the students on the receiving end, he thought gleefully.

Of late, he had taken to asking the students to work out the most complex numericals in the class and taking the students to task for the smallest misdemeanour. Left with no leader after Vipin, the class began to dread his periods. They now maintained scrupulous discipline in all his classes.

What little bluster was left in some of the rowdy students had soon disappeared after Suresh's death. Ah! God was finally looking in his direction, Saransh smiled self-righteously.

CHAPTER – 15

Restlessly, Professor Shantanu strode across the side of the swimming pool that had stood silent witness to the ghastly murder of a promising young boy. He stared intently into the water, almost willing the cool waves gently lapping at the sides to speak up.

It was late evening. No one was about, which was a good thing; for anyone watching would conclude that the good professor had finally lost it.

Why would Suresh come to the pool so early in the morning? The post-mortem said that the time of death was around 5 a.m.

Had Suresh set up a meeting with someone at the pool? And had that someone turned out to be the murderer himself? This could be a possibility. But then, Suresh had been wearing swimming trunks. Surely, he would not set up a meeting and go for it dressed in swimming trunks? Unless the meeting was conducted in the swimming pool... no — this was too farfetched.

Or, had he been unable to sleep, and so had decided to take a swim to relax? That was a possibility, given Suresh's feverish investigations.

Professor Shantanu felt a pang of guilt go through him. Had Suresh embarked on this entire investigation having been inspired due to the professor's own attempts to investigate the murders? This was an uncomfortable hypothesis, which he would rather not face, the professor decided.

He needed to speak to Inspector Bisht immediately; perhaps

the latter had some clue.

"I have told everything to Singhal Saab," Mr. Bisht sounded defensive.

"I understand that there is a lot of pressure upon you. But I'm not trying to belittle you or anything," Professor Shantanu spoke placatingly.

"Well, what do you want to know?" Mr. Bisht spoke grudgingly.

"Suresh was dressed in swimming trunks, right?" the professor asked.

"Yes," Mr. Bisht said.

"Were there any signs of anyone else who had been swimming at that hour?" the professor queried.

"No," Mr. Bisht said.

"And did you not find anything at all to indicate someone's presence?" the Professor persisted.

"No. It is only the signs of struggle that indicate murder," Mr. Bisht paused.

"The murderer perhaps never expected Suresh to struggle. He had probably hoped to make this death look like suicide too. But he was not entirely successful, for Suresh did put up a strong fight," Mr. Bisht continued.

"But did you not find fingerprints?" Professor Shantanu asked.

"No, the killer wore rubber gloves, I think...," Mr. Bisht spoke thoughtfully.

"What about bits of skin, hair, or something that could have been caught in Suresh's hands or nails," the professor probed.

"No, nothing," Mr. Bisht was glum.

"Anyway, thank you officer. Please fax me the details of Suresh's call records too," Professor Shantanu said.

There was silence.

After a while, Mr. Bisht said, "Sir, I don't mean any disrespect, but now I have to keep everything confidential and I just can't keep giving out such information."

"Oh. I see," Professor Shantanu was disappointed.

"As it is, I am not supposed to discuss this case so freely with anyone. But I have done so. And not only that, I have given you a copy of Vipin's and Gurpreet's call records as well. If my superiors learn of it, I will surely lose my job," Mr. Bisht said.

"Right. I'll have to do without it then," Professor Shantanu said. He suddenly understood that the police officer had shared information with him earlier at Singhal's bidding. But now, with the third murder, things were definitely getting out of hand for Mr. Bisht too.

Back at his lab, Professor Shantanu asked Naresh, "Did Gurpreet's call record reveal any clue about why she went up to the hostel roof?"

"No sir," Naresh looked apologetic.

"That is not good," the Professor looked unhappy.

"Are you sure you have talked to everyone in the list?" the professor queried.

"Of course," Naresh assured.

"And there was nothing?" the professor kept prodding him.

"No," Naresh replied.

Professor Shantanu was quiet.

Naresh handed back the call-record list.

There was a long silence whilst the professor stared

unseeingly at the list.

Inspector Bisht refuses to send details of Suresh's call list. But I suppose it too would have revealed nothing," Professor Shantanu was uncharacteristically gloomy.

Naresh was quiet.

"I do think the matter is very complex." After a while, Professor Shantanu said this reflectively.

"Why do you think so, sir?" Naresh asked dutifully.

"Till the murders of Vipin and Gurpreet, the matter seemed somewhat straightforward; but now with Suresh…I don't know…," the professor seemed to be speaking aloud to himself.

"On the other hand, it could be the case of a psychopath…," Professor Shantanu pushed his fingers through his rather thick unruly hair in frustration. He was no nearer to any conclusion.

Naresh kept quiet.

The professor described Suresh's findings about all the files that the latter had copied from Mayank's laptop.

"So what does it indicate?" Naresh said.

"It indicates that Mayank has been researching into various methods of murders and suicides, etc.," the professor paused.

"I see," Naresh said.

"It also indicates that Mayank was... what do I say... er... somewhat perverted...," the professor spoke hesitatingly.

"So what does it all add up to?" Naresh said.

"Well, it's quite evident that all the murders have been made to appear as suicides. This indicates that the murderer has a psyche of playing games," the professor paused.

"He enjoys creating doubts in the minds of others. It is like a sport for him," he continued.

Naresh remained quiet.

"It points to a mind that is devious and yet curiously creative in a warped way; and a mind that is perhaps full of black humour... It is probably Mayank...," once again, the professor seemed to be speaking to himself.

"I'm sure Mayank will do something now which will incriminate him ... I have instigated him enough during my last talk with him, I think ...," the professor continued.

"It seems to me...," Naresh paused, a strange expression on his face.

"Yes, go on, my boy, don't dither in the middle of a conversation." Naresh was sometimes too slow, in matters other than his research, thought Professor Shantanu.

"Well, sir, I think that Vipin and Gurpreet died because of each other and Suresh drowned accidentally," Naresh's face was deadpan again.

"But evidence has it that Suresh was murdered," Professor Shantanu spoke in an irritated tone; Naresh was being uncharacteristically stupid, he thought.

"With due respect, sir, you know how our policewallahs are. Their deductive abilities leave a lot of room for improvement," Naresh paused.

"In fact, I'm quite sure that Vipin and Gurpreet committed suicide," Naresh stated emphatically.

"Even after knowing everything, you are saying this? What ...?"

Suddenly, a piercing scream filled the air, cutting Professor Shantanu in mid- sentence.

It came from the Central Workshop in the adjacent

building.

Professor Shantanu and Naresh rushed there. It was from the Machine Shop, they surmised.

Rapidly they entered.

Kanika was rooted to a spot, seemingly paralysed. She stood horrified, her mouth open in a scream that was now soundless; staring in the direction of one of the lathe machines.

They followed her gaze.

Sprawled transversely atop the massive lathe machine was Mayank. Death had transformed his countenance into a monstrous facade of his former self. Blood was splattered all over the lathe.

Immediately, Professor Shantanu rushed towards Kanika and led her out of the Machine Shop. She was shaking so badly that she was barely able to walk.

Gopal Das Singhal urgently sent for Professor Indresan and Professor Shantanu.

There was an uneasy stillness. No one was able to speak.

After a long silence, Singhal said, "What should we do now?"

"We can only hope that Inspector Bisht is able to crack the case as soon as possible," Professor Indresan spoke hesitatingly.

"What do you say?" Singhal addressed Professor Shantanu.

"I have to admit I'm flummoxed. As per my findings, Mayank was the most likely culprit. But… but now I have to rethink my entire hypothesis," Professor Shantanu looked troubled.

"Yes, but meanwhile, what should be our stand?" Singhal asked.

"Well, we just have to ensure that there is as much normalcy as possible, given the circumstances," Professor Shantanu said.

"Er... should we declare a one-week holiday for students?" the director proposed.

There was silence.

"Yes, that is a good idea. But I think we would have to confer with the police officer first. Maybe he would want everyone to be available in the campus. Who knows who all he has listed as the prime suspects?" Professor Shantanu said.

"Yes. You are right. I can only pray to God that this unholy mess is resolved soon," Singhal sighed deeply.

After a pause, he continued, "Well, I think you both are doing a great job of maintaining a semblance of routine. I would expect that there should be no slackening whatsoever, given the latest developments," Singhal instructed.

"Yes. I will see to it that everything goes on as usual," Professor Indresan reasserted his leadership.

Later, in his office, Professor Indresan found Col Akash, Professors Mritunjaya, Girish Shukla and Ramesh Bhardwaj waiting for him.

"Sir, both students, and the faculty are deeply disturbed," Professor Bhardwaj hesitatingly broached the topic that had brought them there.

"Yes, *woh kya kehte hain,* this is very serious, very serious," Col. Akash shook his head gloomily.

"We all know it is serious!" Professor Mrityunjaya was irritated. "That is why we are here to discuss our future strategy," he continued.

"Yes, well, I have just taken the management's inputs. And he would not like the institute to be closed or anything. So, all of us must ensure that we maintain our academic schedule. Needless to say, counselling will remain a top priority," Professor Indresan said.

After more deliberations in the same vein, the meeting ended.

Professor Shantanu was back in his lab.

Naresh was away in the city for some work, he had said. Of late, Naresh was staying out for long hours. Perhaps he had a girlfriend, Professor Shantanu reflected. Anyway, it was good that the boy got out of the lab more frequently now. It was not normal for a young boy to be cooped up in the lab all the time with an old professor.

He fished out his writing pad. Sadly, he struck out the name of Mayank from the list of suspects. That left Ramadin, Saransh and Mohit.

It was bizarre the way the murders were occurring in such quick succession. First Vipin, then Gurpreet, then Suresh, and now Mayank. Based on everything, he had almost concluded that Mayank was the perpetrator, and now he too was dead. What was he to make of everything now?

He sent for Ramadin, Saransh and Mohit one by one. The respective conversations provided no headway.

All that he could gather from them was that Mayank was persona non grata for everyone concerned, particularly the students. But then, the moot question was, would anyone go so far as to kill him? And if so, why? More so, was it linked to the first three murders? Neither Saransh nor Mohit were able to give him any clue regarding these questions. Ramadin claimed to know very little about Mayank.

Perhaps one of them had something to do with Mayank's death, the professor suggested. The response was predictable. Ramadin was flabbergasted at such a suggestion, Mohit was belligerent and Saransh non-committal. However, none of them had any alibi either for the time that Mayank was murdered. But that, in no way, indicated their involvement in the crime. As Mohit pointed out, there were scores of students who wanted Mayank dead and had no alibi either — however, that, in no way, implicated them.

He let all three leave.

Professor Shantanu felt as though he had got into a frightful muddle.

And then of course, there was the missing Deepak.

There was also the curious fact of Mayank's murder being so blatantly in-your-face. So, was it a different murderer this time?

In the earlier homicides, the penchant of the killer had been to commit murders in such a way that it created the illusion of a suicide. But this particular slaying... this was a brutal murder — straightforward, plain and simple. The question was — why?

If it was the same murderer, which in all likelihood it was, was he losing his nerve? Or did he not care now to deflect the investigation in the direction of a suicide? Or was he becoming jittery due to something, and so, acting in an unplanned manner? Or was he getting ready to flee, and so did not care anymore? Or was he so confident that he was now throwing a challenge?

Professor Shantanu had no answers.

A group of students had gathered in the canteen.

The mood was ominous all around.

"This is terrible, really terrible," a third year Electrical student

said.

"Yes," Nitish was gloomy.

"Mayank sir was bad. But... but he did not deserve to die," said another student.

"Yes. And that too like this," a second year Electronics girl spoke softly.

"It is horrible," another girl concurred.

"This is really awful. What is happening in the campus?" Nitish said.

"We really don't feel safe any longer. Who knows when and where the killer will strike next?" the third year Electrical student looked fearful.

"Yes, but why is someone doing all this?" a third year Mechanical girl asked.

There was a menacing silence.

"It must be some psycho. There is no other explanation," Nitish said, who felt that some of the sleuthing capabilities of Suresh had got transferred onto him.

"Yes. It must be a psycho," the second year Electronics girl said whilst a shudder seemed to pass through her being.

"But our resident psycho is... er... already...," the third year Mechanical girl pointed out.

"Yes," Nitish conceded.

"Which other psycho can it be?" the third year Electrical student said.

"You know, this one must be a real psycho. Real psychos don't let anyone come to know that they are psychos. They keep the dark part of themselves properly hidden. In real life, they appear totally normal," a third year Mechanical boy said.

"Gosh! Have you done a Ph.D on psychos?" Nitish looked at him in surprise.

"By that logic, poor Mayank sir was not really a true psycho. Foolishly, he let the whole world see that he was a nut case. I mean er... peculiar," the second year Electronics girl said.

"Yes," the third year Mechanical girl nodded.

"So that brings us back to square one. Who is it?" the third year Electrical student said.

"Maybe Saransh sir?" Nitish said.

The group fell silent.

"You know, none of us liked Mayank. But for him to go like this... it's terrible," Rakesh, the Electrical lecturer said.

The other faculty members sitting in the staffroom nodded.

"And you know, he was easily the best warden MIST had, or could ever hope to have," the Mechanical lecturer, Ashish pointed out.

"As long as it was the students, it was a different matter. But now, with faculty being targeted, I don't know... it seems no one is safe anymore," Mona, the Electronics lecturer spoke hesitatingly.

"Arre, come on. Don't be a scaredy rat," Rakesh admonished.

"No. I'm not being a scaredy rat or anything. I'm just being very realistic. Who knows where the killer will strike next?" Mona looked nervous.

At this, a few lecturers glanced anxiously at each other.

"In fact, I'm thinking of taking a few days' leave," commented Vinita, the Computer Applications lecturer.

"Yeah, sure. When the ship is sinking, it is the rats that abandon it first," Rakesh was sarcastic; though he himself had secretly thought of taking leave.

"So what should we do?" Ashish asked plaintively.

"Just sit tight and keep your fingers crossed," Rakesh responded.

"You know it is only the people associated with the hostels who are being targeted. Remember, all the three students were hostellers and Mayank was, of course, the warden," Rakesh continued.

"So?" Ashish asked.

"So we need not worry," Rakesh was triumphant.

"And what about us? Are we the next target?" the warden of the first hostel block suddenly spoke, looking distressed.

"Who knows?" Rakesh said.

Everybody remained quiet.

"What has Inspector Bisht to say about Mayank's death?" Professor Shantanu asked Gopal Das Singhal.

Gopal Das looked quizzically at the professor.

"I had been intent on escorting Kanika out of the machine shop and ensuring her well-being; and so did not closely examine everything," the professor explained.

"Well, not much. He was killed by one of the machine shop tools," Gopal Das was morose.

"I suppose the killer simply yanked out one of the tools displayed on the walls of the machine shop," Professor Shantanu said.

"Yes. Exactly."

"Has the tool been found?" Shantanu asked.

"Yes. It was lying adjacent to the lathe machine."

"Any fingerprints?" even before making the query, Professor Shantanu knew it was pointless.

"Wiped clean," Gopal Das was glum.

"Which tool was it?" the professor asked, out of academic interest.

"Something called a pipe wrench, I think," Gopal Das said.

"Ah yes. Probably a heavy-duty one, and made of cast iron... evidently enough to do the job," Shantanu muttered absently.

Gopal Das recalled Bisht's description of the brutal violence, and shuddered involuntarily. Mayank's head had been battered so viciously that the skull was smashed.

"What was the time of death?" Professor Shantanu asked.

"Bisht says that it was sometime early in the morning," Gopal Das said.

"Of course, one need not wonder what Mayank was doing in the Machine Shop early in the morning. He was always about —somewhere or the other," the professor said.

Singhal nodded.

"Come to think of it, all the deaths occurred sometime after midnight. Does it have some significance?" Professor Shantanu seemed to be talking to himself.

Gopal Das was quiet.

"Has Inspector Bisht got any leads?" Professor Shantanu asked.

"I don't think so. Today, he will question all the workshop technicians and attendants. Let us see what he is able to establish," Gopal Das paused.

"I hope to God that this stops now. I simply cannot believe

that four deaths, murders — to be precise, have happened. It is incomprehensible. And for what? What could be the reason? What is the link between them?" the chairman was evidently distraught.

"I did seem to have an inkling of the link. But it was all conjecture. And now probably I will have to rethink everything...," Professor Shantanu said, frustrated at his own lack of insight into the matter. Ordinarily, he prided himself on his astuteness. However, he seemed to be failing this time.

"So, what was the link?" Gopal Das asked.

"Well, Vipin's and Gurpreet's murders seemed to be linked, I had assumed..." Shantanu said.

"And Suresh?" Singhal queried.

"Suresh was investigating the matter. So...er...maybe...," the professor spoke hesitatingly.

Singhal interrupted and asked, "And how do you explain Mayank?"

"Yes. Mayank is a puzzle. All my investigations pointed to him as being the murderer. But now...," the Professor looked troubled.

"But why was Vipin murdered in the first place?" Gopal Das asked.

"Yes, this is the most vexing issue. I am sure that as soon as I can establish the real motive behind Vipin's murder, I will have arrived at the killer's identity."

"So, haven't you established anything yet?" Gopal Das was disappointed.

"Several people hated Vipin. And I have questioned all of them. But somehow I am not convinced that they would have killed him ...," the professor paused.

"There is Ramadin, Mohit and Saransh. I have questioned them yet again after Mayank's death. But somehow I am not certain that either of them could have carried out such dastardly acts," the professor continued.

"What about them?" the chairman asked.

"Well, Ramadin is a mess worker of the boys' hostel who was present in the hostel the night Vipin was murdered, and curiously enough, he had visited the girls' hostel too, the night Gurpreet died," the professor explained.

"Then, it is clear!" Gopal Das exclaimed.

"Not really. He has no clear motive and he has a plausible explanation for his presence in the hostels on both the nights."

"What about Saransh?" Gopal Das asked.

"Saransh is a lecturer and is somewhat strange... I must admit I am a bit unsure about him. I'm inclined to think that he is also a bit of a psychiatric case like Mayank... and now, with Mayank dead, perhaps... I don't know..." the professor's voice trailed away.

"But why do you suspect him?" Gopal Das asked.

"Vipin and his cronies took it upon themselves to trouble Saransh in every lecture. In fact, Vipin's shenanigans often hit below the belt. So Saransh had ample reason to hate Vipin," Professor Shantanu said.

"And Mohit?" Gopal Das asked.

"Mohit is a second year student who was treated badly by Vipin. And Mohit is a rather aggressive boy who is capable of violence, I think," Professor Shantanu said.

"So, these three are my major suspects," Professor Shantanu

continued.

Gopal Das was quiet.

"Perhaps one of them could have killed Vipin. But the other murders? No, I don't think so! And it has to be the same person who has killed everyone...," Professor Shantanu paused.

"Or does it?" he shook his head in frustration.

"And then there is Deepak and 'Enigma'...." the professor seemed to be speaking to himself.

Gopal Das looked distressed. It was not good that the professor was so bewildered. And, who were Deepak and 'Enigma'? He wanted to ask; but Professor Shantanu spoke again, "I think I'm going round in circles. I will apprise you as soon as I am able to arrive at some conclusion. Meanwhile, do let me know how Mr. Bisht is progressing," the professor strode off intent on action.

Gopal Das leaned back in his chair. He needed a strong cup of coffee. And then he would call Inspector Bisht for a meeting. He pressed the buzzer to summon his peon.

Back at his lab, Professor Shantanu began going through all the files that Suresh had saved on his laptop. He was sure that there must be something here that he had missed or had not realised the significance of. What was it? And it was probably that crucial something which had led Suresh on to some further clue; or perhaps even to his tragic death. After all, the basis of Suresh's investigations were these files.

He clicked open the various folders. There was all the gruesome stuff from Mayank's PC. There were links to poor Gurpreet's blog and her *Facebook* profile. The password to her *Facebook* account was helpfully stored, so the professor was easily able to log onto her account. An unusual aspect of her account was that her mailbox was overflowing, with mails to her numerous virtual pals... and too many mails to 'Enigma'. Professor Shantanu began to see their history. This friendship with 'Enigma' began immediately after Vipin's death. This was odd.

He needed to find this person. Was this a fake account? Or was the person known to Gurpreet in real life? This was proving to be a real problem.

If only Suresh was here... he would have easily hacked into 'Enigma's' account.

Now there was no way to determine his identity.

Professor Shantanu decided to leave it for the moment.

Suddenly, he noticed that in one of the last mails, there was an exchange of cell phone numbers between Gurpreet and 'Enigma'. Excited, Professor Shantanu quickly jotted Enigma's number and then dialled.

To his immense disappointment, the recorded message at the other end returned that the number did not exist.

Saransh stood before his mirror. The spiked look definitely made him look good. The new fairness cream he was trying out seemed be working as well. Was he imagining it, or was his skin colour a shade lighter? Just a slight change; almost imperceptible, really, but Saransh was sure that the miniscule improvement had definitely occurred.

Things were improving for him all around. He was looking better, the students were behaving themselves in his class; and he had heard that some jobs in government engineering colleges were soon going to be advertised.

Except... except for Professor Shantanu. He had had great respect for the professor before these incidents. But that was before the professor had begun to unnecessarily pick on him. How could he treat him in that way! He was not some criminal to be subjected to the kind of questioning that the professor had subjected him too. This was unfair. After all, when the police were investigating everything, why did the professor need to get involved in it too? Why not stick to his research?

Something needed to be done. Of course, God was on his side. After Vipin and Gurpreet, Suresh too had died. That was good. That over-smart Suresh, always hacking into other peoples' laptops, spying on them, and even trying to be a student leader... served him right. He was up to no good.

Then an appalling thought struck him. Had Suresh hacked into his laptop too? Saransh was suddenly apprehensive. He recalled the nature of files that he had saved in certain hidden folders. A sense of shame went through him. It would be terrible if his tastes became public. No... no, that was not possible. Suresh had no reason to hack into his laptop. And even if he had, it made no difference now. He was dead — and whatever he knew was gone with him — lost forever. And that was how it should be.

But then, Suresh had been a prime *chamcha* of Professor Shantanu. Had he revealed something to the professor? Was that why the professor had started questioning him repeatedly? Perhaps something really needed to be done, to set Professor Shantanu on the right track.

Mayank too had started probing into the deaths. Really, what had got into these people? Why couldn't they stick to their own business? Why couldn't they simply do just what they were supposed to do, instead of poking their nose into things that did not concern them? Well, if they didn't, they would have to pay for it, wouldn't they? Vipin, Gurpreet, Suresh, Mayank — all had paid... who would be next? He looked up at the ceiling and seemingly through it. No doubt, God would soon reveal His grand design....

CHAPTER – 16

Professor Shantanu breathed in the crisp mountain air as he strode briskly on the Mussoorie road taking his usual early morning walk. This was the best part of working at MIST, he reflected. There was lush greenery on either side of the gradually winding road. The road had been cut into the mountainside and it moved steadily uphill. It had rained about an hour ago. The foliage all around was freshly washed, the mud was wet, and as a result, a divine fragrance pervaded the atmosphere. This delightful aroma was characteristic of this area and Professor Shantanu was absolutely in love with it. If he were a poet, he would have written reams on the glory of nature, he thought with a smile.

He had reached the famous Radha-Krishna temple located on the side of the road adjacent to the mountainside. On the other side of the road, there was a deep chasm. At this hour, there were not many devotees, he noted. This temple was one of its kind; here no visitor was permitted to make any kind of offering, be it humble or ostentatious. On the contrary, every visitor was offered complimentary prasad and tea. It was a mandatory stop for every tourist visiting Mussoorie. Apart from darshan, there was the opportunity to buy precious and semi-precious gems, jewellery and other knick-knacks from the temple premises. On most days, business was brisk, which probably accounted for the effusive hospitality offered to everyone.

A little ahead was the Sakya College. Professor Shantanu had often thought of visiting the college. He had become even more interested in it after hearing Pierre's account of the academic ambience of the college. He would love to talk to the monks studying there. But somehow, he had never got round to it. He walked on; it was almost time for him to turn back towards MIST. But the ambience was so intoxicating that Professor Shantanu decided to walk for another kilometre.

There was nothing else now on the sides of the road, no sign of habitation; it was pure untouched nature at its best. As he walked, his brain mulled over the vexing happenings in the institute. There was something he was overlooking, something so obvious that he was probably not relating it to the murders, he thought.

Suddenly, he heard a movement close behind him. He turned to see what it was. Before he could turn completely, a heavy object hit his head and the force of the blow threw him off the side of the road into the gorge below. Desperately, Professor Shantanu clutched at the sides of the hillock. There was nothing to hold on to. His mind was blanking out rapidly and he slid helplessly to the bottom and passed out.

It was uncharacteristic for Professor Shantanu to be late, thought Professor Indresan as he looked at his watch. And the peculiar thing was that nobody knew where he was. This was strange.

Then a horrifying thought struck him. Had something untoward happened to him? Professor Indresan began fidgeting with his hair.

Immediately, he called Col Akash and instructed him to trace Professor Shantanu. The security guards were instantly put on the job and they got into action.

Professor Shantanu lived in one the guesthouses located within the campus. He lived alone, for his wife had passed away a long time back and he did not have any children.

Within an hour, the guards reported that he was not to be found anywhere. Apparently, the guesthouse cook had served him tea, and then he had left for his customary morning walk. There was no way that Professor Shantanu would not return in time from his walk, particularly when he knew that there was a meeting scheduled at 9 a.m.

Fearing the worst, Professor Indresan instructed that the guards and the chief security officer should go and look thoroughly all along the path of Professor Shantanu's usual walk. He knew that the Professor normally went a little beyond the Sakya College. Immediately, he reported the matter to the chairman.

An hour later, the chief security officer reported that the professor was not to be found anywhere.

Immediately, Gopal Das Singhal sent for Inspector Bisht. The latter arrived with his team, including sniffer dogs.

Much later, Gopal Das Singhal said to Professor Indresan, "Mr. Bisht has reported that Professor Shantanu was found in a deep gorge a little ahead of the Sakya Temple."

"I hope he is all right," the director was genuinely concerned. His fingers snaked up to his hair falling over his right ear-lobe.

"I don't know. He is admitted in the hospital and is yet to regain consciousness," Singhal was pensive.

There was silence. There were no words forthcoming from either of them. The multiple murders and the terrible mishap of Professor Shantanu had caused a disquiet that refused to let up.

"We will know what happened only after he becomes conscious. Maybe, maybe he slipped and fell...," Gopal Das spoke wishfully.

"Yes. It had rained heavily, and the ground on the sides of the Mussoorie road is awfully slippery," Professor Indresan concurred appeasingly.

The thought running through both their minds was that it was most likely a vicious murderous attack; but neither wanted to articulate it, until confirmed by Professor Shantanu himself. Till then, it was best to keep their fingers crossed.

"I have been getting too many calls from parents who are asking whether the matter has been resolved," Professor Bhardwaj spoke gloomily.

He had just entered the director's office.

"Well then, handle it. You are the dean. This is your job," Professor Indresan spoke testily.

"But sir, it is becoming increasingly difficult for me to assure them and pacify them. Four murders is no joke," Professor Bhardwaj raised his voice. This was uncharacteristic of him. Evidently, the pressure was getting to him.

"So, what do you want me to do?" Professor Indresan challenged softly.

"Er... nothing, sir. But what should I tell them?" The dean was flustered. It would not be wise to antagonise the director.

"Tell them we have taken all possible steps to ensure the safety of all the students; and the police are on the job; they are investigating... Do I have to tell you everything?" Professor Indresan was irritated. Unconsciously, he pulled at a lock of hair from behind his right ear.

Professor Bhardwaj had already said all these things, but parents were far from being satisfied. But he thought it better not to argue the point, seeing the director's cantankerous mood.

"Well, how is Professor Shantanu?" Professor Indresan turned towards Col Akash.

"Sir," Col Akash straightened to attention.

"He is much better, I think. Woh kya kehte hain, luckily, he did not fall too far below into the gorge. A little to the left or right, and he could have very easily slipped into the deep end of the gorge. God is kind," he continued.

"Yes. Thank God," the director felt genuinely relieved.

At this trying time, Professor Shantanu was the only one who could be relied upon to take care of things. Professor Indresan sighed.

At the hospital, Professor Shantanu had just regained consciousness.

The attending doctor asked softly, "How are you?"

"Er... fine," Professor Shantanu mumbled.

"What happened?" he asked after a pause.

"You were hit at the back of the head and the impact of the blow caused you to slip and fall down the gorge at the side of the road," the doctor explained.

"Oh!" the memory of the blow came back to the professor.

"Luckily, the blow has not caused any serious damage. There was some mild concussion, which will take a week or so to heal...," the doctor paused. "It seems you have a tough skull," he smiled.

The professor gave a feeble smile. Then a thought occurred to him. "Do people know about this?"

"Yes, your people at the institute know that you are unconscious and in the hospital," the doctor said.

"But do they know the cause?" the professor asked.

"What do you mean?" the doctor asked.

"I mean, do they know that I had been hit at the back of my head?" the professor asked impatiently.

Puzzled, the doctor looked at Professor Shantanu. Was his diagnosis of there being nothing wrong with the professor really correct? The latter seemed to be talking about irrelevant things.

"Tell me doc!" Professor Shantanu spoke urgently.

"Er no…I don't think so," the doctor was intrigued at Shantanu's persistent questioning. "Well, good," Professor Shantanu breathed deeply and relaxed.

"Er…I think I will run some more tests to ensure that everything is in order," the doctor said.

"Yeah, no problem. But just ensure that you keep all information about my injury and condition etc. to yourself," Professor Shantanu said. "It should remain confidential," he further emphasized the point.

"Right," the doctor reassured him, though he was puzzled by the request.

"I mean, don't tell anyone I was hit on the head. Just say that I accidentally slipped and fell," Professor Shantanu reiterated forcefully.

The doctor nodded.

"We will keep you under close observation for a week to ensure that you are perfectly alright," the doctor said.

"Yes," Professor Shantanu closed his eyes, tired all of a sudden.

"What is this? The doctor was initially hesitant to tell me about your condition!" It was early the next morning. Inspector Bisht had just arrived after learning that the professor had regained consciousness.

"Er... what?" Professor Shantanu was groggy with the effect of all the medication he had been given.

"How did this happen? I need to know," the police officer's voice softened seeing the professor's condition.

"Ah yes. I told the doctor not to give out this information," the professor said.

"Why?" Mr. Bisht was perplexed.

"It is because of all the events preceding my accident," Shantanu explained.

"Well, perhaps that was the right thing to do," Mr. Bisht conceded.

"Well, what happened?" he asked again.

"I was hit on the back of my head with some heavy object. The blow caused me to fall into the gorge and I was perhaps left for dead," the professor said.

"Oh, that is terrible. This means..., Mr. Bisht paused.

"It is quite clear that the murderer wanted to somehow harm me; perhaps even kill me," Professor Shantanu spoke evenly.

"Yes. You are right," the police officer looked troubled.

"Have you got any clues about the identity of the murderer?" Professor Shantanu asked.

"No," Mr. Bisht said mournfully.

"I think we had better deduce something fast or else who knows when and where the killer will strike next?" Professor Shantanu said "Though it is quite obvious that I am the intended next victim," the professor continued wryly.

"Yes, you are right. I will depute a constable here at the hospital for your safety. Perhaps the killer will make another attempt," Mr. Bisht said.

"But why this attack on you? What is the motive?" the police officer ruminated aloud.

"Yes, I too have been grappling with this question ever since I realised what had happened," the professor said.

Inspector Bisht remained silent.

"Why would the killer try to eliminate me or injure me? It is not as if I know the identity of the killer, and so he is trying to get rid of me," the professor paused.

"Is it because the murderer thinks that I have some vital clue or some evidence that points in his direction? Is that why he attacked me?" Professor Shantanu asked, though he already knew that he had hit the nail on the head.

"Yes. Yes Professor; that must be it. Think. Just think hard. What have your investigations established till now?" Mr. Bisht spoke excitedly.

Professor Shantanu did not respond.

"Please think. I too am desperate for some leads in this unfathomable case," Mr. Bisht spoke plaintively.

Professor Shantanu closed his eyes in an effort to concentrate.

The police officer waited patiently.

After a while Professor Shantanu said, "I'm sorry. I am not able to recall anything."

"Oh. Well, I better get going. In case you remember anything, give me a call immediately," Mr. Bisht got up.

"This case has become very serious now," he continued.

"And... and do be careful," Mr. Bisht added as an afterthought.

Professor Shantanu lay back wearily.

The chairman, along with Professor Indresan, entered Professor Shantanu's room. They had been waiting for the police officer to leave, and then meet the professor. Apparently, Mr. Bisht had wanted to be the first person to speak to the professor as soon as he regained consciousness. And he had wanted to meet the professor alone.

The other deans, heads, faculty and students who had been waiting to see the professor were requested by the doctor to leave. The latter was concerned that the professor needed to rest and so many people would cause unnecessary mental stress.

"How are you?" Gopal Das Singhal asked.

"Er... fine," Professor Shantanu spoke softly.

"It is by God's grace that you are safe," Professor Indresan looked distressed. His nervous fingers pulled at stray strands of hair above his right ear.

"Yes. You really gave all of us a big scare," Gopal Das nodded.

"Particularly after all these murders, I... we thought..." Professor Indresan lost his breath in mid-sentence.

"Don't say such things," Gopal Das censured.

Professor Shantanu closed his eyes.

"I think the professor needs to rest," Gopal Das spoke softly.

"Yes. We should leave," Professor Indresan concurred.

"Yes. We have ensured that he is safe and will be fine. And

that is all that matters," Gopal Das Singhal said.

Professor Shantanu drifted off into a drug-induced fitful sleep.

"Hey, you know what? Professor Shantanu is in hospital!" a third year student of Electrical said.

"Oh my God! What happened?" a third year Computer Science student said, worried that her favourite professor was in hospital.

"I don't know. Apparently, he was out for his usual morning walk, but slipped and fell in the gorge a little ahead of the Sakya Temple," the Electrical student disclosed.

"My God! That is awful," a third year Mechanical student said.

"But how could he have slipped?" the Computer Science girl queried.

"Yes, that is weird. He goes for his walk everyday and so it's not as if the path is new for him," the Mechanical student pointed out.

"Er... perhaps it was because it had rained, and so, the side of the road was slippery and so...," the Electrical student postulated hesitatingly.

"But Professor Shantanu has been going on the same road for years and he is well aware of how slippery the sides of the roads become after the rains. After all, it is not the first time that he is experiencing the rains of Dehradun," the Mechanical student argued.

"Yes. That is right," the Computer Science girl agreed.

There was silence all around.

"Perhaps, er... someone tried... tried to kill him," Nitish who was quiet until now, spoke what was in everyone's mind.

Everyone looked at each other apprehensively.

But no one spoke.

"Thank God, you are fine!" a visibly worried Naresh exclaimed at the sight of Professor Shantanu lying on the hospital bed.

"I had come yesterday, but you were still unconscious," Naresh paused.

"And I have been waiting all morning to see you. But naturally, my turn had to come after the police officer, the director, etc. And then when I looked in, you were asleep," Naresh continued somewhat petulantly.

The professor gave a ghost of a smile. He had just woken up. Although loathe to admit it, he had been waiting for Naresh. For the umpteenth time, he reflected that if he had had a son, it would have to be a clone of Naresh. After gaining consciousness, Naresh was the one person he had looked forward to seeing.

"Tell me, are you really fine?" Naresh looked anxious.

"Yes, my boy," Professor Shantanu whispered.

"Thank God the fall did not cause any serious injury. It could very easily have caused brain injury...or a coma...," Naresh's voice trailed away.

Touched at his concern, the professor held out his hand. Comfortingly, Naresh enveloped it with both his hands.

Soothed considerably, the professor closed his eyes. Now he could rest. Naresh was by his side.

But there was something troubling him, something... before

he could identify what it was; the drugs pumped into him took over and the professor drifted off to sleep.

CHAPTER – 17

"These college people are in deep shit," Mohit said to his roommate.

"Er... yes," the roommate wondered how he could get his room changed. But if he requested the warden, then Mohit would come to know of it and then God alone knew what he would do to him.

"Yeah. Isn't it great that Professor Shantanu too almost died?" Mohit gave a ghoulish grin.

Inspite of himself, the roommate was shocked. "Really, you should not say something like this," he protested feebly.

"Are you on my side or theirs?" Mohit was irascible.

What was happening to his friend? the roommate wondered. Before his very eyes, Mohit seemed to be morphing into some sort of unrecognizable fiendish devil. "Er... of course, I'm on your side," the roommate forced a weak smile.

"Good. Now as I was saying, this bloody professor had it coming to him. The audacity of him calling me and literally accusing me of the murders!" Mohit was indignant.

The roommate could only stare at Mohit in bewilderment.

"Infact, all these damn teachers should be done away with. Isn't it fantastic that Mayank sir was murdered — and in such a way that he must have suffered? Serves him right for torturing us hostellers with his constant spying and his bloody rules and regulations," Mohit was vehement.

The roommate managed a nod, lest Mohit got upset.

"And serves Suresh right too. The chamcha of the bloody

professor! Pretending to be a student leader, when all he cared about was himself," Mohit paused.

"You know, I had gone to Suresh also for help with regard to my short attendance but he too did nothing. And of course, he is dead now," Mohit gave a chilling smile.

The roommate wondered if he should take leave and go home until everything returned to normal. Yes, that was the best way to escape and remain safe too.

The next evening, Pierre was sitting at the bedside of Professor Shantanu. He was quite distressed at this unfortunate turn of events. He considered Professor Shantanu to be a friend of his and was quite appalled at this unexpected mishap.

"Do you know what the poor Tibetans are facing now? Pierre took recourse to his favourite subject in an attempt to divert the professor's mind as well as his own.

"What?" Professor Shantanu managed a ghost of a grin. Trust Pierre to make this naive attempt to distract his attention from the gruesome events that were almost becoming the norm at MIST.

"The Chinese government has launched a massive spy attack on all the major computer networks across the globe to spy on all kinds of activities across India, UK and US. And their main focus is of course to spy on all Tibet-related activities. All systems related to the Dalai Lama have been infiltrated. They are now able to have prior information of all his activities. In fact, it is the largest cyber spy attack of its kind in the world," Pierre was indignant.

"And what do they hope to gain by doing this?" inspite of himself, the professor became interested.

"They will ensure that the Tibetan government-in-exile remains isolated. They came to know of Dalai Lama's impending visit to South Africa and then pressurised them to deny him a visa. They are doing many such things," Pierre was passionate.

"Ohh," the professor was surprised.

"And to top it, the Chinese have alleged that a Dharamshala based group has instigated the wave of self-immolations in China," Pierre was indignant.

"That is preposterous," Professor Shantanu said.

"I know. In fact, China is preparing for some kind of war against Tibetans," Pierre spoke in an appalled tone.

"If all this is true, then it is really terrible," Professor Shantanu whispered. He was still weak.

"Of course it is true. It is all there in the news. But since you have been out of circulation, I mean, sorry…" Pierre stumbled.

"No, no, go on. It's ok," the professor encouraged him.

"Well, it is certain that Tibetans will not take this lying down. Enough is enough. And it is high time India comes out in support of the Tibetan cause."

"What do you mean?" Professor Shantanu asked.

"I mean that this sort of thing is virtually the last straw and perhaps this is what is needed for the Tibetans to swing into action," Pierre was indignant.

"Action? What do you mean?" Professor Shantanu asked.

"I think...," Pierre lowered his voice. "That some sort of militancy is going to take place soon."

Pierre had surely got carried away, thought Professor Shantanu.

"Yes. Remember, I had told you that there are some fringe

groups who are chafing at the advocacy of peaceful protest by the Dalai Lama?" Pierre paused.

Well, they are no longer willing to subscribe to this traditional view. And they are ready to take some drastic action," he continued in a rush.

"What do you mean?" the professor asked.

"I mean, they are soon going to do something big... and... some Indians are sure to be involved in it either directly or indirectly," Pierre hesitated.

"And 2012 is the do-or-die year for them. China invaded Tibet 60 years ago and they think it is now or never," he continued.

"Really?" the professor said.

"Yes. The Tibetan Youth Group is advocating militancy because of China's unwillingness to negotiate honestly. This anger will soon be mobilised and lead to a violent struggle," Pierre paused.

The Professor looked uneasy.

"An armed revolt within Tibet might be coordinated from outside, using routes and communication channels that people in exile use to keep in touch back home," Pierre continued.

"Are you serious?" the professor was stunned.

"Of course. You see, now the voice of the Tibetan people is not enough to force the Chinese to change their stand. The support groups all across the world will have to mobilise international opinion also in this regard. Only then something can happen. A tougher line towards Beijing is necessary to protect Tibetan culture, language and religion," Pierre was in his element now.

Professor Shantanu had no clue what Pierre was actually

talking about.

"And not only that; I am pretty sure that someone from MIST is also involved... in fact, it may be, may be...,"

Naresh entered. He was carrying fresh flowers and fruit.

Professor Shantanu beamed.

Pierre's favourite theme was soon lost in the ensuing conversation.

"Thank God, Professor Shantanu seems to be recovering," Professor Bhardwaj said.

It was the first period; and a group of heads and deans were standing in the main corridor of the academic block as part of their morning round for monitoring classes.

"*Woh kya kehte hain*... it could have become serious, very serious. Shantanu is lucky," Col. Akash joined the group.

"Yes. That is true," Professor Dinkar concurred.

"But, how could he have slipped like this?" Professor Girish Shukla asked.

"Yeah, that is strange," Professor Bhardwaj nodded.

"Did he slip or... or was there some foul play involved?" Professor Mritunjaya asked hesitatingly.

"Well, the director said that the professor simply slipped. But I am inclined to disagree," Professor Mishra said.

"Really? Why?" Professor Bhardwaj asked.

"Arrey! Why would he need to be admitted for a week if he had just slipped? And why is there a bandage around his head?" Professor Mishra said.

"Well, that could be because the fall caused injury to his head and for that he needs time to recover," Col Akash said.

"Well, perhaps you are right," Professor Mishra conceded.

"Yeah, of course, he must have just slipped. Otherwise why would the director not tell us if there was something else?" Professor Bhardwaj said.

"Yes. Perhaps the murders have made me jittery and I'm getting silly ideas," Professor Mishra smiled self-deprecatingly.

"Yeah. I think these murders have made all of us a bit fanciful," Professor Dinkar said.

"Yes, particularly for something to happen to someone as nice and upright as Professor Shantanu, it is unthinkable," Col Akash said.

"Yes. Why would someone want to harm him?" Professor Bhardwaj asked.

"But... but wasn't he investigating the matter?" Professor Mishra asked.

"Well, yes, he was...," Professor Bhardwaj conceded.

"So...so perhaps he found out something and so...," Professor Mishra's voice trailed away.

"Oh come on; again you're going back to square one. Now don't be ridiculous," Col. Akash chided him.

"Anyway, let's take our rounds as we are supposed to do, and stop discussing such implausible things," Professor Girish Shukla said.

Professor Shantanu looked around his room in frustration. This forced confinement was getting on his nerves. It had been three days since his accident. And now he was itching to get back to his lab and resume his normal routine. But the doctor was adamant about keeping him under the mandatory one-week observation.

The question that plagued him constantly was, who could have carried out this dastardly attack upon him? Professor Shantanu believed himself to be a nice and genuine human being. He also had a somewhat exaggerated notion of himself being universally liked by everyone. Hence, it was incomprehensible for him to accept that someone could go to the extent of actually harming him.... .

Of course, it had to be a depraved individual. The same one, no doubt, who had carried out all the murders. Obviously, the murderer believed that the professor was closing in upon him; hence the attack. Little did the culprit know that the professor had no clue about the perpetrator of these horrendous murders.

Professor Shantanu shook his head in frustration. How could he be so dense? What was he missing? Where had his intelligence disappeared? If the murderer believed that the professor knew something, then obviously he had to know something. What information was he supposed to have which was related to the murders? What did he know — but was unable to comprehend and grasp?

Oh God! What am I missing? Professor Shantanu felt like tearing his hair out in aggravation.

Naresh entered.

"I really am very stupid," Professor Shantanu said in an irritated tone.

"Why?" Naresh was puzzled. It was abnormal for the professor to be agitated.

"I'm supposed to know the identity of the murderer," Professor Shantanu said.

"But why?" the professor seems to have lost it, Naresh thought.

"Well ... er ...," Professor Shantanu paused. He remembered that no one except the doctor and the Police Officer knew that he had been attacked; and so it was natural for the poor boy to be puzzled.

Should he confide in Naresh? the professor debated.

"Why are you supposed to know the identity of the murderer?" Naresh interrupted his thoughts.

"Er ... I was just thinking I ought to know because er ... given the fact that I have been investigating the matter since the very beginning, it should have been unravelled by now," Professor Shantanu spoke hesitatingly.

Naresh was quiet. The professor had too much time on his hands here at the hospital, he thought.

"Incidentally, have you given any thought about who could be the murderer?" the professor questioned.

"No," Naresh paused.

"And I do think that you should give up pursuing this matter. And take a long, peaceful holiday away from the institute now," Naresh spoke emphatically.

The professor looked surprised. He rarely, if ever, took leave from teaching and research.

"All this is not good for your health. You should leave the investigation for the police — for those who are meant to do it," Naresh continued.

Professor Shantanu started to protest; but before he could speak, Naresh reiterated, "You really should take care of yourself."

Professor Shantanu smiled, overwhelmed at Naresh's concern for his well-being. For the umpteenth time, he wished the latter was his son.

"Come on now, close your eyes and rest," Naresh ordered.

The next day, Inspector Bisht visited Professor Shantanu.

"We carried out a thorough search of the area but have been unable to find the weapon which was used to attack you," Mr. Bisht said.

"Even if you had found it, most likely it would not have had any fingerprints," Professor Shantanu spoke wryly.

"Our killer is too clever," the professor continued.

"Yes. The doctor says the wound indicates that it was a heavy iron object, maybe an iron rod. Evidently the attacker took it back with him," Mr. Bisht said.

Professor Shantanu remained quiet.

"Do you know who it could be?" Mr. Bisht asked.

"I thought you were going to tell me," Professor Shantanu gave a feeble smile.

"Obviously it is the murderer," Mr. Bisht spoke reflectively.

"Brilliant!" Professor Shantanu said.

"You have a right to be sarcastic," Mr. Bisht responded. "But this case has me puzzled. I came because I thought perhaps you might have recalled something; anything which could give some clue," he paused.

"You know, this case could be the first black spot in my career," the police officer looked depressed.

Professor Shantanu felt contrite for his sarcastic remark. After all, he himself was no nearer to understanding the case given all his so-called brilliant intellect. Then why take it out on the hapless police officer?

"I'm sorry. I think that these murders and the attack upon me have made me somewhat perturbed. Do not take my remark seriously," the professor said.

"It's okay, I understand," Mr. Bisht spoke softly.

"Didn't you get any leads from Suresh's and Mayank's cell phone records, laptop details etc.?" the professor asked.

"No...," Mr. Bisht hesitated. "Everything seems run-of-the mill," he spoke in frustration.

"Maybe you should look again," Professor Shantanu suggested half-heartedly.

"Well, there is no harm in going through everything again," the police officer left rapidly.

"Er... sir, may I come in?" a diffident Nitish peeped into the doorway of Professor Shantanu's hospital room later in the afternoon.

"Yes, of course," the professor was glad at the intrusion. This forced and somewhat solitary confinement was getting on his nerves.

"I'm sorry to disturb you," Nitish mumbled. "The doctor was loathe to allow me in."

"No. It's all right," the Professor was glad that the doctor had started permitting at least a few visitors.

"Well, tell me why you wanted to see me," the professor asked.

"Er... sir... actually I don't know how important it is," Nitish dithered.

"Don't worry about its importance. Just tell me," the

Professor prompted.

"Well, actually, Mayank sir had forced me to hand over all the contents of Suresh's laptop," Nitish paused.

The professor was surprised. He had not known this. Then he remembered Mayank's words about gathering clues on his own...

"Suresh had kept a copy of all his stuff on a back-up hard disk as well, you see," he explained.

Professor Shantanu nodded.

"Mayank sir...er...threatened me and I was so afraid that I...I gave him a copy of all the files," Nitish was apologetic.

"It was the same stuff that Suresh had given to me, isn't it?" Professor Shantanu asked.

"I don't know. Actually, I have brought a copy of it for you also, so that in case there is something extra, or something that had been missed earlier, you can see...," Nitish's voice trailed away as he handed over a CD.

"I've also brought along my laptop as I thought you might not have yours at the hospital,' Nitish added helpfully.

"Right. Insert the CD and show me the contents," Professor Shantanu said.

Nitish quickly did as instructed.

Rapidly Professor Shantanu scrolled through the contents. There seemed to be nothing new.

The professor lay back frustrated. "Thank you Nitish. You did the right thing," he said.

Nitish left.

CHAPTER – 18

Professor Shantanu switched on his laptop. Now what was the last thing he had been looking at before the attack? He opened Internet Explorer and clicked on the History tab. It was blank. This was strange. Normally the History Tab showed details of navigation even as far back as three weeks. And he never ever deleted the contents of his computer history. Then what had happened?

It was a week later, and Professor Shantanu was back at MIST much against the advice of the doctor and the hospital authorities. They felt that some more rest would do the professor a world of good. But Professor Shantanu was more than fed up with the forced confinement.

He had had plenty of time to mull over all that had happened and was keen to be back at the scene of crime and sort out everything. Though lying in bed, all he did was think about the murders, yet his formidable intelligence seemed to be failing him. Or perhaps it was the blow on his skull which made thinking painful — in a literal sense.

Now that he was back at his guest house, what he needed to do was retrace his steps just prior to the attack on him. No doubt the murderer believed that the professor was closing in upon him, which was why the attack had taken place. But what had he learnt, that the murderer was afraid to let him live? What did he do the day before the attack? Ah yes, he was going through the files that Suresh had given him. He had also gone through Gurpreet's *Facebook* profile.

He opened the folder that contained the files that Suresh had copied onto his laptop. The folder was empty. Professor Shantanu was shocked. He went to the Recycle Bin — this too was empty. Where did all the files go?

Was there some virus in his laptop? Or had someone hacked into his laptop the way Suresh had hacked into Mayank's laptop? Or had someone opened his laptop and accidentally or deliberately deleted the contents of the History tab and Suresh's folder? It could not be an accident. It had to be deliberate; for only things pertaining to his investigation into the murders were missing. Details of his research, notes etc. were intact. Rapidly he went through all his other folders and files — they were untouched, Professor Shantanu noted.

In that case, the person would have to know his password to open and access the contents of his laptop. As a precautionary measure, Professor Shantanu had ensured that his laptop was password-protected. He became perturbed. This was too much!

Suddenly, he recalled that he had noted Enigma's cell phone number from Gurpreet's Facebook mails on his notepad. He looked through his drawer; his notepad was there. But the page where the cell number was noted was missing — it had been roughly torn out.

Immediately he opened Gurpreet's *Facebook* profile and went to her mailbox. He would copy the phone number again. Surprisingly, all mails since the day Vipin was murdered had vanished. Gone too were the mails Gurpreet had exchanged with 'Enigma'. In fact, there was no mention of any 'Enigma'. He put in a search for 'Enigma'. The site returned that the profile was no longer in existence.

Professor Shantanu started to feel increasingly agitated. The murderer was onto him. He had not only deleted everything on his laptop, but had accessed Gurpreet's profile and deleted all the recent mails. Perhaps those mails had contained some vital clue.... .

And then this 'Enigma' had deleted his own profile as well. Who was he? Did he know the murderer? 'Enigma' had mysteriously appeared around the time of Vipin's murder and had disappeared now...perhaps he had disappeared right after Gurpreet's murder, who knew? What was his significance? He was known only to Gurpreet. No one else had heard of him...

Earlier Deepak seemed to have disappeared; and now 'Enigma' had disappeared. Vipin, who could have told him something about Deepak's absence, was dead. And Gurpreet, who could have told him about 'Enigma', was also dead. Suresh, who could have easily hacked into 'Enigma's' *Facebook* account, was also dead. He could have had another student hack into 'Enigma's' account, but the account itself had been deleted.

Now there was no doubt that 'Enigma' was an important link in the murders. Deepak, by virtue of his unexplained absence, was important; more so since he was close to the deceased Vipin. Kanika too had thought that there was something peculiar in Deepak's absence. And then there was the uncharacteristic behaviour of Deepak's parents, Brigadier and Mrs. Kalra...how did all this add up?

A dull ache began at the back of his head right where he had been hit. Professor Shantanu wondered whether he should take an extra doze of his prescribed painkiller.

This entire business had turned into a cipher to break all

ciphers. Was it the doing of a serial killer as Suresh had surmised? The only psycho left after Mayank was Saransh. Was he the murderer? Or was it that obnoxious, nasty Mohit? And what about Ramadin?

Ramadin could have murdered Vipin and Gurpreet; but why murder Suresh and Mayank? Ramadin was motivated by hatred for Vipin; but what was his motivation for murdering Gurpreet?

Mohit may have murdered Vipin, perhaps Gurpreet and Suresh too; and maybe Mayank perhaps... Mohit's motivation was revenge — or was it pure wickedness in all the cases?

And Saransh — he could have definitely murdered all four. He had that peculiar kink in his personality...

He recalled that Nitish had given him the CD of all of Suresh's files. Immediately Professor Shantanu inserted the CD into his laptop. At first glance, all the files appeared to be the same as those already saved by Suresh. It contained the same old copied contents of Gurpreet's blog. There was Mayank's net downloaded x-rated files and details about murder weapons, murders that appeared as suicides. And the link to Gurpreet's *Facebook* profile — which he had already checked, and which contained nothing about 'Enigma' now. There really seemed nothing that could give him some sort of lead.

Frustrated that he was getting nowhere, Professor Shantanu switched on the television. Mindlessly, he switched channels whilst his brain grappled with the murders. Most of the news channels talked about the planned visit of the Chinese Premier to Dehradun two days later. There were detailed reports about the Military Academy and other institutions of Dehradun that were readying themselves to put forward their best foot for the Premier. It was a historic occasion and marked a distinct upswing in Indo-China relations, the T.V. channels proclaimed.

After a while, Professor Shantanu decided to fish out the notepad he had used while at the hospital. What he had scribbled on the notepad was a flowchart giving the sequence of events. There were question marks at two crucial places. The first was at the murder of Vipin and the second was at the attack made upon him. He was sure that as soon as he could determine the reason for Vipin's murder, everything would fall into place.

The dull ache at the back of his head had turned into a throbbing pain. Professor Shantanu grimaced as he swallowed a couple of extra painkillers. Perhaps he should call and ask the doctor about the pain. But then the doctor had categorically cautioned him to take it easy; and would no doubt berate him for straining his mental faculties so much, so soon after the injury. But Professor Shantanu could not help it, he had to get at the bottom of it all.

He decided to increase the medication on his own, without consulting the doctor.

Something had woken him. But Professor Shantanu was not able to recall what it was. He looked at the bedside clock. The radium hands indicated half past two. Was it some sound? He got up. His head swam. Professor Shantanu sat down on the bed for a moment to get his head back to normal. A little later, he got up gingerly and carefully checked the doors and windows of his room. No, there was nothing untoward. No it was something… some memory… had the blow on his head impaired his ability to recall things? The professor hoped not.

He lay back and decided to go back to sleep. Just then, he heard some sort of a muffled sound. Was the murderer trying to attack him again? Maybe fatally this time? A frisson of fear went through his entire being.

Cautiously he got up again. Perhaps he should wake up Naresh who was in the adjacent room. Two people would be more than a match for any intruder, more so when one of them was young.

Naresh had decided to stay with Professor Shantanu for a week to take care of him. Professor Shantanu had protested vigorously, but all to no avail. Naresh was adamant about not leaving the professor alone, so soon after being hospitalized. Professor Shantanu had been moved at this open show of care and affection by Naresh. When one was physically unwell, one really needed someone by one's side, he realised.

Supporting his suddenly aching head with one hand, Professor Shantanu warily approached Naresh's room. He could hear some sound. Was the intruder in Naresh's room? Was he going to attack Naresh, mistaking him to be the professor?

Professor Shantanu became alarmed. He walked up to Naresh's door. Should he scream aloud? As he debated, he suddenly realised that the muffled sounds were words ... It seemed that Naresh was talking to someone over the phone. So this was probably what had woken him, Professor Shantanu sighed with relief. Maybe to the mysterious girlfriend! the professor thought and smiled. He turned to go back. Then something unusual about the emanating sounds caught his attention. The words seemed to belong to some strange language.

Professor Shantanu paused for a couple of minutes. He did

not really want to eavesdrop; but inspite of himself, the professor was rooted to the spot. He really did not know that Naresh spoke any other language apart from Hindi and English. Naresh's mother tongue was Hindi too, as far as he knew.

His head was really pounding now.

The professor strained hard to make sense of the softly-spoken words wafting from the room. He was bemused; the language did not resemble any of the Indian languages he was familiar with — it was neither Bengali, Bhojpuri, Gujarati, Marathi nor did it sound like any of the South Indian languages. Was it some foreign language? It did not sound like French, German or Spanish — the only foreign languages that he recognised. This was certainly peculiar. And yet, the professor could not bring himself to barge into Naresh's room at that time of the night and ask for a clarification.

Professor Shantanu decided to let it rest for the moment and went back to his room to get some sleep. The hammering in his head was unbearable now and the professor rapidly gulped down a couple of painkillers and a sleeping pill.

First thing in the morning, he asked Naresh whether he knew any other language apart from Hindi and English. Naresh laughed off the query. Reluctantly and somewhat embarrassedly, Professor Shantanu admitted to having eavesdropped outside Naresh's room the previous night.

Naresh was surprised on being interrogated. But when the professor persisted, Naresh became alarmed. The professor seemed to be losing his mind. What had the injury on his head done to him? "Sir, I think that the injury on your head coupled with the medication that you are taking is causing you to either hallucinate or have such vivid dreams that you are mistaking them for reality," Naresh spoke emphatically.

Was what Naresh saying true? Professor Shantanu was confused.

"I really think you should go far away from MIST for a couple of months to get some real rest," Naresh continued forcefully.

At this, Professor Shantanu stopped his questioning. Could it be that Naresh was right? The murders, his feverish attempts to investigate, the brutal attack on him, the medications.... they were all probably getting to his sanity. "I think I'll stay put in bed today," Professor Shantanu replied weakly.

"That would be best," Naresh said. "I'll get back in time for lunch which we must have together," he smiled compassionately.

Professor Shantanu tried his best to take it easy the rest of the day, but his brain would not let up. Somehow, he could not imagine that what he had heard the previous night was merely a figment of his imagination. But then, why would Naresh deny knowledge of another language if it was true? In fact, he thought last night he had heard Naresh mention 'Chinese Premier', but the rest of the words were as good as Greek. But then, could it be that the memory of the news on television had got mixed up in his hallucination?

Professor Shantanu was only too glad when it was lunchtime, and Naresh was back. All through lunch, Naresh made it a point to talk only of mundane, routine matters so that the atmosphere remained relaxed.

"I think you should retire for a nice siesta now after the sumptuous lunch. I have some work outside campus. I'll be back late. So, make sure to have a proper dinner and sleep early," Naresh smiled cheerfully.

Professor Shantanu nodded. He really was feeling rather tired; perhaps it was all the medication.

Later, left alone, as he was drifting off to sleep, Professor Shantanu suddenly remembered what had been bothering him since a very long time now. Whenever he had discussed his investigation and his suspicions about the murders with Naresh, the latter had always been particularly obtuse. In spite of all evidence pointing to murders, Naresh had persisted in trying to convince him that they were suicides. This was completely uncharacteristic of Naresh. He had always known Naresh to have a brilliant intellect — an intellect that was logical, analytical and methodical. Then, to deliberately ignore evidence...

Not only that, Naresh had an element of curiosity within his psyche, which was the hallmark of every good researcher. Then why did he seem not to be interested in the murders at all? This too was unfathomable.

And now, to try and convince the professor that he had been hallucinating last night or had been mistaking dream for reality? This was taking it too far! Admittedly, for a moment he too had concurred with Naresh. But the more he recalled the incident of the previous night and ruminated over it, he became convinced that what he had heard last night was the absolute reality. It was no delusion or dream. He had not so completely lost control over his mental faculties. There was pain, yes — but no other symptom — no delirium, hallucination or phantasm. So why would Naresh allege such a thing? And more importantly, why deny knowing a third language?

There was something not quite adding up here, he thought uneasily. This bit about Naresh had become another piece of the jigsaw that did not fit in smoothly the way it should have...

Unless... unless Naresh knew more than he was letting on? Or maybe Naresh was somehow mixed up in this thing...Of course, he could not be really involved; maybe he just knew something. But then, why had Naresh not shared it with him? Particularly since Naresh knew about his own involvement in the matter? He knew that the professor was anxious to solve the mystery and so if he knew something, he should have definitely shared it with him. Then why?

There was no point in speculating about all these postulations. He should simply ask Naresh. Maybe the explanation would be simplicity itself. Professor Shantanu tried to go back to sleep. But sleep was not forthcoming. When the tossing and turning became too much, he sat up...his headache returned. Determinedly ignoring it, he got up from bed.

He went into the adjacent room where Naresh was staying. He knew he would find nothing; but yet, he had to make sure. Naresh's laptop was lying on the bed. Professor Shantanu switched it on. In all likelihood, it would be password protected and he would be unable to find anything important, the professor conjectured.

To his surprise, this was not the case. There was no need for any password. Well, obviously, Naresh had nothing to hide, the professor thought, relieved. Surely there would be nothing incriminating in the laptop. Or was Naresh too complacent and over-confident that no one would suspect him enough to go through his laptop? Now he was being paranoid, the professor censured himself.

However, he just had to make sure; so Professor Shantanu went through all the files stored on the laptop. There was nothing much, besides details of Naresh's on-going research. Just as the professor was about to give up, he came across a file titled innocuously as T1. Since he had opened all the other files, the professor opened this one too.

Amazingly enough, he found that it was full of details of the Tibetan cause. This looked more like Pierre's laptop, Professor Shantanu thought perplexed. Or had this file been accidently copied from Pierre's laptop onto Naresh's? Surely, this Tibetan stuff was something to be found only on Pierre's laptop. What did Naresh have to do with Tibetans? Just then, a tangential thought occurred to him. Perhaps the language he had heard Naresh speak last night was Tibetan... and... and hadn't Pierre mentioned that he had seen Naresh at the Tibetan Colony on Rajpur Road? Oh God! What did this mean? The professor felt overwhelmed. He supported his suddenly blank and throbbing head with both his hands.

Just then, out of the blue, he had a brainwave. The events became juxtaposed in his mind — Pierre's words, the missing Deepak, Suresh's investigations, the sequence of the murders... Oh God, was it possible? It all came to him in a flash. Suddenly, everything added up. It was crystal-clear really. How come he had not understood it sooner?

Instantly Professor Shantanu dialled Inspector Bisht's number. "Come to the guest house immediately! I know who the murderer is!" he spoke urgently.

Fifteen minutes later, the police officer entered the

guesthouse.

"Arrest Naresh immediately! He is about to assassinate the Chinese Premier tomorrow at the Indian Military Academy!" Professor Shantanu spoke agitatedly, in a rush.

Mr. Bisht was flabbergasted. "With all due respect, sir, I think that you are delusional due to the injury and all the medicines."

"Brigadier Kalra is in charge of security at the Military Academy. His son Deepak is missing. Vipin was Deepak's project partner. Gurpreet was in love with Vipin. Suresh was investigating the murders. Mayank was the prime suspect...only he was not the killer as suspected... and all of them are dead!" Professor Shantanu shouted.

The police officer tried to make sense of what he was hearing.

"Don't dither! Time is running out! Just do as I say. Or else, the result will be a national disaster!" Professor Shantanu was frantic.

The professor had surely gone mad, a part of Mr. Bisht's brain reflected. But could it be true? It was impossible; totally far-fetched. And why would Naresh assassinate the Chinese Premier? And why Naresh?

Professor Shantanu saw the questions flitting across Inspector Bisht's face. "Please, officer, there is no time to waste. Just do as I say! Naresh has gone out of campus — to give the final touches to his terrible plan, no doubt!" he spoke anxiously.

"So, from where do I arrest Naresh if at all I do so?" Mr. Bisht asked, still perplexed.

For a second the professor looked confounded. Then his face cleared. "Let us go to the Military Academy and confront

Brigadier Kalra. He would know the whereabouts of Naresh. And he will also tell us where and how the assassination is to take place," he said earnestly.

Mr. Bisht looked unconvinced.

"I promise I will explain everything on the way!" the professor spoke in a frenzied manner.

Sceptical, but deciding to humour the professor, more so because he had nothing to lose, Mr. Bisht agreed to do as the professor proposed.

Soon they were on their way to the Indian Military Academy.

CHAPTER – 19

"So, the entire plan was to assassinate the Chinese Premier?" the chairman asked.

"Yes," Professor Shantanu concurred.

"But why?" Gopal Das Singhal was still hazy.

"To draw world attention towards the cause of free Tibet," the professor said.

The two were sitting in the chairman's office, at ease after the hectic events of the past week.

Naresh had been arrested and had confessed to everything.

Deepak, who had been held hostage all this while, was rescued from the abandoned, dilapidated temple in the Dhaniyo ka Dhanda village nearby. Surprisingly, he had been within a 5 k.m. radius of MIST. He was united with his parents, Mrs.Kalra and Brigadier Kalra, much to their relief.

"But I don't understand how Naresh was mixed up in all this," Gopal Das was puzzled.

"A couple of years back, Naresh met this girl in Dharamshala and fell in love with her. And she, at one point of time, was a member of the Women's Welfare Association of Tibet."

"You mean she is a Tibetan?" Gopal Das asked.

"Not is — was," the Professor said.

"What do you mean?" Gopal Das Singhal said.

"Well, let me explain from the beginning."

"Have you heard of this Women's Welfare Association of Tibet?" Professor Shantanu asked.

"Mm… I think I have heard of it," Singhal was sure he had

read about it somewhere recently.

"Well, this Association was originally founded in Lhasa and currently has several branches all across India, Nepal and abroad," Professor Shantanu paused.

"Actually, this group has traditionally been involved in peaceful activities related to religion, culture, education, social welfare, public affairs, and environment. Their focus is on children, elderly people and empowerment of women." Out of force of habit, the Professor explained all this as though giving a lecture.

"Then, how are they associated with this assassination plot and Naresh?" This was getting too confusing, Gopal Das thought.

"Well, a few young girls of this group became friendly with some boys of this crazy militant fringe group. This group had broken away from the Dalai Lama's middle ground approach, and had been advocating an extremist approach. The girls somehow became infatuated with militancy, or perhaps were brainwashed into it. And Naresh's girlfriend happened to be one of these girls," the professor explained in a rush.

"I see," Singhal said.

"And she inducted Naresh into this plot?" Gopal Das asked.

"Not really," the professor said.

"Then?" Gopal Das asked. This seemed more convoluted by the minute.

"During the Tibetan uprising in March 2008, this girl, along with others, sneaked into Lhasa via the mountain passes of Nepal to participate in the protests. In the severe Chinese crackdown that followed, she was killed," the professor paused.

"Oh no!" Singhal exclaimed.

Professor Shantanu was quiet.

"Er... why were the protests being organised?" The chairman was not really up-to-date, as far his general awareness was concerned.

"Actually, on March 10, 1959, the Tibetans organised their first uprising against the Chinese invasion of their country. Then on March 10, 2008, Tibetans organised protests to commemorate the 49th anniversary of the original uprising," Professor Shantanu explained.

Gopal Das Singhal waited patiently.

"In fact, Naresh's girlfriend was one of the 140 Tibetan protestors killed in police firing in Garze, a Tibetan majority town in southwest China's Sichuan province near the border with Tibet," the professor continued.

"My God, that is terrible," Gopal Das grimaced.

"Well, that was the time Naresh decided to avenge her death. He was already in touch with that fanatical militant group to which she belonged. After that, it was simple enough for him to convince them to participate in the plot to assassinate the Chinese Premier," Professor Shantanu said.

"You mean, he was the mastermind?" the chairman was awe-struck. The nondescript, soft-spoken, mild-mannered, bespectacled young man he knew as Naresh seemed hardly capable of such a vicious and intricate plot.

"Yes," the professor said sadly.

"And when news came of the impending visit of the Chinese Premier to Dehradun, particularly the Indian Military Academy, they had their plan cut out to precision. Gopal Das Singhal began connecting the dots.

"Yes. The entire plan revolved around the assassination of the Chinese Premier during his visit to the Indian Military Academy. This was their best bet to instantly grab the world's attention towards the Tibetan cause," Professor Shantanu said.

Gopal Das listened avidly.

"Naresh realised that in order to actualise his plot, he had to find a way to infiltrate the Indian Military Academy. He, along with his group, began analysing the security system of the Academy," Professor Shantanu said.

"And?" the chairman asked.

"Soon they had their breakthrough. They learnt that Brigadier Kalra was incharge of the security arrangements at the Military Academy, and he had a son who was studying at MIST. This was their eureka moment and well, the rest was obvious," Professor Shantanu explained.

"I see," the chairman nodded.

"There was only one way to manipulate the Brigadier and that was by kidnapping his son Deepak," Professor Shantanu said.

"So, is this why Naresh took admission at MIST?" Gopal Das asked.

"Yes," Professor Shantanu spoke sadly.

"But, Naresh did not have to join MIST for this!" the chairman was still distressed at his institute's needless involvement.

"You see, the purpose was three-fold. Not only did MIST give Naresh an opportunity to get close to Deepak unobtrusively and kidnap him without rousing any suspicion, it gave him impeccable credentials and also provided him with the perfect alibi. After the assassination, he would be back in the campus, complete his research project in a couple of months, and vanish in due course, with none being the wiser," Professor Shantanu expounded.

"But why not assassinate the Premier during his visit to different organizations in Delhi?" the chairman asked.

"Well, for one, the security arrangements at all locations in Delhi where the Chinese Premier was scheduled to visit were more stringent and almost impossible to breach. Secondly, there is a sizeable population of Tibetans in Dehradun, which could provide logistical support to this group. Thirdly, members of this group could easily mingle amongst the local Tibetans without raising any suspicions," Professor Shantanu explained.

"But I always thought that Tibetans were a peaceful lot. How did this turn-around come about?" Gopal Das asked.

"Well, this turn around hasn't really come about. Thank God!" the professor said.

"Still, I want to know!" Gopal Das said.

"It was only a marginal group from among some of the Tibetans," Professor Shantanu explained.

Singhal nodded.

"They decided that something extreme had to be done to draw the attention of the world towards the troubles of the Tibetans. India was increasingly becoming pro-Chinese, and so was the rest of the world. And the self-immolations were having no impact," Professor Shantanu paused to catch his breath.

"After all, in the eyes of India and the world, billions of dollars worth of trade is the priority," the professor elaborated further.

"Yes, that's true," Gopal Das Singhal always appreciated the fact that the economics made the world go around.

"This mad fringe group believed that terrorist activities could achieve the biggest impact at the lowest cost. In fact, they have founded a guerrilla movement and have given training in guerrilla combat and warfare technology to numerous Tibetans," the professor paused.

"They were planning to simultaneously enter China and carry out an armed struggle. They were ready to sacrifice up to 200 of their own people for this cause," Professor Shantanu elaborated.

"My God!" Gopal Das thought all this was too to be true.

"Exactly! They were also inciting the Tibetan youth to indulge in underground activities, spy on railway, water resources, power grid projects, military command areas, and barracks within Tibet. They had already created a 'Free Tibet Movement'," the professor described in detail.

"How were they able to do all this?" Singhal was puzzled.

"Support to this movement was being provided by a few fanatical members of the Congress Party of Tibet, Women's Welfare Association of Tibet, The Free Tibet Organization and National Party of Tibet," Professor Shantanu explained.

"My God, there are so many groups!" Gopal Das Singhal was surprised.

"Yes; but these organizations were not really aware of what was going on in the sidelines. It was merely an extremist handful, who sort of got together and put together this dastardly plot under the instigation of Naresh," Professor Shantanu elaborated.

"You have really done your homework, haven't you?" Gopal

Das was impressed.

"Well, I am a researcher at heart. Once I understood the entire conspiracy, I was determined to find out everything. I have been up most nights this past week, piecing together everything," Professor Shantanu smiled.

"But I should have understood it all much earlier. Brigadier and Mrs. Kalra's behaviour, and Pierre's information about Naresh visiting the Tibetan Colony should have put me onto the right track," the Professor became morose again.

"How could you have known?" the Chairman tried to pacify Shantanu.

Professor Shantanu looked unconvinced. "I was blind, blind to what was right under my nose..." he mumbled.

"But why the murders?" the chairman suddenly realised that the professor was not tackling the most important issue.

Professor Shantanu took a deep breath.

"What went wrong in their strategy?" Gopal Das Singhal asked.

"Things started to go wrong for Naresh and his accomplices' right from day one of execution of the scheme — in fact, right from the time they kidnapped Deepak in order to blackmail his father Brigadier Kalra," Professor Shantanu paused.

"Naresh and his co-conspirators had planned that with Deepak in their custody, they would simply compel Brigadier Kalra to reveal all the security arrangements at the Military Academy. They would also coerce the Brigadier to enable them to sneak into the Academy and lie in wait at a vantage point from where they would carry out the assassination," the professor elaborated.

"Then?" Gopal Das was all ears.

"Well, you will have to blame the spirit of research amongst our students which stymied the entire plot," Professor Shantanu said with a touch of pride.

"What? How do you mean?" Gopal Das had no clue what the professor was referring to.

"Well, Deepak was almost fanatical about his research project which involved the development of a car engine that ran on alternate fuel. He was looking at the entire gamut of options ranging from fuel extracted from the Jatropha plant, to some other bio-fuel combinations," the professor gave details.

"That is great!" Inspite of himself, Gopal Das Singhal felt a surge of pride at the work being done by the students of his institute.

"The ill-fated Vipin was Deepak's project partner and close friend. He knew that Deepak would not go on a long leave without telling him. The bright boy that Vipin was, he refused to buy Brigadier Kalra's story that Deepak had gone to Singapore to tend to some problem related to his grandmother," Professor Shantanu paused.

"I see," Gopal Das said.

"Yes. Vipin was convinced that there was something seriously wrong" the professor said.

"But, how did he know it was Naresh?" Gopal Das asked.

"On the last day that Deepak was in the campus, he told Vipin that he was going with Naresh to meet some students at IIT Roorkee who were also working on some engine design which used bio-fuel," Professor Shantanu said.

Gopal Das was quiet.

"Knowing about Deepak's project, Naresh had, in fact, used this ruse to lure him out of the campus. Subsequently, he kidnapped Deepak with the help of his gang," the Professor said.

Singhal stared at Shantanu, not being able to believe what he heard.

"When Deepak did not return and there was no word from him, Vipin asked Naresh about their visit to Roorkee. Naresh admitted that he had accompanied Deepak to IIT Roorkee. But that was all; he had no idea why Deepak was on leave," Professor Shantanu said.

Singhal waited patiently.

"Then through some of his contacts at IIT Roorkee, Vipin managed to find out that Deepak had never visited the IIT. This straightaway cast a suspicion on Naresh. You see, Vipin too was a researcher of sorts," the professor paused.

"Not knowing the gravity of the situation, Vipin foolishly confronted Naresh with this fact. Naresh managed to somehow fob off Vipin for the moment. That was when Vipin realised that Naresh was lying. And that was Vipin's ruination...," Professor Shantanu clarified.

"Oh!" Gopal Das said.

"There was too much at stake and at this late stage of the plot, Naresh and his militant cronies knew that they could not allow their assassination plan to go awry. After all, a very large cause — that of free Tibet — was at stake. There was only one solution — Vipin had to be eliminated before he caused any real trouble," the professor was despondent.

Singhal listened patiently.

"The next night, Naresh murdered Vipin in cold blood and tried to make it look like suicide. He was banking on the fact that an engineering student committing suicide was fairly acceptable and it would not arouse great suspicion," Professor Shantanu spoke gloomily.

Gopal Das shook his head sadly, "If only it had ended at that."

"Well, that was not to be. Gurpreet's actual attempted suicide gave rise to fresh complications," Professor Shantanu said.

"Yes. But surely she need not have been murdered," Gopal Das said.

"I know. But once Naresh learnt that Gurpreet had visited Vipin on the night of the murder, he knew that he had to find out the extent of Gurpreet's involvement in Vipin's life," the Professor paused.

Naresh used a two-pronged approach to trap Gurpreet. On the one hand, he began making anonymous calls to Gurpreet trying to scare her into revealing all that she knew about Vipin. On the other hand, Naresh created a virtual avatar of himself named 'Enigma', on *Facebook*, and became friends with Gurpreet. Soon, 'Enigma', who was really Naresh, became her closest confidante," Professor Shantanu elucidated.

"My God! This is really devious," Gopal Das was startled.

Professor Shantanu nodded. "Vipin's murder combined with the anonymous threatening phone calls from Naresh, sufficiently terrified poor Gurpreet. This led her to confide all her fears to her new best friend 'Enigma', who was actually Naresh. You see, 'Enigma' had smoothly slipped into the void created in Gurpreet's life due to Vipin's death," he gave details.

"This is really very convoluted," Gopal Das said.

"Yes. Then one day the unfortunate Gurpreet recalled that the deceased Vipin had told her about his suspicions regarding Naresh. Stupidly, she discussed this with 'Enigma', not knowing that she was talking to Naresh himself. And thus she signed her own death warrant," the professor was glum.

Gopal Das shook his head in dismay. "And what about Suresh?"

"I think I am to be blamed for Suresh's death," the professor was gloomy.

"Why, why do you say that?" Gopal Das was perplexed.

"As you know, I was carrying out my own investigations into the murders. And well, this really bright boy Suresh was simultaneously investigating the entire thing. In fact, I took Suresh's help to hack into Gurpreet's *Facebook* account and thus inadvertently egged him on to get further interested in trying to find the identity of the killer," the professor said.

Gopal Das was quiet.

"You see, I could have very easily prevented Suresh's death if I had any intelligence. Suresh had not only led me to Gurpreet's blog, but also opened her *Facebook* account for me, and I... I failed him. I just thought that it would be an exercise in futility. There would be no purpose in trying to determine the identity of all of Gurpreet's virtual *Facebook* friends. I did not consider it to be serious enough," Professor Shantanu berated himself.

"But you had no way of knowing," Gopal Das spoke sympathetically.

"But I should have known!" Professor Shantanu's voice rose. "But instead of me, it was Suresh who soon deduced that

'Enigma' was really the id created by Naresh. Suresh was planning to follow it up, but before he could do so, he… he…,"

There was silence.

"Naresh and his deadly group concluded that a few more murders were easily justified in pursuance of their noble cause — that of free Tibet," Professor Shantanu was bitter.

"I see," Gopal Das said. There was no accounting for the warped thinking of fanatical people, he thought.

After a long pause, the professor spoke, "And poor troubled Mayank. Again, I was the one to lead him to his death." Professor Shantanu knew that this guilt would not go away for a long, long time.

"How can you say that?" The professor was being too hard on himself, reflected the chairman.

"You see, I goaded Mayank to breaking point. I thought that as a result of my provocation, Mayank would do something thoughtless and would unintentionally provide conclusive evidence that he was the murderer," Professor Shantanu revealed.

"I really believed that Mayank was the murderer — that he was actually a serial killer…," the professor continued.

Gopal Das waited for the professor to continue.

"Of course, I was wrong!" Professor Shantanu said.

Singhal looked on sympathetically.

"Mayank did get goaded; but as a result, he decided to find out the identity of the culprit and thereby clear his own name. He caught hold of Nitish, terrorised him so much that the latter quickly told him everything he knew. Nitish also handed over a soft copy of all of Suresh's files dealing with his investigations.

It contained details of Gurpreet's blog and *Facebook* account. After that it was simply a case of putting two and two together," Professor Shantanu described.

"Er... who is Nitish?" Gopal Das asked.

"Nitish was Suresh's closest friend and knew everything, except the bit about 'Enigma' being Naresh," Professor Shantanu said.

"And er... what did Mayank put together?" Gopal Das was puzzled.

"Mayank also concluded that 'Enigma' was important. He followed the virtual trail left behind by Suresh and managed to unearth that 'Enigma' was Naresh," Professor Shantanu said.

"Oh! And then?" Gopal Das asked.

"Mayank imprudently confronted Naresh directly, not realising that he was dealing with a dangerous homicidal maniac. In a fit of rage, Naresh did what he does best...," Professor Shantanu's voice was toneless.

"Well, thank God it has all ended. It could have been worse, had you not caught on that Naresh was the murderer," the chairman spoke compassionately.

Unconvinced, Professor Shantanu stared blankly into space. "I was too late," he mumbled. The institute had paid too heavy a price in the form of the lives of innocent students and faculty, he thought.

"Well, at last we can get back to academics." Professor Shantanu said.

A fortnight later, he was almost back to normal and feeling relatively better. He had come to terms with Naresh's betrayal.

"Yes. In fact, I will go back to IIT. The excitement that has happened here is enough to last me a lifetime," Professor Indresan said.

It was late evening and they were sitting in the director's office sharing a cup of coffee. Professor Indresan had called for this interlude ostensibly to thank Professor Shantanu.

"Well, I cannot say anything about your going back. But we should consider ourselves fortunate that a national crisis has been averted," Indresan commented. Professor Shantanu was sombre.

"Yes. RAW — the Research and Analysis Wing — has been called in, I believe?" Professor Indresan said.

"Yes. All efforts are being made at the highest intelligence and diplomatic circles to ensure that this does not have detrimental implications. After all, a hundred thousands crores worth of business is at stake. India-China relations are on a distinct upswing. And this could have ruined it all," Professor Shantanu said.

"I'm still not clear how and why the murders took place," the director looked perplexed.

It was obvious that Professor Indresan had as usual forgotten a few vital links in the entire plot. Professor Shantanu decided to patiently explain it all over again.

"How did Naresh plan all this? And more importantly, how did he commit all these murders?" Professor Indresan asked again.

"Well, to begin with, Naresh really was an academically brilliant boy. Soon after completing his engineering, he was working for Siemens. After the tragedy of his girlfriend, he left his job and joined this militant group. Soon they learnt of the proposed visit of the Chinese Premier to India, which was decided well in advance as these visits normally are," Professor Shantanu paused.

"I see," Professor Indresan nodded.

"As you know, they kidnapped Deepak with the intention of blackmailing his father Brigadier Kalra into helping them to assassinate the Chinese Premier during his scheduled visit to the Indian Military Academy," Professor Shantanu said.

"Ah yes, I know," Professor Indresan said.

"Well, it was Deepak's project partner — Vipin — who began causing problems," Professor Shantanu paused.

"Hm ..." Professor Indresan mumbled.

"Vipin was really intelligent. And this intelligence was his undoing. He became suspicious that Naresh had something to do with Deepak's absence," the Professor was forlorn.

"So, Naresh had no choice but to get rid of Vipin." Professor Shantanu was glum.

"But how did he do it?" Professor Indresan was puzzled. He began toying with a curl dangling over his right ear.

"It was quite simple for him really. Since Naresh lived in the boys' hostel, no one questioned his presence. He simply walked into Vipin's room late that night, locked the room from inside, took the sleeping Vipin by surprise, and easily overpowered the groggy boy," Professor Shantanu explained the modus operandi. "Gurpreet had already slipped a bit of poison into Vipin's coffee due to which he was somewhat woozy, you see," he said.

"Oh God!" the director said. Unconsciously, he began pulling at his curl of hair, winding it tightly around his right index finger.

"Then Naresh strangled Vipin to death with a rope that he had carried along for the purpose. Subsequently, he tied Vipin to the ceiling fan with the help of the latter's bedsheet. Of course, Naresh kept the rope with himself to deflect suspicion of it being murder. He also deleted all sms and call records from Vipin's cell phone. Once the dastardly deed was done, Naresh simply jumped out from the balcony of Vipin's room onto the balcony of the central lobby of the apartment. He then strolled out, with none being the wiser," Professor Shantanu elucidated.

"Ah, hence the post-mortem report which said that the murder occurred due to garrotting by some corded rope-like material. And the deep-cut somewhat V-shaped ligature marks proved that death occurred due to strangulation and not due to hanging," the director recalled.

"Exactly," Professor Shantanu said.

"And Gurpreet?" Professor Indresan asked.

"Gurpreet was in love with Vipin whereas he regarded her as his best friend. Although in love with Kanika, he routinely confided in her," Professor Shantanu clarified.

"Ah... these young people...," Professor Indresan said wistfully. In his days, there had been no scope for such things. Softly he stroked the lock of hair.

"Well, Gurpreet did not realise the importance of what Vipin had told her about Deepak going with Naresh. It was only after Vipin's murder and when I questioned her about Deepak that she realised that something dangerous was afoot," Professor Shantanu paused.

The director listened avidly.

"Not realising that Naresh was the culprit, she innocently asked him for help in trying to make sense of everything that was happening. She did not know whom to trust," Professor Shantanu paused.

"Naresh knew that he could not allow Gurpreet to live, or else sooner or later, some suspicion would fall upon him, before he was able to execute his larger plan. So Naresh swore her to silence, convinced her that her life too was in danger and told her to meet him on the girls' hostel roof late after midnight, when he would explain everything. And the rest we all know," Professor Shantanu said sadly. Gurpreet had been a good girl.

"But how come he entered the girls' hostel without exciting any suspicion?" How could such a thing happen at his institute? the director wondered, mortified.

"Yes, Naresh really is quite crafty. He knew that the area at the rear of the girls' hostel was not well-lighted. He had also observed that there were jutting pipes and parapets located on the walls towards the back of the hostel. After that, it was simple really. He just climbed using the back wall of the girls' hostel. Since he probably climbed up sometime after midnight, he was not observed by anyone," Professor Shantanu expounded.

"This was so unnecessary," the director said.

"But why would she ask for Naresh's help? What was her link with him?" Professor Indresan was baffled. This did not seem to fit.

"Naresh created a profile of himself called 'Enigma' on *Facebook*. As 'Enigma', he managed to become Gurpreet's closest friend through *Facebook*. She trusted him completely, confided in him, and even agreed to meet him on the roof that fateful night not knowing that she was actually speaking with Naresh," Professor Shantanu said.

"Oh!" This was a nasty underhand move, thought the director.

There was silence.

"Er... and Suresh?" Professor Indresan asked delicately.

"Suresh was investigating the murders. Whatever he found out, he gave me in the form of soft copies of various files, etc. No doubt Naresh went through all of them on the sly, by accessing my laptop. He concluded that the assassination plan could still go awry, and so decided to do away with Suresh."

"Oh!" Naresh was a nasty beast, thought the director.

"The night that Suresh deduced that 'Enigma' was really Naresh, he was troubled. However, he was not really sure that it was 'Enigma', aka Naresh, who could be the murderer. The entire night Suresh could not sleep, as he was grappling with the puzzle. He went for an early morning swim to calm his agitated mind," Professor Shantanu paused.

The director was agog.

"Naresh had been keeping a watch on Suresh all this while. He knew sooner or later Suresh would be able to determine Naresh's culpability. Seeing him go alone for the swim, Naresh saw his chance. He took the swimming Suresh by surprise, and forcefully held his head under water until he drowned. Suresh put up a brave struggle; but he was no match for the fiendish Naresh." There was a catch in Professor Shantanu's voice.

"That is awful," Professor Indresan shook his head sorrowfully.

There was silence.

"And I suppose Mayank too was eliminated because he learnt that Naresh was the killer?" Professor Indresan said. He had begun to see the pattern in the crimes.

"Yes. Absolutely," Professor Shantanu concurred.

After a long pause, Professor Indresan asked delicately, "But why the attack on you?"

"Well, my intelligence did kick in — rather too late, I'm ashamed to say. And I realised that I needed to find out the identity of 'Enigma'. I had jotted down the cell phone number given by 'Enigma' to Gurpreet on my note-pad. The number was, of course, no longer operational."

"So?" the director asked.

"So, like I said, Naresh was in the habit of snooping around my laptop and other things like notepad etc., behind my back. He saw 'Enigma's' cell number written on my note-pad. Earlier, he had already noted the other details on my laptop. Based on these facts, he realised that I too was closing in," Professor Shantanu said.

"Oh!" Professor Indresan exclaimed.

"In fact, he often dissuaded me from investigating the murders, and even tried to convince me that the earlier murders were suicides. At that time, I did wonder how a boy as intelligent as Naresh could arrive at such a wrong conclusion. But there was no way that I could be suspicious of Naresh…," Professor Shantanu looked forlorn.

Professor Indresan was quiet.

"In fact I should have become suspicious after noting that Deepak's name was missing from the list of Vipin's friends that Naresh had compiled for me," Professor Shantanu paused.

"Given Naresh's meticulousness there was no way he could have overlooked listing Deepak's name. Not only that, he reported that there was nothing of importance in Vipin's and Gurpreet's call-list either." The professor continued remorsefully.

"There was no way you could have suspected Naresh — none of us could have!" The director exclaimed in an attempt to soothe the professor.

"Anyway, soon Naresh decided to eliminate me too, and so attacked me. Then he deleted his profile of 'Enigma' from *Facebook* and all other files that Suresh had given me, from my laptop," Professor Shantanu said.

Professor Indresan looked distressed.

"Unfortunately for him, I survived," Professor Shantanu spoke poignantly.

"And when did you realise about him being the er... killer?" Professor Indresan's voice caught in mid-sentence.

"The night when after returning from the hospital, I overheard Naresh speaking in a strange tongue. Upon being confronted, he tried to convince me that I was delusional — that was when alarm bells went off in my head," Professor Shantanu's voice quivered.

The director was quiet. He did have an inkling about the affection that the professor had had for Naresh.

"I have been sheltering a devil under my wing...," Professor Shantanu's voice trailed away.

There was a long silence.

"So Naresh did it all for love..." The director asked.

"Not completely. Naresh was also extremely upset with the Chinese occupation of land in J&K, their claim over Arunachal

Pradesh, and their recent forays into Ladakh. He said that any self-respecting Indian would have attempted to do what he did in order to reclaim the Indian sovereignty and self-esteem," Professor Shantanu revealed.

"Clearly he was delusional," Professor Indresan said.

"Mm... I suppose so...," Professor Shantanu said reflectively.

Visions of Naresh flashed through him. The innocent face, the beguiling eyes behind the spectacles, the rational intellect, the lover, the idealist, the son he never had... was it possible that he still felt love for Naresh?

In spite of all that had happened, would he ever succeed in letting Naresh move out from the corner that he had come to occupy in his heart?

Ah, such maudlin emotions might well be his undoing one day, Professor Shantanu mused as he gazed out at the serene, cloud-kissed hills of Mussoorie.